Praise for Author Jessica Eissfeldt

"**I find Jessica Eissfeldt's books sweet and gentle** and often wonderfully atmospheric, too. **They tell stories I can enjoy** and relax with and lose myself in, **a special gift** during times of stress, whether personal or collective."

—Mary Balogh, *New York Times* bestselling author

"**Jessica Eissfeldt's talent** for combining compelling characters, unique stories and charming settings **guarantees I'll be reading far into the night.**"

—Karyn Good, romantic suspense author

"**Jessica Eissfeldt writes with heart.** A reader can **get lost between the pages** of history and then come back to today with her contemporary stories. Whether you're **wanting to escape** for a brief time or a long time, these novellas and novels are **fun to read.** You have so many choices."

—Annette Bower, award-winning sweet romance author

GET YOUR FREE SWEET ROMANCE HERE!

Will Sara find true love?

Before she was Jake's boss, Sara was a savvy TV reporter determined to not give up on her dreams, or true love...

Don't miss this **exclusive collection** of **three sweet** contemporary **romance** novellas I wrote **just for you!** Includes:

- **Passport to Romance & Relics** – prequel novella, Sara & Todd's story

You won't find this collection available in any store! But it's yours FREE when you sign up to hear from me.

Go here to get started:
www.jessicaeissfeldt.com/yourfreegift

Hidden treasure of the Heart

Hidden treasure of the Heart

Book 1 in the Passport to Romance & Relics series

JESSICA EISSFELDT

Hidden Treasure of the Heart: A novel
Jessica Eissfeldt

Copyright © 2022 by Jessica Eissfeldt. All rights reserved.

Print Edition
ISBN: 978-1-989290-40-8

This is a work of fiction. All names, characters, places and events are either used fictitiously or are products of the author's imagination. Any resemblances to actual people, living or dead, business establishments, incidents, events or locales is purely coincidental.

ALSO BY JESSICA EISSFELDT

Sweet Historical Romance:

Sweethearts & Jazz Nights

Dialing Dreams
Shattered Melodies
Fancy Footwork
Unspoken Lyrics
The Sweethearts & Jazz Nights Boxed Set:
The Complete Collection

Love By Moonlight

Beneath A Venetian Moon
Beside A Moonlit Shore
The Love By Moonlight Boxed Set: The
Complete Collection

Sweet Contemporary Romance:

Prince Edward Island Love Letters & Legends

This Time It's Forever
Now It's For Always
At Last It's True Love
The Prince Edward Island Love Letters &
Legends Boxed Set: The Complete Collection

Passport to Romance & Relics

Hidden Treasure of the Heart
Lost Treasure of Love
Secret Treasure of Us
Passport to Romance & Relics: The Complete Collection

Collections

Love & Lattes: A Sweet Romance Short Story Collection
Pieces of Me: A Poetry & Lyrics Collection

Romantic Comedy

Love, Your Fangirl
The Keys to Love

Chapter One

New York, NY

VANESSA EISENZIMMER RUSHED up the Manhattan subway steps as fast she dared in a skirt suit and heels—an outfit she only wore on special occasions—and tried not to sound like a dying camel, but it didn't work.

She made a wry face as she dodged other Thursday morning commuters. Was she out of breath because of nerves or because she hadn't been to the gym lately?

She checked her watch and winced. One minute after ten o'clock.

Kali, her boss at the Women of the American Revolution Museum, wouldn't be pleased.

And if Kali happened to mention it to the museum board, that wouldn't look good, either. Only last month, Vanessa had finally gotten their approval for her fundraising gala and silent auction idea.

She'd started to work on the event right after she'd gotten the go-ahead. But she knew that if this event in two weeks didn't help the museum reach its monetary goals for this fiscal year, it would have to close. She'd lose her job, too.

She swallowed and did her best to suppress the flutter of nerves in her stomach. That's why this promotional video *had* to be perfect. She muttered the opening lines to herself as she rushed along.

Kali and the board expected her to be the spokesperson in the short video and then post it on social media. Except they hadn't checked with her to see if she was comfortable in front of a camera. They'd simply assumed she'd do it. She'd been too distracted by arranging gala details to explain otherwise.

She hated being in the spotlight.

But if it meant saving the museum, well, she'd just have to get herself on track. Even if the thought of the whole world seeing her on camera made her nauseous.

She darted a quick look left and right before she jaywalked across William

Street, toward the little museum tucked away on Cedar Street in what had once been an 18th century merchant's house. The small two-story red brick home had blue shutters and wide windowsills.

She smiled. Some days it was easy to imagine this part of Lower Manhattan as it must've looked in the 1700s. Other times, like today, with the Dunkin' Donuts nearby and the honk of yellow cabs, it was a bit harder.

Her fascination with the past was something her ex-boyfriend had never understood about her. He spent his time doing auditions on Broadway, hoping to be discovered. They'd never shared the same appreciation for this historic city.

A horn blared in her ear, and startled her attention back onto the sidewalk in front of her. She caught herself just before she tripped—darn heels—and then took a second to pause on the steps of the small house.

She could see her boss through the six-by-six window. She inhaled, exhaled and then pushed open the door.

"Vanessa." Kali looked at the clock on the wall above the stone fireplace. "Glad you could make it."

Vanessa opened her mouth before she closed it again. Pretty useless to argue with a native New Yorker like Kali. Especially when she was dealing with her husband's difficult health issues. So Vanessa just nodded and smoothed her hair away from her face.

Kali gave Vanessa an appraising look. "I see you listened to my suggestion, anyway. I think that powder blue will work well on-camera. Sets off your dark brown hair. Jill, you agree?"

Kali beckoned to someone else standing on the other side of the room. "This is Jill Wood, the same gal the Met used for that video series on Impressionist painters last month that caused such a sensation. She'll be doing the filming."

"Yep, I think what you're wearing'll work great." Jill extended a hand to Vanessa. "Nice to meet you."

Vanessa shook it. "You too."

Kali clapped her hands. "Well, if you don't need anything else, then," she checked her watch and tried to hide a worried look. "I have an important conference call to make. Vanessa, don't leave anything out, ok? We need the Friends of the Museum, and the general public too, to have a compelling reason to buy a gala ticket. Half the funds we need are coming from ticket sales, remember."

Vanessa pressed her lips together. "Right. And the other half from the silent auction at the gala." She gave a quiet sigh of relief as Kali went down the hall and into her office. She liked her boss, but the other woman could get intense at times.

"So," Jill said, "we're all set up in over here."

Vanessa's palms grew clammy and she had to remind herself it was only a five-minute video. Piece of cake. She muttered the opening lines to herself one last time.

She followed Jill to the space she'd set up by the stone fireplace to film, and felt herself relax. This didn't *look* very intimidating.

She took a seat on the Louis XIV chair and squinted as Jill flicked on a bright rolling light before she headed over to a small camera set up across from the chair. "Ready?"

Vanessa nodded and settled into the chair. Jill cued her just before the red light blinked on.

"The American Revolutionary War era is filled with stories of heroics and bravery, bloodshed and bitterness. But what some people might not realize is the extent that women across races and tiers of Colonial society played in helping win the War of Independence."

Vanessa paused, wet her lips and gathered her thoughts before she continued with the rest of her speech about the gala and the exhibit. At least she wasn't forgetting her lines and blanking out like she'd been afraid she might. She lifted her chin and spoke the final lines.

"That's why the Women of the American Revolution Museum needs your help. This display we are creating is about female spies of that era. They might not be as well-known as their male counterparts but are, nonetheless, people who played just as important of a role in the fight for independence. With your help, their voices will be heard, and their acts of bravery not forgotten. Please donate, or purchase a gala ticket today."

The red light blinked off. Vanessa breathed a sigh of relief and stood.

"That was great, Vanessa. We won't need to do any retakes."

"That's a relief." Vanessa chuckled. "Thank goodness I won't have to look into another camera lens for a very long time."

Los Angeles, CA

JAKE FORD ADJUSTED his aviator sunglasses and grinned as the wind ruffled his wavy brown hair and the open collar of his maroon safari shirt. It was good to be back in California. Lots of sunshine, and not so many monsoons. With both hands on the steering wheel of his Jeep, he did his best to blink away jet lag from the thirty-hour trip he'd just completed. He'd been over in Myanmar, on the hunt for an ancient jeweled scepter rumored to have been a love token for an empress.

Not that he'd actually *found* said relic. He sighed. Seemed he never did. Yet somehow, he got his hopes up every time.

He rubbed the back of his neck and winced. Must've slept on it wrong during the flight back.

He stifled a yawn, glad he'd taken the doors off the Jeep and rolled back the canvas top. He certainly couldn't complain, though. After years spent piecing together his acting career doing hundreds of commercials and bit parts, he'd gotten a break landing that TV host position with the Travel Channel. Which had led to this—his dream job hosting *Passport to Romance & Relics.*

He grinned. Who else was lucky enough to get paid to travel around the world and investigate the romance and history behind some of the most legendary relics in the world?

Passport to Romance & Relics was the #1 rated show on the Globetrotter Network right now. Pretty phenomenal for its first season, which had just wrapped. The pilot had done better than even his executive producer, Sara, had hoped.

A combination of determination and sheer good luck? Then again, he'd never been one to trust much to luck, really.

He fiddled for a moment with the woven bracelet he always wore on his left wrist. The silver hematite beads woven into the jute braid always made him feel grounded. Centered.

Ever since he'd gotten it from that

Buddhist monk at Angkor Wat during his very first backpacking trip abroad after college graduation from Stanford, he'd never taken it off. He smiled faintly. Maybe he was a bit of a believer in luck, deep down somewhere.

With some of the close calls in adventure travel he'd had over the years, maybe he'd be remiss not to be the tiniest bit superstitious.

Even with the risk and danger, there was nothing better than adventure. The thrill of the chase. The hope that somehow, some way, somewhere, maybe even just around the next corner, was the real relic discovery that would put his career on the map at last. Would—

His cell phone rang. He pressed the enable call button on the steering wheel.

"Jake Ford speaking. How can I help?"

"Jake, this is Sara."

"Oh, hey, Sara. How was your trip with Todd to Bora-Bora?"

"That snorkel experience you recommended was absolutely amazing. Best moment of our honeymoon, ever."

Jake chuckled. "Glad that it lived up to expectations. The tropical fish in those waters are something else, aren't they?"

"*You've got that right. I'd never seen anything like that electric blue before. Of course, Lake Mendota in Madison isn't exactly prime scuba water. But all joking aside, Jake, I called because I wanted to discuss a bit of business.*"

"Sure. Just picked up my Jeep from long-term parking and am on my way back from the airport now, so I have a bit of time to chat. What's up?"

"*Listen, Jake...*"

Jake's stomach dipped at his boss's tone.

"*The ratings have come back in for the season finale.*"

"And?" Jake couldn't keep the eagerness from his voice. If those finale ratings matched anything near the rest of the season's episodes, the show'd be #1 for a lot longer.

"*I'll be honest—it's totally bombed.*"

Jake's gut clenched and he swore under his breath.

"*I know. None of us could've predicted this.*"

Jake sighed and his mouth turned down. "You're right about that."

"Listen, can you swing by the studio? There's...something interesting you might want to see."

Jake stifled another yawn as he forced cheer into his tone. "Sounds good. I'll head over there right now."

He checked his rearview mirror and both side mirrors before he crossed six lanes of traffic. He hit the accelerator to narrowly avoid a Massarati that blared its horn at him.

He resisted the urge to roll his eyes—Los Angeles. Seemed people cared more about their external status than their internal character. Sometimes this city really wore on him. He thought, fleetingly, of the tiny fishing town he'd grown up in outside of Bangor. At least there, people stated things how they were. No one took it personally.

Here, it seemed to him, everything was personal. But that was Hollywood, he supposed. Big egos and big dreams didn't exactly make for a combination that created happiness in the long term. A view his ex-girlfriend, Laura, didn't seem to share. But that was part of why they'd broken up.

He shook his head. Maybe he'd been here too long, been single too long.

Forty-five minutes later, he'd made it across town and pulled into the parking lot of the TV studio.

He parked and got out. He stretched for a second before he grabbed his cell phone and the car keys then headed inside the building.

The blast of cold from the air conditioner washed over his skin. But the usually welcome sensation made his grip tighten around his car keys. Had Sara talked to the network execs? What would happen now that the finale had bombed?

He took a big breath and nudged those thoughts aside. Whatever happened, he could handle it. Besides, things couldn't be all bad news—Sara hadn't fired him.

His heart a little lighter, he started down the hall toward Sara's office. She poked her head around the doorframe as Jake approached. "That was quick."

"Traffic was pretty light today, a miracle in itself." Jake said. "So what's this big mysterious thing you wanted to show me?"

"You'd better see it to believe it. Come on in."

At five o'clock, Vanessa's phone buzzed. She grinned as she read the notification on the screen. A social media post from her favorite TV show.

Didn't catch that last episode? Passport to Romance & Relics re-airs its season one finale tomorrow night at 9/8 central on the Globetrotter Network. Exclusive cast interview to follow show!

She was still grinning as she locked up the museum and stepped out onto the sidewalk at rush hour. But even the blaring car horns, the shouting and swearing of a bike messenger who'd gotten cut off by a jaywalking father with a stroller, and the press of so many strangers, couldn't dampen her mood.

She'd done it—the video was completed, approved and posted. She lifted her chin as she descended into the subway station, and caught the 5:10 train back to her tiny studio. It'd taken seven years in this city, but she'd landed her dream museum job. She just hoped this video, and by extension, the gala, would help make the difference, and she could keep it.

On the street outside her apartment, she fished out her key from her purse. After she'd wrestled with the slightly battered security door, having to pull the knob upward as she turned the key hard to the right, the old oak door finally decided to pop open.

She stepped into the worn Art Deco space, with its scuffed brass mailboxes and its chipped penny round black-and-white tiles on the floor.

She didn't care that this building charged an astronomical amount for the rent. She loved her minuscule space here—it was all hers—and worth every scraped-together dime.

What was better than living in a piece of real New York history? Nothing, that's what.

Her mind drifted back to her exhibit idea—female spies had really gotten the attention of her boss.

Vanessa's heart flipped—so many brave, courageous women who people knew hardly anything about. With this exhibit, she aimed to change all that, share with the public as much as she could to give a voice to these lesser-known historical women. She also wanted a way to make it interactive. Give people something they could really feel, experience, live.

She didn't want people to dismiss history as part of the dusty past. She wanted to make it come alive. The question was, how? Because if people didn't know their history, how could they appreciate their future?

The glint of light off the bank of mailboxes caught Vanessa's attention, and she eyed them with a heavy heart. The last time she'd opened hers, Eric had sent her an actual letter, months after their breakup, finally apologizing for his behavior.

She took a breath. Thank goodness things with him were over and done with.

She selected the tiny mail key from her key ring and walked over to the box with the ornate Apartment 14B written in neat black ink in the center of the small brass door.

A few muttered curse words accompanied by the jingle of keys and rattle of the doorknob told her someone else was trying to get into the building.

The gust of warm July air that blew across the nape of her neck told her the other person had succeeded. She glanced over her shoulder.

"Oh hey, Melissa," she said to the other woman who'd walked in. "Thought you were the downstairs neighbors who'd lost their key again. Had to let them in twice last week."

"Nope, my key just jammed more than usual. My God. The traffic out there today is horrendous. Wait. Why am I complaining? It's nearly always like that." She laughed and then blew out a sigh as she jutted her chin in the direction of the bank of mailboxes. "Don't tell me that jerk of an actor ex of yours tried to sway you with an actual pen-on-paper love letter again?"

"I hope not." Vanessa laughed. "But I *am* going to check my mail, yep."

"A momentous occasion," Melissa said as she hoisted her second-hand orange Hermes bag over her shoulder and leaned against the doorframe. "So. How'd the video go?"

Vanessa flashed a thumbs up. Melissa nodded solemnly then gave her a playful salute. "I understand. Well, I'm starved, so

I'd better head up to my hot plate to make something a little more healthy than instant noodles. Text me later? Show starts at eight o'clock tomorrow; we're still on, right?"

"Wouldn't miss my armchair travel opportunity." Vanessa grinned. "With the stress at work lately, I *definitely* need to squeeze in some fun. See ya."

Her friend turned and left, the faintest hint of Chanel in her wake. Vanessa sighed and turned her attention back to the mailbox. She took a deep breath then turned the key and opened the small brass door.

There was something inside. She winced. If Eric had—

She frowned as she looked into the dimly lit cavity and pulled out what looked liked a brand new manila envelope.

She checked the mailbox's interior. Nothing else, not even one of those bright orange flyers for that new pizza place a few blocks down that kept the neighborhood mailboxes—and sidewalks—carpeted with advertisements.

She shut the mailbox door, pocketed the key and then hefted the envelope in her hand.

It was light. Almost as if nothing was in there. But she read the address; definitely her name on the front, typed in neat font on one of those white mailing labels.

No return address, though.

She flipped the envelope over, put a fingernail under the flap, and tugged upward. With a small tearing sound, the manila paper gave way.

She peered inside.

JAKE STEPPED INTO the large office. Palms swayed outside the floor-to-ceiling window. If he squinted, he could just catch the sparkle of sunlight off oceanfront.

He had to admit his boss had a great office. Not that he had designs on her job. He was perfectly happy being the TV host and the co-producer of *Passport to Romance & Relics*; executive producers didn't spend as much time in front of the camera as he'd like. His ex had never been supportive of that. She'd always been pushing him to go for the biggest titles, the most prestige...

Truth was, with his double major in acting and ancient cultural studies, well, he had to admit being in front of the camera was more fun than being behind a desk. Still, with his hand in the administrative side, he had a part in deciding the creative direction of the show, which he liked.

"What's up?" Jake said as he tucked his aviator sunglasses into his shirt pocket.

"Listen, Jake, like I said, the network execs aren't happy about the season one finale. Apparently the jeweled scepter wasn't a big draw." She sighed and pinched the bridge of her nose. "It's so hard to predict what will or won't capture viewers. We're re-airing the finale along with that special cast interview to try and jump-start things. But we need to do something more."

Jake sat on the arm of the leather chair in front of Sara's desk. "So what are you thinking?"

"This." Sara flipped her laptop around on the smooth polished glass surface of her desk. "It just came into the show's email inbox."

Jake raised his eyebrows. "A needle and thimble?"

"That's what I thought at first..." Sara continued as she sat down behind her desk. The bright pink cuff bracelets on her wrist jangled as she pointed to the photo. "...until I read the email."

"Okay," Jake said.

"This needle and thimble," Sara said, "were used to sew one of the first American flags."

"So Betsy Ross had them?"

"No," Sara said. "I have reason to believe they're connected to Agent 355."

"What?"

"The woman who emailed the show said these Revolutionary War artifacts might've owned by Agent 355, the still-unidentified woman in George Washington's spy ring."

Jake rubbed his jaw. "How do we know this is legit? I mean, remember the time we got an anonymous tip about the whereabouts of a lost silver mine in New Mexico and it turned out to be a ploy to get a restaurant some advertising footage? They'd faked the documents and everything."

Sara nodded. "Don't think I hadn't thought of that. But I discussed it with a few experts and they all think it could be the real deal."

She continued. "Because in this case, the person who sent the photo said she is a descendant of Robert Townsend, another of Washington's spies. Provided the family tree link and everything." Sara's blue eyes sparkled with excitement as she looked from Jake back to the photo.

"Hmmm." Jake leaned forward to examine the digital image more closely. "Well," he said, "I can see how viewers might like the idea. Very American heritage." It was a close-up shot. The thin silver needle was woven through a piece of red material. Beside it sat a white porcelain thimble.

He reached out a finger, as if to trace the objects, before he remembered that of course, he couldn't. It was only a photo.

Jake gave himself a mental shake. He was always doing that. Getting more than a bit over-enthusiastic and then ending up disappointed.

Just like in his love life. His heart ached for a moment as he recalled the rejection in Laura's eyes. He'd really thought Laura was the one for him. Smart, funny, intelligent. Got his sense of humor and didn't mind being an accomplice to the occasional practical joke he played on his friends.

She'd broken off their engagement a year ago. She'd claimed he was gone too much—and that he loved freedom and travel more than her. The relationship imploded right after the Travel Channel show was cancelled, and he'd gotten this position. But would their relationship have ever really worked in the long run?

He gave a mental sigh. She wasn't a big traveller and well, with that Travel Channel hosting job, he'd been gone pretty often. But with this position, he was gone even more—over 200 days every year. Guilt nudged him. Their relationship would've become even more long-distance than it already had been, and—

"—the flag, then?"

"Oh, uh—" he fiddled with the jute bracelet on his left wrist and flushed "—sorry. What did you say?"

"You know that idea you pitched awhile back for doing an episode about a search for the first American flag?"

Jake nodded. "The higher-ups at the

network didn't think it had enough oomph."

"But now," Sara said as she tapped a finger on the screen, "with this whole 355 angle, it just might. Besides, no one's ever found this flag, either. And the network's agreeable."

"Wait." Jake paused. "You're saying that if we do something more U.S.-focused for the second season opener, it might give the show the boost it needs?"

Jake ran his hand across his stubble as excitement built inside him. "*The Lost American Flag* or something like that would be a good working title..."

"Unfortunately," Sara leaned back in her chair and pinched the bridge of her nose, "it's not just about boosting the ratings."

Jake's stomach plummeted.

Sara met Jake's gaze, her tone resolute. "What I'm saying is you have thirty days to get a top-notch episode about this filmed and in to me, or the network axes the whole show."

Vanessa reached into the manila envelope and pulled out a folded sheet of thin and brittle paper.

It looked old. Really old. She'd been trained to handle antique documents, so, if she had to guess...from the 18th century.

Her heart thudded, and she knew one thing: she had to examine this document properly.

She took the stairs two at a time to her fourth-floor walkup. After she kicked off her heels and dropped her purse by the door, she took off her suit jacket and tossed it over the back of the couch.

She'd need to look at this more closely. Hmm. Even if preservation gloves decreased tactile feedback a bit, she'd use them. She always kept a spare set in her kitchen, if anyone could call the minute space a kitchen. Still. It had a window above the sink that overlooked a tiny patch of grass at the back of the building, which made all the difference.

She pulled on the white gloves then rummaged around under her kitchen sink until she found the last remaining new garbage bag and pulled it from its box.

She spread it on the kitchen table that doubled as her home office. Then she placed the manila envelope, along with the folded antique paper, on it. Next, she darted over to her couch and picked up the table lamp on the side table. She plugged it in near the kitchen table and put it next to the workspace she'd created.

She turned the piece of paper over. A faded red wax seal was pressed into the page. She winced a little as she very slowly and carefully removed the seal and then unfolded the page.

New York   2 September 1780

My love,

I find this prison of my mind akin to those iron bars that now detain you, dearest. I had hoped my signal would have prevented such circumstances as these. Nonetheless, I have spoken with 721, who has promised to speak to 711 about a re-trial...

I can only pray that the extent of your involvement will not become known, though I fear 'tis too late for that, and the fault is entirely mine.

Please know that you are the intended of my heart, no matter what Father has in store for my wedding plans. Every stolen kiss has been worth every second of danger, for I have not yet begun to love you as I intend.

I shall fight for freedom — and you — as long as I still draw breath.

355

Vanessa's heart pounded as she skimmed the lines again. 721? 711? 355?

Did this letter....have to do with the Culper Spy Ring? She knew about the nation's first spy network, of course. How could she not, what with working on an exhibit about female spies during the Revolution.

She studied the page again. If she remembered correctly, these numbers stood for names. Her mind whirled. This *had* to be a letter to do with the Culper Spy Ring.

It was George Washington's secret circle of six people: five men and one woman, who worked undercover when the British occupied New York City during the Revolutionary War. Apparently, the spy network had been named after Culpeper, Virginia, where Washington worked as a young man.

In fact, the origins and identities of the Culper agents had been so well-hidden that the final male Culper ring member wasn't identified until 1929: Robert Townsend.

Vanessa tapped her finger against her chin. Agent 355, though, was still unidentified... What if she added this letter to the female spy exhibit?

After all, it fit right in. Some who said 355 had been a relative of one of the five men in the circle, also speculated that she'd been Robert Townsend's sister Sally, who had helped her brother with spy efforts.

Others thought 355 could be Loyalist Meg Moncrieffe, who decided to become a spy after Aaron Burr rejected her.

Still others theorized that a widow named Elizabeth Burgin had been 355 because she helped patriots escape the British prison ships in New York Harbor.

None had been able to prove it, though. In fact, no known correspondence from 355 had ever been found.

Until now?

Chapter Two

At the museum on Friday morning, Vanessa's chest tightened as she crossed the wide wooden floorboards in the narrow hallway that lead to her office.

Sure, the big filming event she'd dreaded had finally wrapped, but then this whole double booking of the event space had come up yesterday.

She had to figure out what to do about a replacement location for the gala. She flipped through the desk calendar—only thirteen days til the event.

She swallowed hard. There was so much riding on the gala... She made herself take a deep breath, then two. There had to be something...somewhere. Right? She straightened the collar of her mauve polka dot blouse. There *had* to be.

Her mind flitted back to the letter again. Could the document somehow prove 355's identity? Her heart jumped. If *she* was the one to finally discover this long-debated piece of historical intrigue, it would mean so much for the museum, and for her own career.

Vanessa frowned. Who'd sent it to her? And why? Besides that, who was 355 writing to?

Vanessa had left the letter at home but made sure it'd been safely stored. The exhibit wasn't about Agent 355 specifically, and somehow, she didn't want to show the letter to anyone else yet.

It felt too special, private, somehow. Even though she was probably committing several cardinal sins by not bringing it directly to the museum here, she couldn't quite bring herself to move it. She would. Soon.

"Good morning, Vanessa," Kali said as Vanessa gave her a half-wave when she passed the break room; the small space had been part of the larder, original to the house's 18th century construction.

"I hope everything went okay yesterday with that conference call," Vanessa said as she paused to take a breath before she stepped over the threshold—she wasn't a big fan of tight places. But usually, being in the break room didn't bother her. She grabbed her favorite aqua-and-white mug from the cupboard and glanced at her boss.

"We'll see what my husband's specialist says this afternoon." Kali's lips compressed and she stirred creamer and two sugars into her usually black coffee. Vanessa noticed the dark circles under the other woman's eyes, and put a hand on her arm for a brief moment. "Hang in there. If you need anything, just let me know."

Kali cleared her throat and straightened her shoulders. Gave Vanessa a thin smile. "While I appreciate your offering, that won't be necessary. But thank you."

That was as enthusiastic a response as she was going to get, Vanessa thought to herself as she selected a drink pod, fit it into the machine, put her mug underneath and then pressed brew. But that's just how her boss was, with all her stress, right now. Vanessa loved her job too much to let that get in her way.

"You're welcome. So, uh, I know the gala deadline's looming. Which is why, first thing this morning, I'm going to get right on calling more venues about a replacement location."

"We haven't had any luck so far." Kali clenched her fingers even more tightly around her mug. "I don't know what we'll do if we can't find a new venue." She rubbed her temples. "The date is coming up fast. Remember, it needs to be somewhere historic."

"It's too bad they only let us know yesterday that our first choice here in the city got double-booked by accident," Vanessa murmured, more to herself than Kali.

"That's life," Kali said in a clipped tone. "Keep me posted. I'll be in my office." Without another comment, she left the room.

Vanessa's stomach knotted. If they didn't find something, and fast, they were all going to be sunk. She took a fortifying sip of her mocha and hurried to her desk. After she checked her email—no responses from the queries she'd sent—she checked her phone and noticed a message from Melissa.

Just saw your video. It's on all the socials. You did a great job. Oh, and don't forget our

Passport to Romance & Relics *watch party tonight. We can both catch the season finale now, PLUS a cast interview—what's better than that? ;) I'll bring the popcorn.*

Melissa was such a great friend. Always had her back. They'd met several years ago, after they'd both shown up for a viewing of the same apartment.

Sounds great. Vanessa sent a smile emoticon too then turned to her computer screen again.

A few hours later, after Vanessa called what seemed like every venue in a twenty-mile radius of the city, she sighed and flopped back in her chair.

Between bar mitzvahs and birthdays and baby baptisms, nothing was available.

She massaged her stiff neck muscles—a headache was beginning to build. She needed to *think*. She got up and headed over to grab a coffee refill. They needed some place historic. Something related to the Revolution.

If they were talking about female spies, and the American Revolution, why not think a bit farther afield? After all, the Revolution took place all across the 13 colonies...

She stepped into the break room and selected another coffee pod. Too bad this museum was too small to host the event. Place was pretty historic.

She glanced at the exposed stone wall by the kitchen sink. A few of the stones had come loose when they'd redone the counters in here.

Hmm. Where else might work? The coffee maker beeped and she poured herself a cup. What about that historic site in Morristown, New Jersey? George Washington was headquartered there for part of the Revolution. Might be the perfect spot, with that Colonial-style house, other preserved buildings, and extensive grounds. Granted, it was a bit farther from New York but the gala attendees were coming from all over the country anyway.

She rushed back to her computer to look up the contact information.

But just as she sat down, Kali leaned around the doorway.

Vanessa's eyes widened and her smile faded as she looked at her boss's face. "Are you okay?"

Kali's complexion had drained of color,

HIDDEN TREASURE OF THE HEART

her lips were set and her usually neat hairstyle was in disarray. "Vanessa, I've been called away. I'm not sure how things will develop or how long I'll be gone. At least a few weeks. It seems his condition is worsening at a much faster rate than the doctors anticipated. So I'm going to have to test your mettle, because I need to take a leave of absence."

Vanessa tried to stifle a gasp.

Kali nodded. "You're in charge now—head curator. Guess you just got a promotion." She laughed tiredly. "But with such a small speciality museum here, and only the two of us running this place, I have every confidence in your abilities." Her phone buzzed and she jumped. "I need to go. Keep me informed about the gala and your exhibit plans."

Vanessa nodded mutely as she watched her boss leave. Now what?

FRIDAY AFTERNOON, JAKE propped his feet up on the rattan footstool on his apartment's back patio and cracked open a pineapple-mint iced tea.

The sound of the surf whooshed in his ears as he leaned back against the blue and white striped cotton canvas of his deck chair.

His eyes drifted shut and his mind wandered. So good to be home. It'd been too long since he'd been in one place for more than a few days. Bonus points for not having to live out of a suitcase at the moment, either.

A chance to sleep in his own bed was a nice change of pace from mud-and-brick huts with spiders as big as dinner plates that watched every movement in the purple twilight.

People asked him how he did it: survive all those conditions in far-flung locations. He chuckled to himself. The trick was to pretend that what you'd gotten, and where you were, was exactly what you had wanted in the first place.

His smile faded. Laura used to say his optimistic, fun-loving attitude was a mask for his fear of deeper intimacy. He shifted in his chair. He didn't see it like that. People liked to smile, laugh. Besides, he was capable of being serious.

His phone vibrated on the teak coffee

table beside his canvas deck chair. He opened one eye.

It buzzed again.

He opened both eyes and glanced at it. One of his cameramen, Bryce. Jake better respond. He read Bryce's text. *Great idea about the lost flag. I'm totally on board for that. Was just tossing some research leads back and forth with one of our writers, and she came across this video.*

Bryce had attached a link. Jake scrolled to it. Hmm. Looked like it was from an organization called the Women of the American Revolution Museum, based in New York City. He cocked his head. He'd never heard of it, and he'd spent a fair amount of time in New York at one point.

He tapped the screen and the video played.

After the short clip ended, he couldn't help but spend a moment longer than necessary looking at the woman who'd delivered the museum fundraising message.

Big green eyes. Long, glossy dark-brown hair. She looked like an actress. She'd delivered her lines well, too. And something about the intelligence in her eyes tugged at him...

He rubbed the back of his neck. It'd been a year since Laura had broken things off with him. He hadn't met anyone since who'd caught his interest. But now...? His pulse thudded. Was he actually ready to start dating again?

His lips curved up in a smile as he looked at the women's image a moment more—he'd certainly noticed *her*. She seemed to love history as much as he did. Knew her facts, too. And gorgeous, to boot... Maybe this was an indication he was ready, after all.

He brought up Bryce's text and typed a reply. *Interesting video, man. Thanks for sending it along. I can see how she might have some insight into 355. Could be an interesting layer to add to our episode. Twenty-nine days and counting.* He added the crossed fingers emoticon and then hit send.

He tried not to let worry gnaw at his gut as he put his phone back down and settled again into his deck chair. What was he going to do if the show tanked and really did get taken off the air?

He had to admit, the sense of job security it had given him had been a huge relief after such a long time doing bit parts and shampoo commercials. He'd gotten a lucky break, as they said in the business.

But after he'd landed that host position on the Travel Channel, the show's funding got cut and he'd been out of a job two seasons in. Was the past repeating itself here?

He took another sip of his drink and watched the pinks and purples of sunset fade into the water.

This new episode had to be phenomenal.

Would they be able to find enough information, get enough solid leads, interview enough experts to tie things all together in an exciting and interesting way for viewers?

He took another sip of his drink. It really had to be compelling. He wasn't sure that just a flag would be captivating enough...

The question was, what would be?

FRIDAY EVENING, VANESSA sighed in relief

as she stepped into her apartment and slipped out of her black patent leather ballet flats.

She rubbed her feet for a moment, glad to be able to stop rushing around—at least for a little while. Doing all that research on the venue had really gobbled up a lot of energy and time today.

But she wouldn't be getting much sleep this weekend. She had to put in a good chunk of hours over Saturday and Sunday, what with the gala stuff and Kali's additional workload now shifted to her. For tonight, though, she could let herself relax a bit.

She flicked on the lights and padded barefoot across the faded pink hall throw rug and into her kitchen.

The black and white linoleum was cool under her feet. She rummaged around in her apartment-sized fridge and surveyed the options. Half a case of lemon-lime soda. Tuna casserole leftovers. And that box of Pad Thai she'd picked up for lunch and already eaten half of.

She opted for the tuna casserole and also took out a block of cheese. She grated it on top of the tuna before she popped it into the microwave. Friday night and she was here in her apartment. Alone yet again. What had happened to her love life?

She hadn't really dated since Eric. But all at once, she found herself remembering the good times with him.

Those first few months where everything seemed golden, untouchable. That sparkle in his eyes every time he'd looked at her. How she'd cuddled into the warmth of his arm around her shoulder as they'd sat on her couch over there and watched the pilot episode of *Passport to Romance & Relics*.

Her eyes strayed to her sofa.

He'd said the show hadn't really been his thing, and she'd pretended to be fine with that. But she'd secretly been disappointed.

She'd guiltily really wished he'd been a bit more like... Jake Ford. Her lips quirked up at the thought. Not that she had any idea what the TV host was like in real life, of course, she reminded herself.

But Eric hadn't been someone with an adventurous spirit. She wished he'd been able to display a bit more courage, had a bit more willingness to step outside his comfort zone, believe in his convictions passionately. Instead, he'd been a homebody content to color inside the lines.

She sighed as the microwave beeped and she rummaged for a fork in the silverware drawer. She sat down at the kitchen table and began to eat.

Maybe she'd just been dating the wrong type of man?

She winced as she took another forkful of tuna. Then again, the breakup wasn't entirely Eric's fault. She did have the tendency to get caught up in her work; put on professional blinders, so to speak. More than one guy in her past told her she overanalyzed things. Obsessed a bit much over details. And while those traits were necessary for her job, she knew they weren't so helpful in her romantic relationships.

She moved a noodle around with her fork. Maybe she'd been too hard on Eric, expected him to be more than what he could give? Or maybe they'd just never been right for each other after all.

She took another bite. She couldn't bring herself to settle, so it was probably easier to just be single.

But was it, really? She was only in her thirties. Surely someone out there in the world would appreciate a woman who thought things through, and would share her interest in history.

Make that a deep love of history. That's why she'd gone into museum studies, after all.

Vanessa's undergrad degree in linguistics came from New York University—she hadn't been happy with any of the college programs back home in Kansas—but then she'd ended up surprising herself with wanting to get a masters.

So she'd chosen museum studies because she'd always been passionate about history. But how was it *her* fault if men found her intelligence intimidating?

She stabbed a stray noodle with her fork. The last straw with Eric was when he'd forgotten to show up for the very first exhibit she'd designed and curated herself. Even though she'd reminded him twice and he *knew* how important it'd been to her. He'd claimed he'd mixed up the dates of her exhibit with his 'sure thing big role' audition.

She shook her head and pushed aside

those thoughts. She didn't *need* any man in her life. She was just fine on her own. Independent. Free. She lifted her chin. Yes. There was absolutely nothing wrong with her just because she didn't have a date tonight. She wasn't alone. She had friends. Family. A good job. And maybe that in itself was cause for a bit of celebration, so why not dress up tonight?

She smiled to herself as she finished her dinner and sent a text to Melissa. *Dress up! Thirty minutes to go before the show starts.*

She put her dishes in the dishwasher then headed into her bedroom.

She rummaged through her clothes and pulled out a teal dress that still had the tags on. She slipped into the dress and pulled on a pair of silver matte heels.

She went over to her jewelry box. It sat on the marble-topped dresser she'd gotten for free from the sidewalk when the upstairs neighbors moved out. She pulled out the strand of jet beads her mother had given her. Hmm. Now where was that set of earrings that went with it?

She rummaged around in the top compartment where she kept all her earrings. It was a bit of a jumble. Really sometime she should straighten it all out. Oh, there they were. She picked the pair up but a few others had gotten tangled together with them, including a pair of two-tier garnet drop earrings, which had a row of diamonds between the garnet drop and the base.

The garnet earrings had been a birthday present from her grandmother years ago. As she disentangled the mess, the garnet earrings fell onto the marble dresser with a clatter, and began to roll across the smooth surface.

But before she could scoop them up, her apartment buzzer sounded. That'd be Melissa.

She dashed out of her bedroom as she slipped in the jet earrings, and answered the door.

"I brought popcorn, like I promised," Melissa said. She had on a mauve wrap dress. "Oh, and I brought some chocolate brownies too—freshly baked."

"Mmm, smells delicious. Thanks—come on in. You're right on time. I'll get the drinks. Let me just turn on the TV."

A minute later, Vanessa returned with

a drink tray and took a seat on the couch beside her friend. "Love your dress, by the way."

"Thanks. Sample sale in the garment district my brother told me about. He texted me during a lull in the stakeout he was on in the area. But you didn't hear that bit of hush-hush info from me."

"Nice."

The show hadn't quite started yet, so Vanessa turned down the volume on the current commercial. She chewed on a cuticle for a second before she finally blurted, "Do I overanalyze things?"

"That's a question out of left field," Melissa said as she reached for the bowl of popcorn on the coffee table in front of the couch.

She finished the handful of popcorn she'd grabbed before she said, "Don't tell me. You've been moping around up here feeling sorry for yourself and wondering where all the good men are."

Vanessa sighed. "Guess I'm letting stress get the better of me." She rubbed the tight spot at the base of her neck. "My boss just took an emergency leave of absence and now I'm pretty much running the place. I'm excited about the opportunity but kind of stressed about it too."

"I can understand that. But I mean, think how stressful finishing your masters' was. And then job hunting. And then your first few years at the museum adjusting to the job role. And you nailed all of it."

"You're right. Thanks for that reminder. Guess I'm just over-thinking things again," she joked.

"Aww." Melissa leaned over and gave her friend a quick hug. "You've been thinking about Eric again, haven't you?"

Vanessa opened her mouth to protest but Melissa crossed her arms. "If anything, Eric wasn't deep enough for you. He didn't really know you. He was so busy worrying about his image as a rising star—" she rolled her eyes—"that he couldn't see what he was neglecting: you. Don't worry. You'll find the right man."

She nodded at the TV. "Ooo, it's starting. Time for some eye candy."

Vanessa secretly couldn't help agreeing—her stomach tingled every time the opening credit montage rolled.

Tonight was no exception when she saw that glint of adventure captured in the close-up of Jake Ford's blue-green eyes moments before he dove, shirtless, from the top of a waterfall in the jungles of Ecuador.

The music swelled.

Vanessa couldn't help but admire the strong muscled lines of his back before the camera panned out and then cut to the next scenes in the show's opening sequence.

Jake driving an open-top Jeep across the Sahara, looking all serious and sexy in his dark aviator sunglasses. Jake landing a helicopter on a glacier in the Arctic Circle. Jake grinning like a kid at Christmas as he plucked a gold coin from a sandy cave floor in Jamaica and exclaiming, "That's amazing!" to an archaeologist beside him.

With one more grin for the camera, Jake's face faded from the screen and the *Passport to Romance & Relics* logo came on right before it went to commercial again.

Melissa gave a happy sigh. "He's just so delicious to look at, isn't he?"

"Mmm." Vanessa made herself sound non-committal. If Melissa found out the size of her crush, she'd never hear the end of it. But the show was more than that—it was a way to see places in the world she'd never been.

"You know," Melissa said after she took a sip of her drink, "I read a blog article just yesterday about how he's been voted Sexiest TV Host of the Year."

"Really?"

"Yep." Melissa grinned at Vanessa. "A bit over half the show's viewers are women in their 30s and 40s." She paused. Frowned. "But I'm a bit worried about the show's future. It also mentioned the ratings really tanked on this season finale. I don't know why, though. I *love* this show."

The last commercial ended and the season finale began.

MELISSA LEFT A couple hours later.

After Vanessa squeezed in another hour of work on her laptop, she yawned and shut her laptop lid. Time for bed at last.

She got out her striped pajama shorts and matching top, but then saw she'd left her jewelry box lid open and went over to her dresser to close it.

But as she did, her bare toes nudged against something smooth and cool on the floor. She glanced down and frowned. Oh no—the garnet earrings. Must have rolled off the dresser when she'd gone to answer the door earlier in the evening. She bent over to pick up the jewelry.

But as she did, the large garnet drop disconnected itself from the earbob.

Grandma wouldn't be too happy with her. She winced. These earrings were how old? She didn't really know. Grandma had said something about getting them from an estate sale in the Hamptons.

Vanessa studied the broken earring. The piece was somewhat unique. There was a tiny metal loop at the bottom of the garnet drop where a second gemstone could be attached, to create two tiers of jewels. But she'd never had the second tier.

She sighed. Where was she going to find someone to fix the earring? She carefully scooped it up. She didn't know any antique jewelry repair shops but in a place like New York, she surely could find someone to—

What was that? She frowned as she cupped the two broken pieces in her palm.

HIDDEN TREASURE OF THE HEART

That was strange. It looked like...

She nudged the garnet drop with a fingertip. The inside was hollow.

She carefully picked up the hollowed-out jewel and looked inside. What on Earth? The smallest scrap of...was that paper?... had been curled up inside.

She rushed to the kitchen as her heart pounded, and grabbed a pair of tweezers from her bathroom. Then she slipped on her preservation gloves, too.

She took the earring over to the lamp by the kitchen table to see it better, and carefully inserted the tweezers into the small cavity.

She held her breath as she very gently tugged out the piece of yellowed paper.

She placed it on the plastic bagging that she still had set out, and whether moments or minutes passed, she wasn't sure, as she lost herself in the precise set of steps needed to unfurl the page.

At last, she grabbed a magnifying glass from that same kitchen drawer where she kept her gloves, and peered at the small, neat lines of script.

It took her a bit of time to discern the words. The writing had badly faded and smeared, as if someone hadn't waited for the ink to dry before rolling up the slip of paper.

"First taste of love is bittersweet
when between those lines
secrets do not retreat."

Vanessa's breath hitched as she quietly mouthed the words to herself.

Some sort of rhyming verse. A poem? Her heart sped up. But what if...it was a riddle?

She shook her head at herself. She was getting ahead of herself. But that didn't stop the speculations that whirled through her mind as she stared at the words on the tiny scrap of paper.

JAKE FROWNED AT the computer screen and sighed. He sat back in the dark red leather office chair and laced his fingers behind his head.

He liked to come to the studio think. With the show wrapped, he had a bit of time to figure out the game plan—but not that much time. He winced as his eyes darted to the wall calendar. He had less than a month to figure out how to provide what his boss, Sara, and the network, wanted.

Not that the flag story in itself wasn't compelling, but he wasn't sure that would be enough to keep audiences around. They had to be glued to their sets, what with the show's fate hanging in the balance here.

His shoulders tensed as he stared up at the ceiling. Well, the flag was a *historical* treasure, so that was something.

Thing was, even if he did his damnedest and came up with the perfect episode, that was no guarantee it'd be a success with viewers.

He opened one of the drawers on the lower half of the desk and rummaged around until he found a feather duster.

Dusting helped him think. He picked up the yellow-feathered plastic duster.

He turned to the knickknack shelf behind him. As he dusted carved soapstone boxes from India, tribal masks from Kenya and an antique globe on a stand from who knew where, his shoulders relaxed and his mind drifted back to that flag. The needle and thimble. Robert Townsend.

Hmm. Since the needle and thimble had been in the Townsend family's possession, the first logical step in his own research should be to look them up. Get some background. He could also draft a reply to the sender of that email... But first, research.

See? Dusting—always helped.

He headed back to his wide-display desktop computer and brought up the search engine.

He clicked on Wikipedia. Looked like Robert Townsend owned a store in what was now Lower Manhattan. Also seemed the Townsend family had been in the New York area for several generations, and were friends with prominent Long Island families.

Jake finished the online encyclopedia entry and turned back to the rest of the results. About halfway down the page, a headline caught his eye:

Townsend and Culper Ring Connected to Lost Pearls?

A surge of adrenaline shot through him. That feeling of discovery just *never* got old.

But then he sternly reminded himself that this could be something that meant nothing. So many hoaxes and fakes out there.

A while back, there'd been a social media fight between a few loyal fans of the show and some Internet trolls who'd claimed *Passport to Romance & Relics* had been just one big fake from beginning to end.

Jake shook his head. The show wasn't faked. Good thing that had died down in about a day.

He held his breath as he clicked on the link.

> *Robert Townsend, a member of the secret spy ring created by George Washington, may have had a few secrets of his own while he worked for Washington during the American Revolution.*
>
> *The shopkeeper, who also worked as a reporter for James Rivington's newspaper called* The Royal Gazette, *had prime opportunity to pass information to his general, because the occupying British frequented the shop*

for everything from buttons to boot laces.

Jake kept reading.

Not only did British soldiers frequent it, but also aristocratic Loyalists came by who wanted to buy ribbon and lace for their latest fashions, or purchase a ream of writing paper.

In fact, Townsend himself would use sheets of blank paper from his own stock to write secret letters in invisible ink. These would be easily overlooked by the British checkpoints into and out of the city, thus able to pass safely on to Washington. His sister Sally also helped her brother in the shop.

But was Townsend's place of business also the intended destination for a cache of priceless pearls earmarked for the patriot cause?

After all, his shop was located on Peck's Slip at the waterfront, and the pearls had supposedly been carried by a French ship.

For some time, Washington had

been in talks with France about sending aid. The Thirteen Colonies lacked arms and monies that European countries like France had in more abundance. But up to that point, Washington had not been successful. Finally, though, Louis XVI agreed to Washington's plea.

But the aid came from an unexpected source. The king of France had, several months prior to Washington's asking for aid, received a cache of large pearls from the Maharaja of India as a diplomatic gift. Louis XVI had planned to distribute these among the favored members of his own court, but decided instead that he would send them on to the patriots, as a gesture of not only good will but also because he knew that the patriots could use the cache to monetize their efforts.

However, after Louis XVI had them loaded as cargo aboard a French frigate bound for the Colonies, they never made it into the hands of General Washington. All trace of the cache vanished from the pages of history.

Were they stolen by pirates? Did the British use them for their own ends? Or maybe they never left France after all...

We might never know the full story. But one thing's for certain: if anyone found those pearls today, their connection to the Culper ring, and to American history, means they'd be worth millions.

Jake's lips quirked. Worth millions, huh? Would these pearls be worth millions of ratings, too? His heart pounded as he scanned the article again.

Hmm. Sally Townsend worked at her brother's shop. Would the Townsend descendant know anything about the lost pearls angle? It couldn't hurt to ask, while they were there about the flag. And if there *was* something more to this whole pearls thing, the viewers would be eager to watch his hunt to find out.

He dug out his phone from a buttoned cargo pocket on his khaki pants and dialed Sara. "Hey, how's it going? Just found a really compelling angle that could tie in perfectly for this flag episode. Robert Townsend and his sister are even involved."

"Send me the link."

Jake did.

"I see what you're talking about. This is perfect."

"This sort of intrigue's the kind of thing the network loves. And the lost jewels angle—okay, lost pearls—would be a big draw for the core female viewership."

"You're completely right. Let's add it in. I'll brief the network execs."

Jake's adrenaline spiked as he hung up. What if he could actually *find* this pearl cache? He'd not only skyrocket the show's ratings, but he also just might get to realize a long-held dream to find lost treasure...

Monday afternoon, Vanessa stood up and stretched as she took a sip from her now-cold coffee.

She made a face and headed to the bathroom to pour it down the sink. It had helped her push through with all this work, but she should probably stop drinking so much caffeine.

She returned to her desk and sat down again. She smoothed down the skirt of her pink striped cotton dress, and studied the spreadsheet she had on part of her screen.

She massaged her temples. At least she'd finally managed to get the venue all lined up in Morristown for the gala spot and had texted Kali about that. The video had gone over nicely, too, and the tickets were selling well.

She'd also reassured her boss that she'd been able to contact existing ticket holders and alert them to the venue location change.

She worried her bottom lip between her teeth. But now it was time to make a last push for more buzz. She'd schedule some more social media posts with the change in venue location and send out a last round of press releases stating the same.

She exhaled slowly as she checked the small desk calendar to the right of her laptop. A week and a half to go before the event.

She allowed a brief smile to flit across her face as a sense of accomplishment filled her. Something else she loved about her job: the reward of tiny little tasks that added up to giant results.

Now she just had to sell the remainder of the tickets, and finalize items for the silent auction. She pulled up her design software and was in the middle of looking for stock photos of Martha Washington when her desk telephone rang.

"Hello, Women of the American Revolution Museum, Vanessa speaking. How can I help you?"

A deep male voice came through the receiver. "Hi Vanessa. My name's Jake Ford. I'm co-producer of a television show called *Passport to Romance & Relics.*"

Vanessa's eyes widened, her throat constricted and her pulse pounded as the phone fell from her grip.

She snatched up the handset again, took a calming breath that did nothing to stop the wild beating of her heart as she said, "Uh, Mr. Ford, um, hello. I'm a fa—I mean, I've heard of the series."

"Well, that's one thing that's easier for me, then. Don't have to explain what we do."

"Right." Vanessa nodded, even though

she knew he couldn't see her. She cleared her throat. "So. What, um, can I help you with?"

"I saw your video about female spies' role in the War of Independence."

"Oh, did you?" Despite herself, Vanessa's voice came out higher-pitched than normal.

"Mmm-hmm. Listen, I'm calling because my writers and I have been gathering research and well, I'll get straight to the point. We want to interview you for an upcoming episode."

Vanessa frowned. "I'm sorry, but why?"

"Oh," Jake chuckled. "The episode we're working on is about an early American flag that might have been sewn by Agent 355."

Vanessa drew in a sharp breath and leaned forward.

"Not only that, we've found a possible connection between the Culper spy ring and a lost pearl cache."

"A lost pearl cache?" Vanessa sat back in her seat. "I wouldn't know where to find it."

"Don't worry, that's my job," Jake said.

"Your expertise is female spies, yeah?"

"Well, I wouldn't say expertise, exactly. But I am working on an exhibit about them, yes." Her mind flashed back to that letter from 355. Since Jake Ford had been doing research on the Culper spies, he might have information about 355 she didn't. If he did, he might be willing to share. And then that might add to the exhibit as a whole...

"Right. We figure that since Agent 355 was the Culpers' female spy, you'd be a perfect addition to our interviewee list for the episode."

"Oh." Vanessa swallowed again. "You mean in front of a camera? On TV?"

"Sure do."

Vanessa's palms grew clammy, and several moments of silence passed. She cleared her throat.

"Your museum is one of the only specialty museums on this sort of thing," Jake added.

"It's not exactly *my* museum," Vanessa blurted. Why was she all awkward right now? She winced. Maybe it was the fact she was talking with her secret celebrity crush. Her cheeks reddened.

Jake chuckled. "Figure of speech. I think you know what I mean." He paused. "My team's already in New York, setting up some preliminaries with another source. I know it's *extremely* short notice, but if you would possibly be available tomorrow, that would be phenomenal. We're working under a, uh, limited time horizon with this episode."

Vanessa drummed her fingers on the table. That was really soon, but in addition to the 355 angle, this was an unbelievable opportunity for more media exposure, what with the gala coming up. And the more media exposure, the more likely those remaining gala tickets would sell.

But her stomach clenched. Could she actually go on camera again? Her pulse sped at the thought. She couldn't just...speak to millions of people. The show reached so many and what if she screwed up? What if she made everyone look bad? What if people thought—

No. She straightened her shoulders. It wasn't about what people thought. It was for the greater good of history, of the museum. And if she could somehow contribute in some small way to that cause, then who was she to refuse when asked?

"All right, Jake. I'll do it."

"Perfect. Thank you so much. My production assistant will send you the details."

Chapter Three

BREATHE. ALL SHE had to do was breathe, Vanessa told herself on Tuesday morning.

She resisted the urge to wipe her sweaty palms yet again on the sides of her powder-blue skirt suit as she paced back and forth in the museum's tiny foyer.

This was such a bad idea. But Kali had loved it when Vanessa'd told her boss Jake's proposition. Kali saw the potential, too, and had agreed this would help raise the museum's profile, and hopefully, the gala profits, as well.

Vanessa took a shaky breath and watched the door. Her heels clicked as she paced faster. What was she thinking? What was she doing? She couldn't—Jake Ford—the show—this was *crazy*.

Okay, so maybe she was overreacting a little. If she kept calm and acted normal, took more deep breaths, everything would be fine. Right?

She really should've asked Melissa to be here with her. Her phone buzzed with her deadline alarm and she jumped. Five minutes before the crew got here.

She started to worry at her bottom lip and then realized she would probably smudge her lipstick, so she made herself stop.

She glanced again at the door and then at the clock. She had a few seconds to make a few more minor adjustments to her hairstyle. But before she could move, the door chime sounded.

Vanessa's heart leapt to her throat. But she made herself take a final deep breath before she opened the front door.

A short woman with curly hair stood on the doorstep. "Hi, I'm Nadine, the production assistant for *Passport to Romance & Relics*. You must be Vanessa." She had a headset around her neck and a clipboard in hand.

"I am. Come on in." Vanessa ignored the ping of disappointment that Jake hadn't been on the step. "I'll just prop the door open and you guys can get all set up."

"Perfect."

Vanessa's gaze darted to the bathroom, just off the front room. Now was her chance.

She crossed the room in a few quick strides and went inside. She never spent long in places quite this small—the tiny, cramped space made her a bit nervous.

She took a calming breath, smoothed some loose strands away from her face and splashed her wrists with some cool water from the tap. She met her own gaze in the mirror. Okay. Things were fine. Going to be great, in fact.

She took a final deep breath, opened the bathroom door and—"Oof!"—bumped into a solid male chest.

"Oops, sorry about that. Thought this was the break room."

There he was. Mere inches away. Jake Ford.

She froze, wide-eyed, her mouth suddenly dry.

There was an apologetic look in Jake's blue-green gaze, and her heart tripped. The television screen didn't do justice to the way his broad shoulders filled out that sand-colored safari shirt. Or how his dark

lashes—

"Hope I didn't startle you badly enough to take too many years off your life."

"Oh." She laughed. He was taller in real life than on TV. Must be nearly 6'2"? His head practically brushed the ceiling. Then again, in all these 18th century houses, the ceilings were pretty low. Why was her mind spitting out all these random useless facts right now?

She needed to get herself together.

Tingles swept through her. She did her best to push them away. They wouldn't do her any good, and distractions like this were definitely not professional.

She cleared her throat. She needed to be strong. In control. "No. It's fine." She took a big step around Jake and into the center of the room, which was rapidly filling up with cameras and other equipment, along with several people who must be part of his team.

She avoided making eye contact with Jake as she addressed the room. "Hi, everyone. I'm Vanessa. Just let me know what you need me to do and I'll be happy to accommodate you. Bathroom's to the right there and the break room's just down the hallway here." She indicated behind her and couldn't help but notice the faint sparkle of amusement in Jake's eyes when she said break room.

Her own lips twitched for a second but she compressed them and looked at everyone else expectantly.

People nodded. Someone began to set up a series of lights and some other pieces of equipment that Vanessa couldn't identify.

Coffee. Surely people would like some coffee as they worked? She knew she needed some. If not for the caffeine boost then for the distraction.

She looked at Jake, who was now across the room in a conversation with someone who she assumed must be one of the camera men. She wasn't avoiding him. He was just...busy. Right. Exactly. She approached Nadine, who now wore her headset and a bright smile.

"Would you or any of your crew like any coffee?"

"Oh, that's nice of you. Thanks."

"Great, I'll put on a fresh pot."

With a quiet sigh of relief, she headed down the hall. This was for the museum, she reminded herself, as she reached past the single-cup pod coffeemaker, and dug out the coffee pot from a cupboard. Then she went through the motions of prepping a pot. For the sake of preserving history. She didn't have to feel nervous or—

"Oh, good," Jake said, as he stepped into the room, phone in hand. "Coffee's just what I need." His phone pinged and he scrolled down the screen.

Vanessa tamped down a flicker of irritation. No, Jake wasn't Eric. But a memory of her ex surfaced anyway. She'd gone with him to auditions from time to time as moral support and all he'd done was ask her to fetch and carry: his costume, his hairbrush, his hair gel.

He'd been on his phone practically the whole time, too. Barely even said two words to her. It was all about him. How hadn't she seen how self-centered Eric'd been? Because she'd *thought* she'd been in love.

Her jaw tightened. Well, she wasn't going to make that same mistake again and allow herself to even think about being attracted to another actor. Television crushes were one thing. Real life, quite another.

She took a breath. Jake was just making a comment. Just being friendly.

"Me too," she admitted, and waved her hand at the machine. "Helps calm my nerves."

He took the coffee pot and began pouring the steaming liquid into the mugs Vanessa had set out. As he did, he glanced around. "Great atmosphere you've got here. All this exposed stonework."

She couldn't help but grin at his enthusiasm. "Thanks. Yeah. This was actually a wealthy merchant's house from the 18th century." He poured the final cup. She picked it up.

He met her gaze as he leaned against the counter near her. "Oh yeah?" He rubbed a hand across his stubble.

Her pulse jumped at the raspy sound. "We don't know who owned it back then." She waved a hand, and almost spilled the coffee cup she held. "Could've been anyone, really. I mean, who knows, right?" Okay, she was babbling. She cleared her throat. She needed to stop it and be professional. "Frankly," she took a breath, "I haven't had time to look into its full history, but we're pretty sure this part is basically the last original bit of the house." She pointed to the area near the sink, and found herself enjoying the chance to talk about the building itself. "But it's looked better. We're still waiting for a masonry person to fix the loose stone by the sink here. Seems like we put it on the bottom of the list, though, what with all this other stuff we've had to do. The fundraising. The gala organizing."

"And your spies exhibit," Jake added.

"Right," Vanessa smiled. "The spies exhibit. Which is what you're here to talk to me about." She swallowed and twisted the mug around in her hands.

"Hey," he said, and his voice dipped a little lower, into a more serious tone, and Vanessa couldn't help the tingle that slid up her spine at the timbre. "I remember I was so nervous the very first time I went on air. You'll be fine."

That was nice of him. "Thanks." She squared her shoulders. "I've done this once before already, so I'm sure I will be."

"So. Whenever you're ready, I think we're all set up out there." He jerked a thumb over his shoulder.

"Right." She took a quick sip of her coffee then followed him out into the hallway and back to the main room.

Everything had been set up. In fact, it looked pretty similar to the video setup for the fundraiser.

She felt her shoulders relax. Maybe this would even be...fun?

JAKE TOOK A deep breath and held it for a moment as Bryce gave the three, two, one countdown. But as the red light blinked on, a surge of excitement zipped through him like it always did and he began to talk.

"So, Vanessa, you're the assistant curator with the Women of the American Revolution Museum. I'd actually never even heard of a place like this before we started researching this episode, so that's great. I love to learn new things."

He grinned and met Vanessa's eyes. That green was much more compelling up close compared to when he'd watched her on his phone screen. He pushed away that thought. Focus on the questions. Focus on the topic.

She adjusted her skirt and Jake couldn't help flicking his gaze to her long legs as she crossed and then re-crossed her ankles. "That's right. We're actually a fairly new museum and started operations two years ago. We only just recently moved into this house about a month ago."

"I can see why. It's got some great historical details. And it's from the 18th century." He paused as a thought struck him. "Hey, maybe this house could be connected with the Culpers. It's in the right spot—Lower Manhattan—after all."

Vanessa's eyes widened a moment, and he thought he detected a flicker of panic at the off-the-cuff question, but she recovered herself quickly. "I never really thought about that. But," she laughed, "maybe so? I mean, you're right. This house *was* here during the British occupation of New York."

"Speaking of the Revolution, we're looking into one of its historical mysteries. I mentioned to you earlier we've found reference to an early American flag that might have been sewn by Agent 355. So, what can you tell people about her?"

"Not much." Vanessa laughed. "Not

even her name. 355 simply means "a lady," according to the Culper codebook, developed by Colonel Benjamin Tallmadge. He assigned numbers between 1 and 765 to various people, places and things. But it's speculated 355 was a member of New York high society, and probably from a Loyalist family, since New York at the time was more Loyalist than Patriot."

"I hadn't realized that."

Vanessa nodded. "While 355's one of the women featured in the exhibit I'm working on, there were other female patriots who played a role in the Revolution."

"Right. Everyone hears all the time about men like Paul Revere, but there isn't as much notoriety around the women, is there?"

Vanessa shook her head. "Back then, spying was considered too dangerous for women. But," Vanessa spread her hands, "that error in judgment was a benefit, because it gave women opportunities to obtain information in ways men didn't or couldn't. British troops often billeted in Colonial households, and while women went about their daily lives, they also picked up bits of useful information to pass along."

"The whole hiding in plain sight thing," Jake said.

"Exactly." Vanessa grinned. "Though sometimes it was just plain hiding. One part of this exhibit will feature a woman named Lydia Darragh. She lived in Philadelphia during the war. In December of 1777, British troops who lived in her house had a secret meeting. She hid inside a closet and overheard their plan to surprise Washington's army at White Marsh. After their meeting, she went out under the guise of delivering flour to a nearby mill. But really, she passed on what she'd learned."

"That's so interesting. I can see why you'd feel the need for an exhibit like this," Jake said. "But going back to Agent 355 and the Culpers for a minute." He leaned forward and caught a hint of Vanessa's floral perfume; it smelled like sweet pea and—He couldn't get sidetracked. "We think there's a possible connection between the Culper spy ring and a lost pearl cache."

"Oh?" Vanessa re-crossed her ankles.

"Is that a story you've come across in your research about female spies in the Revolution?"

She tilted her head. "Actually, no. I've never heard about that at all. But there's certainly quite a bit that could be discovered."

Jake leaned forward. Vanessa didn't seem to be humoring him; Laura certainly hadn't been so open-minded. "So you think it's possible?"

She studied him a moment. "I suppose you could say anything's possible."

"Well put." For a moment, he forgot the next question he was going to ask. Right. Okay. Needed to focus. He cleared his throat. "What's your view on something like the lost pearls?"

"I mean," Vanessa said, "the Culper ring had serious business with helping Washington re-take New York and win the war. What would they want pearls for?"

"That's the thing, though," Jake countered, with a look at the camera then back to Vanessa. "From what I've read, the ring supposedly was going to use the cache to raise funds for the war effort."

Vanessa waved a hand. "Folklore like that is the enemy of solid historic evidence and research."

"I thought you said anything was possible."

"I just don't know how probable it is."

Vanessa's words caused a twinge of disappointment to streak through Jake. But maybe he was taking her comment too personally. With all his TV experience, he should've just been able to shrug it off. But somehow, coming from her...

"The show makes every effort to research the facts," Jake said, careful to keep his tone light. "We talk to as many experts and primary sources as possible to make sure we're as accurate as we can be."

Vanessa's eyes narrowed a fraction of a second before she straightened her spine and replied, "Well, it's my job to make sure that history is taken seriously, and that means taking my work seriously." She said it with a smile for the camera but Jake knew he'd crossed a line.

"Of course," he said, but he could tell it'd done little good. Damn. He hadn't meant to insult her.

As the camera's red light blinked off, Vanessa's shoulders stiffened even more. She did her best to avoid eye contact with Jake. Did he not take history seriously? She pursed her lips and looked at him from the corner of her eye. Maybe he was more treasure hunter than historian.

She stood then glanced at the clock above the stone fireplace. At least they'd be gone in twenty minutes. Then she could get back to her normal routine...

She headed over to her desk, which was tucked into an alcove by the stairway that led to the seldom-used second floor. She needed to put up a few more social media posts about the remaining gala tickets, and then she'd be able to turn her attention back to her somewhat-neglected female spies exhibit.

Guilt nipped at her. Really, that was what Jake had interviewed her about. The least she could do was finish the exhibit planning so she could move on to the next phase in the exhibition process.

Besides that, she also wanted to find out who'd sent that letter to her mailing address.

Hmm. Melissa's brother worked for the FBI, so maybe if she asked Melissa to ask him, he'd be able to trace the letter?

But before she could log on to her computer, Jake approached. She stood and lifted her chin.

"Listen." Jake rubbed the side of his neck. "I think we got off on the wrong foot."

The open, relaxed—and somewhat rueful—expression on Jake's face made some of the tightness in Vanessa's shoulders ease.

"Our signals might've gotten a little crossed." Her lips quirked. "What else can I do for you?" she said, careful to keep her tone professional.

"Forgive me?" Jake's blue-green gaze studied her with a questioning look.

But just as she opened her mouth to respond, there was a scuffling noise followed by a heavy thud, and then a muffled round of swearing.

Vanessa's eyes snapped to the direction of the sound.

She walked quickly down the hall, barely noticing Jake right behind her. She peered around the doorway of the break room.

One of the two camera men looked up from the pile of mortar and dust. A chunk of stone lay on the floor by the sink.

He pulled a face as he looked from Vanessa to Jake behind her. "I swear I didn't do it on purpose. I was just grabbing a glass of water from the sink here and I banged my elbow against the wall. Must have jostled something because the next moment, this was all on the floor." He twisted his mouth and gestured to the rubble.

"That's okay, Bryce." Jake nodded toward Vanessa. "It's what we have insurance for." He turned back to Bryce. "No worries, man." Jake clapped the other man on the shoulder.

Vanessa added, "That's been loose for awhile. Now we have the perfect reason to bug the masonry company to hurry up." She headed to the dusty piece of stone and bent to pick it up. "Let's just put it back for now as best we can."

She walked over to the hole in the wall with the piece of stone in her hand, and started to put the piece of stone back but paused and frowned.

It looked like a whitish yellow piece of cloth in there... It blended in with the mortar dust, and sat in a narrow gap behind where the stone had worked loose.

She reached a hand out and her fingertips brushed the brittle cloth. It looked like muslin. Very old muslin.

"Look at that," Jake murmured as he came to stand next to her.

Vanessa met his gaze, and as their eyes locked, she felt tingles zip up her spine. "This must've been here for..."

Jake raised his brows. "...centuries?" A corner of his mouth lifted, and something about his expression made Vanessa's stomach flip. Oh. This was exactly the same expression he wore when she saw him on the show every week.

Except—her breath caught—it was happening right now, to her, in real life.

She exhaled slowly and realized neither she nor Jake had broken eye contact. From behind them, Bryce cleared his throat.

Jake blinked rapidly and looked like he'd just come back from somewhere far away...alone with her.

Vanessa's cheeks warmed.

"I think we should get a camera on this, Bryce," Jake said.

"Got it." The other man left the room to retrieve his gear.

"So we shouldn't touch anything yet?" Vanessa lowered her voice to a whisper as she looked from Jake to whatever it was wrapped in cloth.

He nodded. "Probably a good idea. Keep as much drama on the screen as possible. Works best, especially for people who aren't in showbiz, to get initial reactions."

"But how do you know this is even anything?"

Jake shrugged. "Best policy to film first and ask questions later."

Vanessa's brows rose.

"Kidding, kidding," Jake lifted his hands, palm up. "I just meant that it's a good idea to get things on film even if we don't end up using them. Because if we don't have something, we can't really go back and re-discover it for the first time."

"Oh. Right."

Bryce had come back into the room and Jake glanced at Vanessa. "Ready?"

She nodded. Jake gave Bryce the word

and with a subtle nod, indicated Vanessa should go ahead and lift out the packet.

She closed her fingers carefully over the yellowed cloth and pulled it out.

"Oh, it feels like..." She put the packet on the kitchen counter and tried to ignore the churn of her stomach as Bryce stepped forward with the camera, no doubt to get a better angle of her.

Under the crumbled strips of cloth Jake reached forward to brush aside, Vanessa saw a dark brown leather cover of some sort of book.

"That's amazing," Jake whispered, his voice low, reverent.

"What's inside?"

"Let's find out."

Vanessa's heart tugged at his enthusiasm. But she put a hand on his arm. "Wait. We need to do this properly. I'll get my gloves, and a pair for you."

Moments later, she returned. Jake slipped on the second pair she gave him. He flashed her a grin, and she couldn't help responding with a grin of her own as they both reached out and, together, opened the book's cover.

"It's not a book," Jake murmured.

"More like some sort of document holder. Looks like there's just one sheet of paper inside. Interesting."

"A piece of history, right here." Jake's blue-green eyes glowed; he looked like he'd just been given an extra helping of cake and ice cream.

Vanessa caught a whiff of his cologne—something like sandalwood—as Jake leaned in next to her to read the page.

12 December 1779

The Floyds' ballroom was magnificently festooned with holly and garland. 'Twould hardly seem a war is waged, from the opulence within those walls. Indeed, I received a number of compliment from many a British officer on my blue moire gown and ear-bobs — Father is most pleased. But it all paled in comparison to when I met him tonight. For he has set my blood afire.

He spoke with such passion, with his whispered words of liberty and independence, and I cannot forget that; no matter how Father's words of Loyalty to the Crown press upon my mind.

Nay, 'tis my conscience that would smite me if I did not follow my heart, if I did not become part of this quest for freedom, for what is right.

One cannot disregard such things and go blindly on with the status quo. One truly cannot. He has shown me that. How I have begun to care for him, I shall admit nowhere but within these pages, for that is what my heart cannot ignore. No matter the cost. I can compare this to nothing else

I have experienced, save the freedom and wild joy I feel in galloping my mare across open meadows.

Vanessa exhaled a breath she hadn't even realized she'd been holding as she read the final words.

"This is...It's..." Jake exhaled sharply. "Wow."

"I know exactly what you mean." Vanessa's hands started to tremble. "From the date and the first-person account, this seems to be a Revolutionary-era document..."

"But what's it doing hidden behind a loose stone in your break room?"

"Good question." She stared hard at the page.

Vanessa removed her gloves and chewed on a cuticle for a second as she studied the page more carefully; her eyes darted back and forth over the lines.

"I *thought* this handwriting looked familiar. It matches a—" Vanessa paused and shifted her weight as Jake met her gaze, his expression intense "—love letter I have from Agent 355."

Jake glanced at Bryce, who immediately zoomed in for a close-up. He met Vanessa's gaze again. "We need to talk."

Tuesday afternoon, the humidity didn't dampen Jake's mood as he wove his way through a group of Wall Street bankers on the Manhattan sidewalk. "I know, right? That's what she said." Jake couldn't help but feel more than a little tingle of enthusiasm as he relayed his conversation with Vanessa to Sara.

And he knew that tingle had more than a little to do with the fact that a certain assistant curator had agreed to help them out more with this episode.

"Yes," Jake said. "I've arranged for the next interview and we'll be heading there..." he checked his silver Rolex Explorer, "early tomorrow morning. Uh-huh... We've discussed it. Vanessa said she realized that if we pool our resources to see what we can uncover about 355 and her identity, it'll help the museum and this female spy exhibit she's working on, as well as our episode. I also think her own professional curiosity about this love letter and diary entry had something to do with it."

Vanessa.

He couldn't help but remember the way her green eyes had lit with an internal fire as she'd explained her decision. She was so passionate about history, about people's lives from other eras.

He smiled to himself. He could definitely relate. Because that's what history was all about. Uncovering the stories behind the names and dates. Bringing it alive for people today, so that they could see the relevance. Not to mention, she was also willing to believe the pearls might actually be out there...

Whoops. Sara was talking. "What? Oh. Yeah. I mean, who knows? Agent 355 was a Culper. So she might be connected to the pearls, too. Mmm. I've double-checked and our budget will cover the costs. Luckily, Vanessa's boss agreed with her reasoning and gave her permission to come along in an advisory and research capacity. Great. Talk soon."

Jake hung up then slipped his phone into the upper pocket of his safari shirt. Gotten love shirts with so many pockets. A side perk of why he'd become an explorer and adventurer.

But was he, really? Sure, he'd renewed

his membership with The Explorers' Club earlier this year, just like he'd done for the past twelve years, but did that make him on par with Sir Edmund Hillary or Amelia Earhart?

He shook his head. He was just letting his insecurities get out of hand. Of course he was a real explorer like they had been. He'd gotten a degree in the field. He'd gotten the passport stamps.

He veered around a cluster of grade school kids in all-matching navy blue uniforms who giggled over a tablet.

Maybe those cries of *fake* on social media had gotten the better of him? He shouldn't be dwelling on this. It'd happened months ago. Just because someone had accused the show of being fake didn't make it true. It didn't make him a fake, either.

He'd done more exploring and been to more countries than most people would go in their entire lifetimes, he reminded himself. That counted for something. Right?

He sighed as he came to a crosswalk and waited for the light to change. If he was completely honest with himself, he'd noticed these doubts creep in right around the time things began to fall apart between him and Laura.

As if her leaving had something to do with his competency in his career, in his abilities to handle his life.

He shouldn't feel that just because he'd failed at love—he winced at the admission—that he was a failure as a person, too. Of course not. It didn't meant that at all.

He shoved his hands into his pocket and crossed the street. The thump of bass from a passing SUV broke into his thoughts. With effort, he pulled his mind back to current events.

He was supposed to meet Bryce and the rest of the team for a briefing. His pulse quickened. Not only that, Vanessa had promised to bring along a copy of Agent 355's love letter, to compare it with this diary entry they'd uncovered.

Hopefully—he fiddled with some change in his pocket—it would provide some insight. Only twenty-five days left til deadline.

Chapter Four

VANESSA OPENED THE glass door and stepped into the bright, airy coffee shop. She smoothed down her windblown hair as she caught her reflection in one of the floor-to-ceiling windows that gave patrons such a great view of the street in the East Village.

The scent of roasted coffee beans and sugar drifted to her. At least she'd managed to get a bit of work done before she'd come over here. She'd even put up a few more social media posts and sold a few of the remaining gala tickets.

Her social media campaign was gaining traction. At this rate, with the gala only a week away, it was looking as if she'd get them pretty much all sold by the event.

She slipped into line behind someone in neon pink leather shorts and a crop-top argyle sweater.

Granted, it'd taken quite a lot of juggling to balance her work duties with being an advising consultant for the show, but the opportunity was too good to pass up. They'd been able to get an office temp in to cover the daily running of the museum, so that was one less thing to worry about.

She looked into the display case. But she wasn't in the mood for cannolis, even if their golden shells sprinkled with powdered sugar did look tempting. She glanced up at the hand-chalked menu board, where a barista had drawn tiny winged hearts around the flavor of the day. But Vanessa settled on her usual latte.

Kali had been very enthusiastic about the show, which was great. It would be good PR for the museum. And it definitely tied to her exhibit project. What would happen if they did discover 355's identity? Her pulse jumped. It would be truly monumental. She'd taken a photo of the love letter to show the team. How Jake would react to it? Her heart gave a traitorous double beat.

She slid her fingers along the smooth edges of her phone, as if to anchor herself to reality, as if to will herself not to get carried away by Jake Ford or any of this...this showbiz stuff.

As she waited for her iced latte, she studied the curlicues of the stamped tin ceiling, a Victorian design.

This wasn't some Hollywood plot. This was part of her work. Real life. And she'd do well to remember that after all this was over, she'd be going back to normal, going back to her quiet life behind the scenes. Just the way she liked it. She shifted from foot to foot. She loved her job. But... it'd be nice to do a bit of travel...someday.

Her eyes scanned the room as she crossed the scarred hardwood to get her drink at the black marble-topped pick-up counter.

As she fit the lid onto her drink and grabbed a striped straw, she spotted Jake and his team.

There. At the back. Looked like Jake was telling a story to Bryce and Nadine. Jake gestured, delivered the punch line, and the others cracked up.

Her heart pinched. After her very first museum exhibit had opened, she'd arranged a small gathering of her friends and family. Eric had failed to show up for the actual exhibit. But somehow, when the time was right—when it'd suited him—he'd shown up at the party, charmed all her friends and stolen her spotlight.

She should've seen his behavior for what it was. Then again, he'd always been charming. And she'd been so focused on her exhibit and its modest success, that she'd failed to see the waving red flag that his charm masked.

No. Her lips pursed. This was not that situation at all. Besides, she had a job to do here. That's what they were paying her for.

She approached the round table. "Hi, everyone."

"Vanessa. Hey." Jake lifted a hand and gave her a warm smile. "You made it." He put down the last bite of his cannoli and shifted his bentwood chair over. Then he stood, grabbed an empty one from the next unoccupied table and put it down at the only available space—right beside him.

Vanessa swallowed and hesitated half a second before she sat.

As she settled into her seat, Jake nudged her and said in a stage whisper, "Don't worry, I won't bite... too hard."

The others at the table rolled their eyes

and shook their heads at him. The corners of Vanessa's lips twitched upward despite her best efforts.

After Jake had introduced Vanessa to the rest of the production team, she pulled out her tablet and placed it on the table, with the photo of the love letter onscreen.

"So. Let's see what you have here," Jake said in a more serious tone.

Everyone else at the table stopped their chatter and put away their phones as Jake straightened in his chair. All eyes fixed on him—her gaze lingered. He really had the respect of his team, didn't he?

"The handwriting matches perfectly," Jake murmured, as he studied the photo that had been taken of the diary entry and compared it to the love letter photo. His brow furrowed and he moved in a bit closer to point at Vanessa's tablet. She caught a hint of sandalwood. Was it his aftershave or—"So these numbers are people's names, right?"

Vanessa straightened. "Yes. They're, um, the numbers replaced people's names. But other numbers in the code stood for place names, like Long Island, and various other words, like war and courage,"

Vanessa said. "Actually, the entire Culper codebook is on display at Washington's wartime headquarters—in Morristown, New Jersey."

Jake's eyes lit up. "Really? I haven't been to Morristown in years. Not since a grade school class trip."

"I've actually never been." Vanessa admitted.

"No? A seasoned history buff like you?" Jake grinned as he met her gaze.

"The museum's fundraiser gala's going to be held there," Vanessa blurted out.

"You gotta go see Washington's headquarters. You'll love it."

"Yeah? It'd be nice to see more places around the world," she admitted.

"I highly recommend filling your passport with as many stamps as possible," Jake said, with a sparkle in his eye.

Vanessa's stomach flipped at his expression. Gah. No. She couldn't get distracted. She ducked her head and cleared her throat. "To return to our topic, in this letter," she said, "355 is referring specifically to General Washington, as well as John Bolton, which was the code name for spymaster Benjamin Tallmadge."

"Mmm-hmm, okay." Jake propped his chin in his hand as he compared the two photos. "So where do these two documents lead us?"

"Well," Vanessa's heartbeat sped up. "That's what's so exciting." She took a sip of latte. "No one's really found anything like this before, written specifically by 355."

"Wow. Really?"

"Up to this point, she's only been mentioned in other agents' correspondence. So if you're serious about wanting to figure out her identity, and to see how that might fit in with these other leads you have..."

"The flag and the lost pearls, you mean?"

Vanessa nodded. "...Then I think the logical next step would be to look into her known associates—the other ring members. Since we know she wrote both of these documents, it gives us more of a base to work from."

"Good point. And so who are all her associates, exactly...?" His brow furrowed as he met her gaze. He looked kind of cute all confused like that.

Vanessa brushed the thought aside

quickly. "Well, there were people who helped the ring, though weren't specifically *in* it. But there were six members." She ticked off names on her fingers. "Robert Townsend, a merchant who owned a store in Lower Manhattan. Austin Roe, a tavern keeper. Caleb Brewster, a longshoreman who ferried messages back and forth between Long Island and Connecticut. Abraham Woodhull, who visited Manhattan pretty often on business. James Rivington, coffeehouse owner and publisher of *The Royal Gazette*."

"And of course, 355 herself," Jake said. "So you're thinking these others might provide some sort of clue as to who she really was?"

"Right."

"That's perfect," Jake said.

"Especially because," added Nadine, "our next expert interview for this episode is already lined up. It's with a descendant of Robert Townsend."

WEDNESDAY MORNING, JAKE held the cab door open for Vanessa as she stepped out onto the street beside him at the Park Avenue address the team had been given for Townsend's descendant.

Vanessa tucked a strand of dark hair behind her ear and smoothed down the front of her mint-green top. Jake noticed her eyes widen ever so slightly and her shoulders tense as she took in the high wrought-iron gate. Her gaze darted from the house, to the camera equipment and back to the house. She swallowed.

"Hey," Jake murmured. "Nothing to worry about. Everyone will be looking at me if there's a screw-up."

Vanessa laughed, and Jake saw her shoulders relax. "Thanks."

He looked at the house. The place was practically a mansion. All big windows, clean lines and glass angles. The only thing remotely old-fashioned about it was the ornate metalwork on the wrought-iron gate.

Well, they'd better get filming, here. No use in wasting footage. Bryce had already hoisted the camera onto his shoulder and unfastened the lens cap.

Jake turned to Bryce. "All set?"

"Ready as I'll ever be." Bryce began shooting.

Jake started his narration, even as a group of nannies walked by pushing strollers. One of the nannies began to whisper and to point to Jake and the team. Probably thought they were filming some movie or something.

The nanny had pulled out her phone and was doing some filming herself. Jake ignored it but couldn't help a flicker of annoyance. Then again, maybe this would help bump up the ratings?

"And so," he said, as he wrapped up his intro to the scene, "let's find out what she has to say."

Vanessa followed a few paces behind him. He'd been happy to see that it seemed after the first little while she'd gotten a bit more comfortable in front of the camera. That was good.

The wrought-iron gate swung open and he went up to the front door, Bryce filming all the while.

He rang the bell and then threw a look over his shoulder at the camera as if to say *Ready to find out what happens?*

A man wearing a tailored gray suit answered the door. "May I help you?"

"Hi. Yes. I'm Jake Ford and I'm here to

speak with Therese Smith. I think she's expecting us," Jake said.

The man's eyes narrowed as his gaze swept over the group on the steps. "Can you confirm, sir, that you are, indeed, the television crew that Ms. Smith—"

"Wiggins, let them in," said a quiet voice from behind him. "You don't need to worry. They're not the paparazzi."

"Quite. I do apologize."

Jake wasn't sure if Wiggins was addressing his employer or the PRR team. Possibly both.

The door swung wide and Jake stepped inside, along with Vanessa and the rest of his crew.

"Good afternoon. You must be Jake Ford." A slim woman in a tailored black blouse and ivory-colored linen pants, stood by a glass-topped hall table. She had streaks of gray in her blonde asymmetrical bob, and a set of thick gold bangles on one thin wrist.

"I am," Jake said. "Thank you for letting us come in."

She waved a hand. "Oh, of course. But you never know who might be out there these days." She turned to the butler.

"Wiggins, we'll need some tea in the east parlor, please."

"Very good, madam. Right away." Wiggins turned and walked down the long hallway lined with abstract prints in bright colors.

Therese ushered them into a large sunlit room a few doors down. Black and white tile underfoot made her heels click, and the faint echo reminded Jake of that time in Spain when he—

"Now," Therese said as she turned to Jake after she'd taken a seat on a small button-back club chair. "What did you have in mind for our chat?"

Jake took a seat opposite her. Vanessa took a chair nearby and got out a notebook and pen from her purse. Bryce and the rest of the team had set up a bit farther away by the door.

"Well, I'm not sure if you had a chance to read over the briefing notes my team sent," Jake said, "but we understand that you want to show us a needle and thimble you have that you think's somehow connected to Agent 355."

"That's right," she said. "It was passed down to me from my mother's father. His mother, my great-grandmother, could trace her lineage all the way back to Robert Townsend." She slipped a hand into the pocket of her trousers and pulled out a key.

She leaned forward and tapped a French-tipped nail against the table's glass-topped surface. "I never liked sewing very much, myself. But my grandfather was excellent with a needle. He studied textiles and merchandising, and ran his own tailoring business, you know. But I'm getting off track, here. Grandfather loved the story behind the needle and thimble, so he had them put in this display case here."

Familiar-looking red material caught Jake's eye. There were the needle and thimble from the photograph.

Therese turned the key in the lock and slid the glass panel aside. Jake indicated for Bryce to get a closer shot.

Vanessa, Jake noticed, had leaned forward in her own chair and watched as the older woman placed the artifacts on the glass top.

Jake wondered if Vanessa felt as curious about all this as he did. "So, what's the story?"

"During the British occupation of New York and Long Island, patriot sentiments weren't looked on very fondly. Any who were suspected of any patriotic acts ran the risk of being dealt with harshly. Possibly even hanged."

"I can imagine," Jake murmured.

"Well, back in the winter of 1779, Sally Townsend, Robert Townsend's younger sister, who was only around 19 years old at the time, had ordered some red wool to be made into a cardinal cloak."

"Cardinal cloak?" Vanessa said.

Therese nodded. "It was a style of cloak popular in the mid to late 1700s. It tied at the throat with a scarlet grosgrain ribbon." She continued. "The fabric shipped from France. After the wool came in at her brother's store, Sally gave it to her friend, who had a similar cloak, and who loved to sew."

Therese took a breath. "So she made Sally a cloak. But *this* material," she indicated the scarlet fabric, "is all that's left of Sally's friend's cloak. My grandfather found it hidden behind a rafter in the attic of the original Townsend home."

"It's not a very big piece, is it?" Vanessa commented.

"Unfortunately, no. At one point, there was a bit more left, but it's disintegrated over time." Therese pointed to the needle. "Do you see how this needle is held in place by the material? Like someone wove it through the fabric to keep it from getting lost?"

Jake nodded.

"Well," Therese continued. "It's never been disturbed from this position."

"It looks like someone cut strips off the fabric deliberately," Vanessa murmured as she looked at the swatch of scarlet wool.

"You're right," Therese said. "There was a trade blockade, and fabric was in short supply at this point in the war. My family always maintained Sally's friend used material from this very cloak, to sew one of the first American flags. And she left the needle there with the material."

Goosebumps rose on Jake's arms. "So where's the flag?"

Therese raised her hands and lifted her shoulders. "Lost to history."

"Unless we find it," Jake murmured, a gleam in his eye.

Therese laughed. "I wish you a lot of luck with that."

"But," Vanessa spoke up, "how did the needle and thimble, and cloak, end up at the Townsend home, if they weren't Miss Townsend's?"

Jake's lips quirked upward. Vanessa certainly knew how to ask excellent questions.

Therese's eyes sparkled. "Family legend has it that there was a knock at the Townsend's one cold, rainy September night in 1780. Sally opened the door and her friend was on the step, drenched and nervous, wrapped in what was left of her red cloak. Apparently, she'd just sewn the flag but the British had come looking for it, and her. So Sally volunteered to secrete the needle and thimble, and the material too, for her friend, in case the British came back. Then Sally gave her friend her own cloak to wear so no one would know what had happened."

Therese stopped speaking, and for a moment, all was quiet. Then she spoke again. "You see..." She leaned forward and made eye contact first with Jake, and then with Vanessa. "My family always believed Sally's friend was Agent 355."

Jake exchanged a look with Vanessa.

Therese held up her index finger. "Let me show you something else."

Jake saw excitement gleam in Vanessa's eyes as she met his gaze. He raised his eyebrows at her. Her mouth curved upward and she tilted her head ever so slightly.

Just then, Wiggins came in with the tea and began to dispense it.

A few minutes later, the woman returned, a manila folder in hand. When she gave it to Jake, she said, "Unfortunately, preservation methods in eras past weren't what they are today. But I've done what I can to preserve what's left."

Jake opened the folder. Three-quarters of a crumbling, brittle page lay inside.

7 D. ber, 1779

Dear Sally,

'Twas delightf f you to drop by for a ride along the bridlepath and my birthday tea Frid. st. Father presented me with a tiful garnet necklace and matching ear-bobs from France. They ar y. Especial. row of diamonds that lies between the garnet drop and the base. I shall em next week to the Flo yster Bay, for t nual Christmas ball ha. en announced. Are you certain you wil d?

My favorite silver needle has been put. od use, for I have com-

> *ple   e finishi   hes on my blue moire silk gown. 'Tis the la   le from Paris, with Chantilly lace edging. When   e meet for Shrewsbury cakes and needlepoint, I shall tell you a   t. And I shall bring your cloak, a   l I have completed it,   turned out beautifully, I   y.*

"This handwriting..." Vanessa murmured.

Jake pulled up the photo of the diary entry and showed it to Vanessa. "Think it's the same?"

"Sure enough, it is," he said as he glanced at her then showed Therese.

Therese laughed. "This is great—solid evidence at last. Sally's friend really *was* 355."

Vanessa smiled. "Your family was right all along."

"What a connection." Jake grinned.

"But if Sally knew who Agent 355 was," Vanessa said, her pen poised above her notebook, "then surely she'd known her name?"

"I'm sure she did," Therese said. "But at some point, 355 must've sworn Sally to secrecy, because there's no record of her name in my family history."

"So." Jake rubbed his jaw. "we haven't gotten much further on figuring out 355's identity."

"But look." Vanessa pointed. "She says 'my favorite silver needle,' so it seems she sewed her own ball gown, as well as Sally's cloak."

"Great observation," Jake told Vanessa.

He was rewarded with her smile. "Which means," Jake said, "we can surmise she used the very same needle mentioned to also sew the flag."

"That's logical," Vanessa murmured.

Jake looked up from the letter and looked at Therese. "Listen, there's...something else." He dug out his phone. "Do you know anything about a lost cache of pearls in connection with Townsend's store and the Culpers?" Jake brought up the article he'd come across earlier. He was about to show it to her but she waved a hand.

"Oh," she said, "that story's been circulating for years and years. There's no solid evidence that points to my ancestor having anything to do with a secret horde of pearls."

Jake's shoulders sagged but he tried not to act deflated. That's what happened with this kind of thing. One thing led to the next; until it didn't. But with the clock ticking toward his deadline...

"Surely it contains a kernel of truth

somewhere?" he persisted.

The older woman shrugged. "None of my family stories mention anything about a pearl cache. I'm sorry."

Jake's brow furrowed as he read the passage again. He noticed Vanessa was studying the antique document more closely.

"Vanessa?"

But she just continued to stare at the letter, and he watched her put a hand to her chest. He studied her a moment, and noticed she looked a little pale.

"I think..." she whispered in a somewhat strangled tone, as she finally brought her gaze to his. "I have Agent 355's earrings."

VANESSA'S HEART POUNDED as she reread the words in the letter. "Those earbobs she got for her birthday." She swallowed hard. Her eyes darted from Jake to Therese and back to Jake. "It describes perfectly a pair of earrings I have sitting in my jewelry box."

Jake's eyes widened.

Vanessa nodded at his expression as she pointed at the description on the page. "Right down to the band of diamonds around the base, that attaches the earbob to the drop."

"Are you sure?"

"Pretty darn," Vanessa said. She fought down a stab of annoyance at his comment. But she'd probably ask the very same thing herself, if she'd been in the same position as Jake.

"But surely garnet earrings were pretty common," Jake continued.

"Coral was popular back then, and more common, than garnets, which are semi-precious. Actually, pearls were considered more valuable than diamonds at one point in history. Particularly in the 18th century. The French kings, actually, brought pearls into vogue. You always hear about DeBeers and diamonds now, but really it was only in the 20th century that diamonds became a thing."

"Huh." Jake tugged at an earlobe. "Well, if I ever get engaged again, I'll have to remember that."

He paused then cleared his throat. "But still, I mean, there were only so many garnet earring designs in the 18th century, I imagine. Not to be annoying but don't you think that's a pretty big, uh," he glanced at Vanessa then back to the page, "jump to make?"

He shifted in his seat, as if suddenly all too aware that the camera was still filming—the cameras. Vanessa's shoulders stiffened. She'd completely forgotten about that.

Heat flooded her cheeks and she tried to pull herself more together, be more professional. She straightened her spine and took a slow deep breath. Tried not to feel the pressure of both being filmed and having to respond to Jake's words all at the same time.

"The way to rule out supposition," Vanessa said, "is to show you."

As Vanessa unlocked her apartment while Jake stood beside her, she couldn't help but feel a thrill.

No, she was not going to notice how the navy blue shirt he wore today brought out the blue in his eyes. She opened the door and stepped inside.

And she certainly wasn't going to admire the way he looked so explorer-sexy as he stood there, shirtsleeves rolled to the elbow, his aviator sunglasses sticking out of the front pocket of his button-down.

She had to focus, and be professional. She smoothed back her hair. But this felt so...personal; how could she?

At least the crew wasn't here—just Jake. He'd said he'd brought along his own small GoPro and would film once she'd retrieved the earrings.

"Nice place you got here." Jake slipped out of his shoes.

"Thanks. Uh, have a seat. I'll just go get the earrings."

She felt herself blush as he sat down on her couch. Good thing he didn't realize quite how many times she'd sat on that same couch and watched his face on television.

"Oh. Can I get you anything to drink?" She paused partway through the kitchen.

"Sure. You got any iced tea?"

"I think I do." Grateful for the distraction, she retraced her steps and headed to her fridge. "Mmm. Doesn't actually look like it. Sorry about that." She stood at the open fridge door and said over her shoulder, "How's a lemon-lime soda?"

"Great." He got up and crossed to the kitchen in a few strides. "I'm not picky."

He stood by the fridge door, his gaze warm as he regarded her. "Can's fine. You don't need to bother with a glass." His sandalwood scent drifted to her.

Vanessa's breath hitched. Suddenly, her small kitchen seemed very, very tiny. His tall form, his broad shoulders, his whole presence, in fact, seemed to fill the entire space. Her pulse sped up. When was the last time she'd had a man here? Not since things had ended with her ex, over a year ago.

She tried to take a deep breath and move away from him a step or two, but as she backed up, she bumped against the half wall that separated her kitchen from the living room area.

The slight jar brought her focus back to the task. Right. The soda. She reached into the fridge and pulled out a cold can from the fridge door.

She handed it to him. As he reached out to take the cold can from her, she was so busy looking into those blue-green eyes of his that she released the can a moment too soon.

"Whoops. Careful there." He caught the can with his right hand. His left hand closed gently around her bare forearm as she'd reflexively leaned forward to try and catch what he already held.

The warmth from his fingers radiated into her skin. Her eyes drifted to his touch on her arm. Those hands... Steering an open-sided Jeep across the Sahara, paddling a canoe across whitewater rapids in Colorado, brushing centuries of dirt and dust from a horde of buried coins...

"I've got it," he murmured, mere inches away from her.

"Thanks," she whispered.

Neither of them moved.

For a moment, she wished this suspended second could last forever. If she looked into his eyes long enough, would she find out all the secrets that she'd wanted to uncover about him?

His eyes held a quality of light that reminded her of diving underwater then looking up to see the blue of the sky mixed with the green of the ocean depths. The blood pounded in her ears and she found herself leaning forward ever so slightly...

Gah. No. What was she doing? Practically throwing herself at him? She stiffened, straightened and cleared her throat. Took a step back.

"There you go. I'll just, uh, be back in a sec." She practically ran to her bedroom and pulled the earbobs from the jewelry box.

Thank goodness that hadn't been filmed. She wasn't sure what the heck had gotten into her self-control. But she couldn't go there. They were just working together. That was all this was.

She just needed to keep things realistic. She couldn't go giving in to some ridiculous fantasy in her head. Especially because she had no idea who the man really was.

All she had was the fantasy. The small slice of him she'd seen on TV. Romanticizing every little thing about him wasn't going to help her working relationship with him.

That's all this was. A working relationship. She'd do best to keep that in mind, because she was certain that was all he saw this as, too.

JAKE PUT HIS half-full soda can on a coaster on the side table. He tried and failed to ignore the buzz in his system that had nothing to do with the caffeine he'd just consumed, and everything to do with this woman who now sat beside him on the couch, a pair of earrings cupped in her palm.

What would've happened back there in the kitchen if she—No. He gave his head a mental shake. He'd recognized that look in her eyes. Knew what it meant. Trouble. His ex had had that same look in her eyes, in the beginning, too.

He shifted on the couch. That same look that meant she'd liked what she saw—a fun-loving celebrity globetrotter.

But what would happen to that perception when the stressful reality of a long-distance relationship hit? When they had to live apart for 200 days out of the year? Trust eroded. Disappointment grew.

Laura had said his fun-loving outlook was a smoke screen for fear of deeper intimacy. She'd been right. He was always afraid something good would break down...like it had between the two of them.

He cast a sidelong look at Vanessa. No. He couldn't allow himself to imagine anything with her. Definitely not. It wouldn't be fair to either of them. Long-distance relationships never worked—just led to pain and heartbreak. Laura had taught him that.

He pulled himself up short. He had to remember that Vanessa was just consulting here. Assisting. Just doing her job. That was all.

He took a breath. Made himself smile in that easy, relaxed way that usually put everyone at ease.

"So this is them?" Excitement prickled along his spine as Vanessa held up the delicate pieces of jewelry. Discovery. It never got old. "Wow," he said. "That's really a piece of history." He chuckled. "Even if it's not related to 355, it's still, like, over 200 years old, isn't it?"

Something flashed in Vanessa's eyes as she met his gaze.

"It is," she said.

Despite himself, a beat of warmth curled around his heart. "History's great, isn't it?"

She looked up at him through her lashes as a small smile curved her lips. "Speaking of jewelry with history..." Vanessa's fingertips brushed his skin as she reached out to touch the silver stones twined inside the braided jute of his bracelet.

He didn't move, almost didn't dare breath. Her touch was light, soft, and it felt good. Too good. His pulse thudded. It felt better than he'd expected.

"Where did you get this?" Her voice was quiet, soft; like her touch. Yet it somehow reached into places inside that he hadn't explored in quite awhile. Oh, the irony.

He studied her. Those big green eyes, fringed with dark lashes, made him forget everything except wanting to be here in this moment with her, wanting to open himself up to her, share more of himself.

"...Angkor Wat."

She said nothing, as if she knew he hadn't quite finished his thought.

He took a steadying breath. "Back in my 20s, I thought I was something else." He shook his head slightly. "Really gonna conquer the world and all that. I think that's why I thought having a double major would help me out. Not exactly what my parents wanted, but—" He paused but then continued. "I was a bit of a mess, actually. Didn't know which way I wanted to go. Just knew for sure I'd be more bored than hell if I got myself some sort of "normal" office job. So I took off. On the first packet ship headed east out of Boston Harbor."

"Spent time in South Africa. Backpacked for awhile through Iran and even swam in the Dead Sea. Which is drying up, you know." He flashed her a smile.

Her lips quirked up in response. "Hadn't realized that. It'd be a neat place to see. Did you float?"

He chuckled. "Yep." he held her gaze, "I eventually found myself in Cambodia, exploring Angkor Wat, I got to talking with some locals. They took me to this remote, incredible Buddhist temple high above the jungle."

He took a breath as he met her gaze. "I'd never really experienced anything like it before. That sense of stillness, peace, during those meditations that the monks instructed me in, was..." he ran his finger under his bottom lip, "something else. I really just..." he shrugged, as if trying to get rid of the slight and sudden discomfort he felt as he exposed this small part of himself to her "...felt that somehow, my outer quest for adventure and exploration was in some way connected to an inner quest that I had felt was never really complete. Like, not until that moment in that temple."

Their knuckles brushed when he flipped his wrist over. He reflexively glanced at the bracelet, then at her, as he continued.

"That's why I wear it. And it's the reason I decided to go down the path I have. It reminds me that true exploration never ends no matter how many countries you visit. Because there's always another part of humanity you can discover, another piece of yourself to explore, another experience you can savor."

"Wow." Vanessa ran a fingertip unconsciously across the bracelet's smooth stones, and in doing so, also across the exposed underside of his wrist.

Jake closed his eyes momentarily at the sensation of her fingertips against his skin. Could she feel his pulse? His breath caught, but the sound of her voice brought him back to his surroundings.

"What kind of stone is it?"

He exhaled soft and slow, as if afraid the moment might burst if he didn't. "Wha—Oh." He cleared his throat. "It's hematite. Supposed to help arthritis. Gotta keep my old bones oiled up or I'm creakier than the Tin Man."

"You're not old."

He laughed. "Yeah. Sorry. I just...guess I do that sometimes."

"Use humor to hide your true feelings?"

Jake clutched his chest and pretended to pull an arrow from his heart. "Got me." He nudged her. "What about you?"

"Me?" Vanessa paused. She looked at the earring in her hand as an excuse not to have to see him watch her with those intent blue-green eyes of his. Eyes that seemed to see far more within her than she'd first thought.

She held up the intact earring. "This. My grandmother gave these to me. She said I... Well, it was one of the last pieces she gave me before she died." She paused and tucked a strand of hair behind her ear. "She was an anthropologist. I was...closer to her than any of my other female relatives." She swallowed. "She passed away when I was a senior in college but I'll never forget that she taught me how important history is. She showed me that in order to know yourself, you need to understand your past, where you'd come from." She glanced at Jake.

A flare of understanding lit his gaze. Vanessa's heart expanded. He knew exactly what she meant without her having to say anything else. But she continued anyway.

"And whenever I look at it, I remember those words, remember all the love and laughter we shared."

Her cheeks warmed and she met Jake's gaze. He smiled softly.

"I guess I also like to imagine what stories it might have to tell. Which is why..." She straightened. Why had she let herself get off on a tangent? They had work to do. "We should get back to analyzing it." She laid the earring on the table.

"So," Vanessa said, "as you can see here, there are 5 diamonds along the band around the top. And," she continued in that professional tone that Jake couldn't help but find alluring, "if you compare that with…"

Her words washed over him. She really knew what she was talking about, didn't she? He rubbed a hand across his jaw.

She was so intelligent. It took a lot of knowledge and a lot of skill and understanding to be that devoted to history.

"…have a match, don't you think?"

He blinked. "Uh," he cleared his throat, "Right. Yes. I totally agree."

Vanessa's lips turned up at the corners. "You have no idea what I just said, do you?"

"Nope. But uh," he cleared his throat again. "I'm sure you're right."

"As I was saying," she fixed him with a mock-stern look, "If you compare the description found in the documentation from Robert Townsend's descendant, with the actual earring here, you'll find that they are a match," she repeated.

As she put down the earring on the coffee table, he couldn't help himself. He gave her a playful nudge and said, "Excellent detective work, Ms. Watson."

"Finally giving credit where credit is due, I see, Holmes," she retorted without missing a beat.

But her expression suddenly shifted and she looked back down at the earring, her voice lowered. "I found something else."

He leaned in closer, near enough to catch the scent of sweet pea. "What do you mean?"

"The earring was hollowed out."

His pulse beat more quickly. "Why?"

"To conceal this," she said, as she held a fragile sliver of old paper. She read the lines aloud.

First taste of love is bittersweet

When between those lines

Secrets do not retreat.

His eyes widened and a huge grin split his face. "Fantastic! It's some sort of riddle."

"QUESTION IS, A riddle about what?" Vanessa chewed her lip a second as she studied the smudged writing. "Oh! Why didn't I see this before?" She turned to Jake. Their knees bumped on the couch.

"What is it?" Jake's eyes sparkled. "What? What?"

Vanessa pulled out her phone and pulled up the love letter. She pointed between the love letter and the riddle. "Do you see the way the f swoops and curves like that?"

He pulled out his phone. Pulled up the diary entry. "You're right. The F in all *three* writing samples match," Jake said.

"How did I not see the riddle's connection to 355 before?" Vanessa said.

"Hey, don't beat yourself up about it. We all miss things. Besides," Jake said, "to your credit, the words on this tiny little slip of paper are pretty badly smeared and faded."

"You're right." Her heart skipped a beat. That was a nice thing for him to say. Her ex would've just said she was overthinking things and had to use that masters' degree somehow and was just thinking too much.

"You do know what this means, right?" Jake's tone grew excited.

"That we have to solve the riddle?" Vanessa tapped a finger against her chin. "I can see what you're talking about. Why would someone encode something like this unless it was important?"

Jake looked like he'd just been handed a winning lottery ticket. "What if it leads to the pearl cache?"

"Now who's making leaps of logic? We have no idea what it means."

"But think about it," Jake said. He jumped up off the couch, animated. "It all fits together." He gestured at the documents. "She was part of the ring. We know the ring needed money. We know the pearl cache was reportedly sent to the Colonies, and intended for the Culpers—well, for Washington. What if this leads us to the location of the cache? We have to at least *try* to figure this out."

"You do make a good point." Vanessa couldn't help but feel a surge of excitement herself. Jake was totally in his element with this stuff, wasn't he? He didn't put up some sort of facade or front. What you saw on TV was what you got in real life. A thrill tripped up her spine.

"How do you think all those great explorers and adventurers accomplished anything? They started from where they were." Jake flashed her a grin.

Vanessa's knees weakened at the sight of his smile. "You're right. Solving this just might mean we'll get the answers we're both looking for."

He pulled out his GoPro and set it up. Craned his neck this way and that to make sure he had the right angle. Winced a little. Man, he needed to get a massage at some point to work the knots out.

"So," he said and turned to her after he'd made the final camera adjustments and began to film. "what do we have, exactly?"

After she'd recapped, they studied the lines together.

"First taste of love is bittersweet," Vanessa murmured. "Taken figuratively, that phrase seems pretty self-explanatory. So I think..." She pressed a finger to her upper lip "...she's wanting us to think perhaps—literally?"

"Could be," Jake murmured. "Some sort of food, or something you eat or drink that you really love?"

"And when people eat or drink something they really love, where would they do that?"

"At home, mostly, in that era."

"Or at a friend's or relative's house if you got invited to dinner."

"Then again, there were restaurants of a sort....Pubs were pretty popular in colonial times, too."

"Restaurants, pubs....Coffeehouses," Vanessa murmured. "Oh, wait. What if taste refers to *drinking* something?" She worried her bottom lip between her teeth.

"Mmm-hmm." Jake's eyes drifted to her mouth. "It could. People drink things at coffeehouses."

"Like coffee," Vanessa said with a laugh. But then her eyes widened. "Of course. James Rivington had a coffeehouse."

"He was also, not so coincidentally, a Culper member."

"And if you think about taste again—" she pointed to the rest of the line "—coffee is bitter, too, before you add cream and sugar."

He grinned at Vanessa.

Their gazes held.

"So," Vanessa said as she hastily cleared her throat and indicated the paper, "what about the last line? Solving it next might help us figure out the more general middle line."

Jake nodded. *Secrets do not retreat.*

For a moment, neither spoke. Vanessa was all too aware of the quiet around them; the rise and fall of Jake's broad chest as he sat beside her, his heat, his pure maleness. He had seen so many things, done so many things. What would it be like to travel with him to a far-flung place or two, holding her suitcase in one hand, his hand in the other, sharing, exploring, discovering so many things... about him, about herself, about the world.

Suddenly, she could see herself with him, at some street vendor in Morocco, surrounded by bright silks in shades of orange and fushcia with the scents of coriander and cinnamon in the air, the flash of his teeth as he grinned at her, those aviator sunglasses in place, their fingers interlaced—No. She pushed the thoughts aside and pondered the words, instead.

After a few more moments, Jake spoke. "If we're going with the Rivington angle for the first line..." He frowned, picked up his phone. "Hmm. Let's look some stuff up," he murmured to himself as his fingers danced across the screen.

"Ah-ha. Okay. Here we go." He showed Vanessa his phone and started to scroll through the article. "It talks about Rivington being in the Culper ring. But...that's not what—Right there." He pointed to the screen, then read aloud, "...*Not far away from Robert Townsend's store, James Rivington's coffeehouse was used to pass information on to the Patriots, since not only did British soldiers frequent it, but also aristocratic Loyalists who wanted to drop hints about who was attending what, and when.*"

"If the British soldiers and the Loyalists frequented it, and the patriots were there too..." Jake said.

"Anyone with their ears open would be bound to pick up some bit of information they didn't intend the other side to hear," Vanessa murmured. "So, secrets mean gossip."

"Bingo," Jake said. "And the *do not*

retreat bit must refer to the British occupation of New York."

"That would make the most sense. After all, the British didn't retreat. Washington couldn't get them to leave—the Battle of Brooklyn was why New York fell. So Washington organized the spy ring—to gain tactical advantage by gathering intelligence."

"Exactly." Jake grinned. Held up a palm.

Vanessa beamed at him as they high-fived. "We make a pretty good team."

She laughed. "So this just leaves the one phrase: *when between those lines...*"

Jake's brow furrowed. "Sounds like something to do with words. From a poem? A speech? This riddle?"

"Could be anything. But, then again... If you look at it more closely, it says *those* lines. Why doesn't it say *these* lines?"

"Because it's talking about some other document?"

"Some sort of correspondence," Vanessa said. "Letters were pretty common."

"Okay, I see your logic. But that's a really wide net to cast." Jake said.

"I don't think so."

"No?"

"If you look back at the first line," Vanessa pointed out, "I think she's being very specific."

"Oh?"

Vanessa nodded. "She says first taste of *love*. I'd say it makes sense that the correspondence she's referring to here must be a love letter. Besides that, in 355's love letter I have, she mentions the very first time she met this...true love of hers." She avoided Jake's gaze. "So what if she met that person at Rivington's coffee shop and put another love letter there?"

"I like how your mind works," Jake said.

Vanessa felt a warm glow at his words. He hadn't once said in this entire thing that she'd been 'obsessed with her work.' Her heart fluttered. "Thanks."

"So let's go check out Rivington's coffeehouse."

Chapter Five

As Jake walked down the sidewalk with Vanessa beside him, he tucked one of his thumbs into the belt loop of his khakis and resisted the urge to whistle to himself.

Now *this* was making great television. He caught a glimpse of a orange-and-blue mural some street artist had chalked on the pavement. Bryce and the others walked a few paces behind them. The ratings for this episode were going to be astronomical. He'd just given an update to Sara via text and she'd been very enthusiastic about their findings, especially the love letter angle, which was a big relief.

He grinned to himself. Sure, they'd chased after treasure before, but somehow, something about this felt different. Felt closer to real, somehow. Like he could almost feel those pearls sliding through his fingers... Then again, didn't he always feel this way when he was on the hunt?

Yep, definitely. But did that really matter? Nope, not in the slightest. His grin widened.

Vanessa gave him a worried glance as they headed along Pearl Street toward the intersection with Wall Street. "You do know that Rivington's coffee house isn't there any more?"

"That's the fun part. We get to figure out what part of the existing building might have what we're looking for."

Vanessa nodded, but didn't say anything else.

This part of Lower Manhattan was definitely older. He could tell by the way the street had narrowed and the buildings had become, for the most part, shorter. Glass and steel structures co-mingled with the decorative brickwork of older buildings.

"I'd guess none of this was here during the Revolution." Jake looked around.

As they neared the intersection, a girl in a neon green T-shirt rushed up to them and shoved a flyer in Jake's direction. He smiled, shook his head and side-stepped

HIDDEN TREASURE OF THE HEART

the girl. She spun around in the opposite direction to confront a gaggle of tourists who ate ice cream cones.

"Nope." Vanessa replied. "These older buildings are from the 1800s. Even the street was renamed."

"Really?" His smiled dimmed slightly.

Vanessa nodded. "During the Revolution, Pearl Street was called Queen Street. But after the war, the Americans decided to take out references to the monarchy."

"Understandable." Jake indicated the upcoming intersection. "Looks like there's a few businesses on the ground floor of these buildings."

They came to a stop where Pearl crossed Wall. "Well," Vanessa said as she looked up from the documents referenced on her phone, "I think we're here. If my interpretation of source material is correct, this current building stands on several Colonial-era lots. Which means one of its entrances should be where the coffeehouse once stood."

He squinted and tilted his head while he studied the building faced with beige stone. "Maybe *part* of the original coffeehouse might still be intact. Under all...that...somewhere." He frowned. This could be trickier than he'd thought.

"It's certainly a spot you wouldn't be able to miss," Vanessa said slowly.

The street frontage where the coffeehouse once stood was now sided in electric blue sheet metal. A sign over the door read *Chiara's Nail Salon & Day Spa.*

"Which, I hope, will work in our favor." Jake swallowed and tried not to think about what might happen if it didn't, as he headed to the entrance.

Vanessa followed him up the steps. The door was painted sunflower yellow. He opened it and a bell chimed overhead.

A petite woman with long black hair barreled out. "Do you have an appointment?"

"Nope, I actually don't," Jake said. "But I was hoping—"

"No appointment, we can't help you." The woman gave him a stern look and shooed him out the door.

Jake's gut tightened.

"We—" Vanessa started to say but the woman shook her head.

"We're very busy. You need to come back later. Make an appointment."

Jake took a calming breath before he threw a glance at the camera. "Well," he addressed his audience, making an effort to keep his tone light, "looks like I'll have to—" Just then, his phone buzzed and vibrated. "—Maybe this is the answer. Let's find out. Hello?"

"Jake. Hi." It was Sara. He signaled to Bryce to stop filming him, so the cameraman turned and began to take some wide shots of the street and the surrounding buildings.

"I have some bad news."

Jake's stomach dipped. "I'm listening."

"Have you checked your social media lately?"

"Not since yesterday," Jake said slowly. His heart rate accelerated. "Why? Should I?"

A pause. Then. "...Just check it."

Jake closed his eyes a moment, took a deep breath and pulled up his social media app.

Can this guy be for real? one commenter said. *He's totally making everything up. No one finds lost treasure that easily. He plants everything beforehand then just acts like it's a real discovery.*

Jake flinched. What? Sure, there were some preparations the team had to make, a bit of pre-planning and some organizing of details, but they never planted anything beforehand. He ground his teeth. The show wasn't fake.

He scrolled further. Faster. His heart sank even more as his free hand tightened into a fist. It was all the same. Hundreds of re-posts and comments and snide remarks.

Near the bottom, he saw someone had tagged him in a video. He studied the background. That was...at Park Avenue, from the other day.

Oh. His stomach twisted. That nanny who'd been with her friends must have posted the video. The tagline of the video read: *Jake Ford A Forgery?*

He swore under his breath.

Vanessa must have noticed something wrong, because she came over to him and put a hand on his arm. "What is it?"

Without saying a word, he handed her his phone.

Her eyes widened as she read the comments and saw the video.

"How can so many people be saying all this? It's not true. Is it?"

Jake felt a dart of irritation. "Of course it's not true." He made an effort to steady his voice. Calm down. He sighed. "I thought the Internet trolls had decided to leave well enough alone after that incident a few months ago. But that's the Internet for you. No delete button. Not only that, you put something up there, people think it must be true just because it's online."

Vanessa nodded.

His lips compressed as he re-dialed Sara. "I see what you mean, Sara."

"This could put all the good work we've done for this episode in jeopardy," she said.

Jake's frown deepened. "We have to look on the bright side of things." He raked a hand through his hair, slumped against one of the graffitied window sills, and closed his eyes. He let the phone drop from his ear as he tried not to let more frustration and, if he was honest with himself, something that bordered on despair, creep in. This whole thing could fall apart right here, right now and he—

"Jake?" Sara said, her voice tinny and far away. "Are you still there?"

He put the phone back up to his ear

and exhaled quietly. "Yep. Still here."

"Listen, if more trolls get wind of this, it could easily blow up even more."

He pinched the bridge of his nose. "So what do you see as a solution?"

"We need to step up the production schedule," Sara said. "That means you have just two weeks to come to some sort of conclusion about this 355 business. Any suggestions? I'm open to them."

"You're right." Jake pushed away from the wall and straightened. He wasn't going to let a bunch of Internet trolls who spread lies about him and the show, get the better of him. Or this historical mystery investigation. He had a responsibility to keep searching, discover the answers. That's what counted. That's what he needed to concentrate on.

He wasn't going to let anything or anyone stop him. Especially because they were going to get to the bottom of this mystery. They *would* find those lost pearls. They would change history. He owed it to himself and his fans to keep going. He was going to make the best damn episode ever.

"I'm not going to let this show go down without a fight. Those trolls—they're just blowing hot air. All we have to do is find the pearls, prove these rumors all wrong. And the way to do that? We make the best episode ever. From here on out, we document *everything.* Every piece of footage counts. We have to let our audience in more than ever before. We fight these lies that way."

He ended the call and took a deep breath. Turned back to Vanessa. "Let's figure out our next step."

VANESSA SWALLOWED HARD at Jake's words. They wanted to film *everything* now? But this wasn't about her. She took a calming breath, and watched as Jake put his phone back into his pocket.

It was admirable of him, really; he didn't let some random people's opinions, or the threat of losing something he'd worked so hard to gain, stop him. Her heart skipped a beat as he met her gaze.

"Where do we go next? Any ideas?" Jake said as they stood on the steps.

Vanessa pulled her brows together. "I'm not sure. If we figured things right, then the love letter, if it survived, should be here somewhere. But it seems like we've hit a dead end."

Jake gestured at the building then folded his arms across his chest. "Certainly looks like that. I mean," he drummed his fingers as he studied the building. "Whole thing's been redone."

"Unless...That's it," Vanessa said as realization dawned. "It's so obvious I didn't even think about it. And the lady said it, plain as day."

"What?"

She grinned at Jake. "I'm going to get my nails done." She pulled out her phone and punched in the number on the sign.

"Good thinking," Jake said. He rolled his shoulders. After a moment, he said, "I'll just—Hmm. It's a day spa, too." He glanced at the camera crew then back toward the building. "You know, we've all been working pretty hard. I don't know about them but I could really use a massage." He rubbed his neck. "I think I slept wrong on the plane flying back from Myanmar. Besides, divide and conquer, right? This is like, research. The more eyes we have in there, looking around, asking questions, the better. If you're getting your nails done, you can look around and ask there. Me and the crew can look around and ask the staff who work with us."

Vanessa's heart stuttered as she nodded wordlessly. She would not imagine Jake shirtless. But despite her best efforts, her mind drifted back to the show's opening credits.

Him diving off the waterfall without a second thought. The way the water droplets skimmed his back muscles, how sunlight glinted off his broad shoulders. The lush jungle around him. His bare feet. That gleam in his eyes as he looked back at the camera right before he jumped...

Her cheeks heated and she avoided eye contact with Jake. "Um, right. Makes sense." She turned slightly away from him. The better to block him from view. Maybe then she would stop this ridiculous daydreaming. He was an actor. She already knew how *that* ended. It was best to stay professional...

Fifteen minutes later, she found herself on a comfortable tufted yellow stool by one of the tall windows as her manicurist chatted away.

But as Vanessa made small talk with the woman, she couldn't help but track Jake's movements as he first directed the crew to another room and then stepped into the day spa part of the building, himself.

She admired his confidence. His efficiency. Even the way he joked and laughed with the crew like they were his best friends. She smiled to herself. They probably *were* his best friends. The man just really loved life. Which was, of course, why he was such a perfect fit as the show's host.

After he left the room, her gaze lingered for too long on the place where he'd stood. Her heartbeat sped up. Her mind slid again to that opening scene. The clean, efficient way he dove off those rocks. The big grin on his face as he'd surfaced in the pool below.

What would it be like to feel that free, that open, that in love with life? He was sort of inspiring, she realized. If he could do that, be that free and open, maybe she could too?

Maybe she didn't have to find herself hiding behind the scenes so often, using history and antique documents as a way to hide herself from the world. Maybe she was selling herself short by doing that?

She paused. Maybe she could learn something from Jake Ford.

Right now, though, she had a job to do. She pulled her mind back to the manicurist. "Do you know anything about this building's history?"

The woman shrugged. "Not really. Just know that it's old. Divided up between various businesses. Guess the owners bought this section of the building years and years ago. Had it totally gutted and completely renovated. Everything got torn out, right down to the studs."

Vanessa leaned forward. "And when they did that work, did they find anything...old? Any papers or artifacts or anything?"

The woman's eyes drifted up and to the left as she thought. Shrugged again. "No."

AS JAKE UNBUTTONED his navy blue shirt and placed it on the sunflower-yellow chair by the massage table, he rolled his shoulders again. His mind drifted back to Vanessa. How she'd turned away from him ever so slightly outside the building.

His heart pinched. Had he done something wrong? Said something wrong to Vanessa?

He lay face-down on the massage table. A moment later, the attendant tapped on the door and he called for the person to come in.

"So," the woman said, "do you have any sore spots?"

He told her about his neck and she set to work.

Then again, why did the thought of if he'd said or done something wrong to Vanessa bother him so much? They were just colleagues. That's all they'd ever be. All they ever *could* be. His schedule was far too crazy, and he was gone for way too many days out of the year, to make anything work...

He shouldn't be entertaining thoughts like this. He really shouldn't. She was a source. That was all. Besides, in not very long, he'd be gone, out of New York. Flying 35,000 feet over yet another continent.

A strange sort of sadness filled him at

that thought. Didn't he deserve to have love in his life? Didn't he deserve the love of his life?

Maybe not. Maybe his kind of lifestyle, his love of freedom and adventure, meant he couldn't have both freedom *and* love?

He sighed. Who would want to be basically stuck in a permanent long-distance relationship with him? Relationships were tough enough without the added stress of long distance.

Why was he thinking this all of a sudden? Oh, he knew *exactly* why. It was all because of Vanessa. His heart thudded as he recalled the way her eyes glowed as they'd unraveled the riddle. The way she was so invested in, and so passionate about, history—just like he was. Warmth surged through him.

He admired her, he realized with a jolt. Admired her intelligence, her diligence, her drive. She basically single-handedly ran a museum. He smiled. She was different than the other women he'd dated before.

His mind drifted to their time in her apartment. That sweet pea scent of hers. Her long legs as she'd crossed them that first day when he'd interviewed her. Her big green eyes. Those long, dark lashes. The fullness of her lips...

As the massage therapist kneaded his back muscles, the tension and stress started to melt away. His mind drifted further and heat filled him. And for a moment, he allowed himself to imagine it was Vanessa's hands on his bare back, her soft touch, her fingers caressing his skin, stirring his soul and touching his heart. Whispering his name. Making him feel things he'd never—

"There you go," the attendant's words broke into Jake's thoughts. He startled slightly and gave his brain a mental shake.

After a minute or two to bring himself back to the reality of the room he was in, he slowly sat up and then stretched. "Thank you." He ran a hand across the back of his neck. "Feels a lot better now." He hopped off the table, put on his shirt and started to button it.

"Oh. I almost forgot. We're doing research for a television show. Do you know much about this place? It looks like it's been pretty much totally gutted."

The woman nodded. "Yeah. The existing structure with the stone exterior's been here awhile. Not sure of the dates. But in the renovations of it, I do know they keep some usable pieces and parts of older, pre-existing buildings. This section where the salon is still has a bit of the original Colonial structure."

"When they did all that, they ever find anything?" He finished buttoning his shirt. "Papers, documents, that sort of thing."

The woman put a hand on her hip. "Not that I...Oh. Wait a sec. A few months after I started working here, I heard one of the owners say that they'd found some sort of antique journal. From, I think something like the 18th century."

Jake's ears perked up.

"I can't quite—hmmm. Think I recall them saying something about donating it to the archives or something at the New York Public Library."

"Awesome. This is great. Thank you. How much do I owe you?"

"You can pay at the front," the woman said.

"Sure thing." Jake paused and pulled two twenties from his wallet. "But I'm feeling extra generous in my tipping today.

Appreciate the information."

The woman laughed. "Thanks much. Well, have a good day."

"You too," Jake said, as he stepped out of the small room and back into the salon.

Vanessa stood by the front door, studying the view out the window. "Hey," he said as he approached. She looked over her shoulder. A hint of...something...flickered in her eyes as she saw him.

"Hi," she said, her tone a little flat. "I guess we hit a wall, then huh? They've completed gutted everything and no one I spoke with out here knew anything about the building's history."

He placed a palm on her shoulder. "Don't give up yet. I have good news."

THURSDAY AFTERNOON, ON the corner of Fifth Avenue and West 42nd Street, Vanessa smiled when she caught sight of the huge stone lions on either side of the steps of NYPL's main branch.

"Patience and Fortitude," Vanessa said to Jake as they headed toward the library's entrance.

"I always thought they were aptly named," Jake replied. "People like us need that when conducting research."

People like us...Vanessa's heart fluttered. Did he...No. It was just a figure of speech. Right?

She tucked her hand into the pocket of her peach shorts. "Exactly." They reached the top of the steps. "I wonder what sort of documents they found at Rivington's?"

"Well, after my production assistant called and arranged things with the manuscripts and archives division here so we could have permission to film inside the library, she didn't tell me, exactly."

"Oh?" Vanessa adjusted the strap on her messenger bag, which contained her laptop.

"Yep. That way my reactions are natural and real." Jake slid Vanessa a glance. "So I'm not sure, myself. But we're about to find that out." Jake gestured for Vanessa to go first through the door. They walked into the entrance hall of the Beaux Arts building together, with the TV crew not far behind.

"Man, I haven't been in here in forever. This place is something else." The polished stone floor gleamed. Tall, ornately carved candelabras gave the area a soft glow, and two large stone staircases sat off to the left and right.

"Oh, that's cool," Jake said as he read the signage. "I didn't know there was a map room in this branch."

"Yeah. I've been in a time or two," Vanessa said. "Lots of historic maps in there."

"I never would've guessed," Jake deadpanned.

Vanessa swatted him on the arm.

They followed the signs up to the manuscripts and archives division on the third floor, and into Room 328, with the film crew not far behind.

Jake headed over to the staff member who approached, and shook the man's hand. "Hi, I'm Jake, and this is Vanessa."

"Jake, Vanessa, hi. We've been expecting you. I'm Aaron."

"Great, and nice to meet you." Jake said. "I was told you're the guy who knows something about what we're researching here today."

"Right you are. I'm originally from Long Island, so I grew up with regional stories and such about the Culpers." Aaron indicated one of the long wooden tables nearby. "I'll be just a few moments," he continued. "You guys go set up."

Vanessa put her laptop on the table, and caught a few snippets of conversation between Jake, Bryce and the lighting guy before Jake sat down on one of the chairs beside Vanessa.

Aaron returned with a very old-looking leather book of some sort.

"This is it, then?" Jake said.

Vanessa's heart warmed when she saw the appreciation in Jake's eyes as he looked at the antique volume. A fellow history lover, for sure. Maybe he was more historian than treasure hunter, after all.

"Sure is."

"What is it?"

"Sally Townsend's diary," Aaron said as he placed it on the polished surface.

Vanessa inhaled sharply. "How does the sister of Robert Townsend end up with her journal at Rivington's coffeehouse?"

Aaron leaned a hip against the edge of the table. "How does anything get anywhere, over time? Items move, shift, as buildings change hands, so... it's anyone's guess. Owners told me these documents were found behind the fireplace mantle when they ripped it out. From what I understand, Sally had a close circle of friends who frequented Rivington's together." He spread his arms wide, palms up. "Some people theorize Sally was Agent 355, so maybe behind the mantle was a dead letter drop location. I mean, apparently, Rivington hid pieces of paper in his own books' bindings to pass messages to Washington. Things he'd heard from Loyalist coffeehouse patrons. So who knows, right? Important thing is, the diary's here today for us to study." He chuckled. "So you think you'll figure out the identity of Agent 355?"

"The question of the day," Jake replied.

"You know, there's folklore from long-time families in the Setauket area of Long Island, that says a woman named Anna Smith Strong was Agent 355."

"I'd heard a little about that." Vanessa looked up.

"It's possible she could well have helped the patriots," Aaron said. "Story goes that she hung pieces of laundry in certain colors on the line in a specific

HIDDEN TREASURE OF THE HEART

order to signal to ring members about various things."

"Like what?" Jake said.

"Well, according to some folklore, the way she hung out the clothes could indicate numbers of ships or troops. In other versions of the story, she used her laundry to indicate which coves Caleb Brewster could safely dock his boat, since his role in the ring was to pass the Culpers' secret messages from New York to Connecticut."

"Interesting," Jake said.

"But there's no real evidence to support it." Aaron continued. "You know, I've always found the Culper spy ring an interesting topic. Read a novel one time about them. In the back, the author's note said it's possible the Culper ring still exists. No one knows what happened to the ring after it disbanded. In fact, the CIA made a statement that the Culper ring 'may or may not still exist'."

"Classic," Jake said.

Aaron stood and checked his watch. "Well, I'd better quit jawing and get back to it. Have a meeting with my supervisor here in a minute. But if there's anything else I can help you with, just let me know." He left.

Vanessa turned back to her computer screen. "I hadn't realized that little tidbit of information about Robert's sister. That'll fit in nicely with the exhibit." She made a few more notes on her research document about the female spy exhibit.

Jake slipped on one of two pairs of white cotton preservation gloves Aaron left. He offered Vanessa the other pair of gloves as she shut her laptop's lid.

"You ready, Vanessa?" His grin flashed, and the second cameraman moved in a bit closer.

"Definitely," she replied, as she put on the gloves he'd handed her.

They opened the book and began to skim the entries.

But a few hours later, when they'd reached the end, Vanessa rubbed her temples. "This doesn't really give us any new or useful information."

Jake frowned as he reshuffled through the last few pages and sat back with a sigh. "Nope. She didn't put any spy secrets in her diary. Mostly mentioned daily chores, parties she attended, visits to family and friends."

"But Aaron was right—she did talk about going to Rivington's more than once," Vanessa mused.

"Looks like it. With the same group of friends. I wonder if this was the only document—"

"Sorry to interrupt," Aaron approached their table again, a file folder in hand. "After my meeting, I got to chatting with my supervisor. When she heard what you two were researching, she wanted to show you this." He opened a manila file folder. Inside lay a sheaf of paper. "She said it was also something donated by the owners of what was once Rivington's coffee house, but the letter had gotten accidentally misfiled, which is why I didn't bring it out initially."

He handed them the folder. "By the way, guys, not to be a party pooper, but we're going to be closing in about 15 minutes here. You're welcome to come back tomorrow, though. And the building itself doesn't close for a few more hours."

"Okay, good to know," Jake said.

Vanessa's heart sped up as she opened the folder. Inside was a single sheet of paper. The handwriting matched the other documents they had uncovered. This had to be from 355.

New York   January 2, 1780

Dearest Nathaniel,

Though I am taking a chance in penning this letter to you, I cannot help the call of my heart, despite Father's insistence I shall follow his wishes for a proper suitor in Lord C— m, whom, as you know, I also met at the Floyd's Christmas fete a few short weeks ago.

I have thought of little else but you and your words, it seems, these past days, in between our meetings. When you spoke of reason, purpose, I must confess, you inspired me to take up my needle.

I ordered sturdy worsted wool in swatches of red, white and blue from Townsend's. I am told it shall arrive in port on the Cignet. But with the blockade in place, I fear it shall be months before the goods arrive.

No matter. For my heart can concede nothing less than this act of rebellion. Sometimes the sharpest instruments of change available to a lady are her needle and her pen. I yearn to do more, such as you do. May this start be enough to make a difference.

In light of these recent activities of mine, I dare not sign my name to this missive, so shall conclude with only:

— my heart is yours —

"Now we know who she was writing to—someone named Nathaniel," Vanessa said, as she typed a few more notes on her laptop then took a snap of the letter, but made sure to turn off her phone's flash app.

"Right." Jake nodded. Excitement flashed in his eyes. "Do you think we can use this guy's name as a starting point to figure out her identity somehow?"

"Mmm. That's a good thought." Vanessa pursed her lips. "But it was a pretty popular 18th century name."

Jake sighed. "You're right. But hey," he brightened, "you know what this letter also means? It lines up with what Townsend's descendant said. We now have actual proof that 355 sewed that flag. She basically says as much right here." He pointed a finger at the lines then glanced back up at Vanessa. "All it takes is one piece at a time til you get the whole picture. The trick is being persistent enough to find all the pieces."

"You're right." Vanessa smiled then lowered her voice. Leaned closer to Jake. "You know what else...?" She held his gaze.

He leaned towards her. "What?"

"...From the letter's contents, it's safe to assume this was the very first love letter from 355 to Nathaniel."

"Which," Jake grinned, "means it must be the right one the riddle pointed us to."

Vanessa's pulse raced at his smile. This was—A flash of movement caught the corner of her eye. It was Bryce adjusting his camera. She blushed. What was she doing, getting all cozy with Jake? She cleared her throat and straightened in her seat.

"Question is," she said as she looked back down at the document and hoped her embarrassment didn't show up too much on camera, "what's hidden in it?"

"And how," Jake said as he looked around the room, "are we going to find that out?"

AS THEY LEFT the library and stepped onto a wide stone patio area behind the building, the film crew followed. Jake saw her dart a glance over her shoulder at the cameras. She seemed a little nervous.

"Well," Jake said in a light tone, "now that they've kicked us out because the room closed, what do you think we should do at the moment?"

"I don't know, exactly. I need to think." Vanessa smoothed her hand over her ponytail and scanned the green space.

The large grassy area in front of them—Bryant Park—was dotted with trees, and stretched out beyond clusters of metal tables with umbrellas. Children laughed and shouted as they wove between trees and tables. People sat on the lawn or at tables. On the grass nearby, a couple lay on a large red beach towel and fed each other strawberries.

Jake nudged Vanessa. "Wanna think together? Over a drink? It's on me." He nodded in the direction of a smoothie kiosk.

"That sounds..." Her breath caught and a smile curved her lips. "Really nice."

The light breeze caught a few strands of her dark hair and tumbled them across her cheek. She brushed them aside impatiently as her phone buzzed.

"Sorry," she looked at Jake then at the cameras again. "I need to take this." She moved a few paces away.

He nodded. "I'll grab us a table."

JAKE GLANCED AT his crew. They'd stopped filming momentarily to consult about set up and framing for the outdoor table shots. Looked like things were under control.

Jake headed to the smoothie kiosk. He hoped Vanessa liked fresh lemons. But judging from the stock of lemon-lime soda in her fridge, he'd take a chance. He ordered her a frozen lemonade, and got himself a pineapple-mango smoothie.

He set down the drinks at the semi-secluded table the crew had chosen—under the shade of a leafy oak near where the patio met the grass. A few pigeons hopped out of the way as he pulled out his chair.

After he took a seat, he overheard snatches of Vanessa's conversation.

"No, he's—" Vanessa laughed. "Melissa, we've just..." A pause. "That's what the analysis said? Okay. I'll tell him—"

Jake took a sip of the cool, sweet drink. He leaned back in his chair. As much as he'd loved his time in Myanmar, he had to admit, shooting this particular episode was a nice change. Good to take a break from wielding a machete through dense jungle in search of a lost jeweled scepter, while trying to avoid venomous snakes and poisonous spiders, all the while making witty remarks to the camera.

He shuddered. He hated spiders.

He flicked through his calendar app and pressed his lips together. This episode deadline was beginning to remind him of an arachnid as it crept closer and closer. Because if this new information they discovered didn't lead somewhere...

"Sorry about that," Vanessa pulled out the other chair and settled onto it.

Jake took a breath and focused his attention on her. "No problem." His heart missed a beat as Vanessa's eyes lit up. "How did you know I like their lemonade?" She titled her head at him as she took a sip and fiddled with the straw.

"I don't investigate mysteries for nothing." Jake raised a shoulder.

"That lemon-lime soda from my fridge."

Jake lifted his brows at her and grinned.

"So." She cleared her throat. "Down to business. That other love letter I showed you, someone sent it to me in the mail. But there was no return address. No way to identify who sent it. That call I took was an update from my friend Melissa. Her brother works for the FBI. She managed to persuade him to run a few tests on the letter. But—" she shook her head "—no dice."

"Nothing?" Jake struggled to hide a look of disappointment.

"Nope." Vanessa took a long drink of her lemonade. "I was hoping if we figured out whoever sent it, they might know more about..." she waved a hand "...all of this." She sighed. "Maybe sending it to the FBI was too much? I mean, lots of people don't have that kind of access. But when I get focused on something, I kind of tend to go to extremes."

"If it makes you feel better," Jake said. "I do the exact same thing."

Vanessa blinked. "Really?"

Jake gave a rueful laugh. He jerked his thumb over his shoulder toward the film crew, who sat chatting, nearby. "Go ask my team—they can tell you all kinds of stories."

She smiled but hesitated for a second, her eyes on his face, before she spoke again. "My ex-boyfriend always told me I spent way too much time obsessing over dumb little details and that I—" she fiddled with a strand of her hair "—was quote unquote too focused on my work."

Jake leaned his forearms on the table and put a hand on her arm. "Can I be totally frank?"

"...Sure."

"I think," Jake held her gaze, his blue-green eyes intent, "that your ex had no idea what he was talking about."

Vanessa's cheeks turned pink. "Thank you," she whispered. "He *was* a little...self-involved."

"What did he do, anyway?" Jake picked up his half-empty smoothie glass and twirled the straw between his fingers.

"Uh, he was an actor."

"Ah, I see." Jake nodded, his tone mock-serious. "You never know, with those types."

Vanessa laughed. The sunlight caught the emerald of her eyes; Jake's breath hitched. The gleam in their depths brought to mind sparkling waters in the South Pacific where he'd first fallen in love with exploration and travel.

"But anyways..." Vanessa's voice

brought him back to the present. "Maybe we should go back over what we do have and know." She tapped a finger against her chin. "There must be more *to* that archived love letter. But what?"

Jake pulled out his phone "Let's start with the obvious."

"Well." Vanessa scooted her chair over next to Jake's as he pulled up the search engine. "It makes logical sense that she'd encode or hide something in this letter using a method the Culper members used," she continued. "We know by looking it obviously isn't a number code." She drummed her fingers on the tabletop.

Jake pointed to the website that had loaded. "Says here the Culpers used not only numeric codes to communicate secret messages, but also something called...a sympathetic stain?"

Vanessa tossed her hands in the air. "Why didn't I think of that right away? It's a special type of invisible ink that's synthetic, actually, and was invented by a doctor named James Jay, before the war—" She laughed and waved a hand. "Sorry, I'm getting a bit carried away."

"No, no." Jake propped his chin on his

hand. "This is fascinating—really. I hadn't realized all these details."

Vanessa sat up straighter. "That first love letter was written on pretty decent paper, and Washington instructed the Culpers to use good quality paper, since the ink wasn't legible on poor quality stuff." Her eyes widened. "Wait a minute. That's exactly what the riddle told us."

"Told us what?"

"The second phrase: *when between those lines*. From the reading I've been doing, Washington told the Culpers to use invisible ink in a certain way. He said to write a normal letter but put the coded information between the lines of the regular text. So that confirms we need to use the invisible ink to read between the lines—literally."

Jake nodded.

"You know," Vanessa added, "some people say Washington coined that phrase 'read between the lines.' Maybe now we know why."

"Impressive." Jake nudged Vanessa.

She nudged him back. "Apparently, the ring started out with just using the number code. But when the British started to get more suspicious about mail the Colonists carried, the Culpers began to use invisible ink."

"Man, I love my job." He shook his head. "This is just like something out of a movie."

"I know, right?"

They shared a grin.

"But if I remember correctly, you have to have the right re-agent for the invisible ink to show up." Vanessa pointed at Jake's phone. "Does the article give the formula?"

"Mmm. No. But—" Jake's fingers danced across the phone screen "—here's a site that does." He showed her the result.

"Good. So all we need to do now is get the letter, apply the stain and see if there's anything there."

"Sounds straightforward enough. Except the part about convincing the archivists here to let us put a possibly damaging substance on a piece of priceless American history."

"Right, there *is* that." Vanessa laughed. "Got a tad carried away with my enthusiasm. Well," she gestured to the cameras, "you're the one with the TV cred."

"And you're the one with the museum

cred," he replied, and they shared a grin.

Jake leaned his forearms on the tabletop. "Between the two of us," he said as he slid on his aviator sunglasses, "I think we can figure out something."

IT HAD BEEN a long day, and so, after Vanessa left, Jake retraced his steps and headed back into the building, the film crew not far behind. Vanessa would appreciate his doing a bit of extra research. That was the great thing about libraries. So much information at your fingertips.

With the letter situation on pause, his mind returned to the diary entries they'd found in the wall. Why had those few pages from 355's own journal ended up in the wall?

It stood to reason that doing a little digging on that particular house itself might yield something. Hmm. Blueprints or a city map might be a good place to start.

He pulled open the map room's heavy oak door. This room was as impressive as the rest of the place. Pale blue walls, with built in bookshelves around the perimeter, and an ornate ceiling. He made a beeline for a staff member, an older woman with a purple streak in her graying hair.

"Hi there. I'm doing research related to the city during the Revolution. Do you have any information on Lower Manhattan from that time period?"

"Anything you're looking for specifically?"

"Actually, yeah. A wealthy merchant's house." Jake gave the address.

"Got a name to go with that?"

Jake shook his head.

"Let's see what I can come up with..." The keyboard clacked as the staff member conducted a search.

Jake looked around the room as he waited. People worked at long tables, and he noticed framed maps on the walls.

"Not much I can tell you, I'm afraid."

Jake's shoulders sagged.

"Looks like the titles and deeds for that particular structure didn't survive. A big fire in the early 1900s burned a good portion of 18th century documents for that area of Manhattan that were housed in archival storage. You might take a look at our maps from that period. Would be your best bet."

"Perfect, thanks."

The staff member nodded. "Let me show you where we keep those."

She came out from behind the desk, and headed to a long, low cabinet and pulled out a drawer and tapped the glass covering. "Here you go. From around spring of 1779."

"This is great."

He turned to the map, and studied the yellowed document, its corners crinkled and frayed. Looked like it'd been hand-drawn.

He scanned it, not exactly sure what he was looking for. He located Townsend's store, which was labeled. Then moved his finger over to the address of what was now Vanessa's museum.

He frowned as he made out the words. "Mason's Teas & Fine Imported Goods," he murmured to himself. "I thought that Vanessa said they didn't know who'd owned the place originally."

Then again, maybe she hadn't thought to look at a map? But she'd also said they'd only moved to their current location a month ago, and she certainly had enough to do now with the running of the museum itself.

"Mason," he muttered again. He rubbed a hand across his jaw. Vanessa would like to know this.

His pulse stuttered. Wait a second. Mason. His mind raced. The diary entries from 355 had been in the house—the same house labeled as Mason's Teas & Fine Imports.

Which meant... had they finally found a last name for Agent 355?

Chapter Six

AFTER VANESSA RODE the sweltering subway partway back to her apartment, she decided to walk the rest. The long blocks and marginally cooler, fresher air would do her head some good. Hmmm. How could she arrange to examine that letter in the archives at NYPL more closely?

As she came up the last of the subway steps and onto the street, her thoughts slowed and she felt her mind relax. Maybe if she didn't think too much about it, a solution might come to her. The blue-and-white umbrella from a hotdog vendor set up nearby caught her attention, and the aroma made her mouth water.

But she made herself flick back through her phone's notes app instead, to review her conversation with Kali after she'd left the library today. Her boss had sounded tired after a long stint in the hospital waiting room.

But at least Vanessa'd been able to give her good work news: all the gala tickets had sold, and the temp had helped Vanessa finalize the silent auction details. That office temp was such a lifesaver in all this.

But Vanessa's stomach lurched when she recalled that Kali had also mentioned it would look good if Vanessa brought a date to the gala.

The gala—Vanessa's palms started to sweat. What if it didn't pan out? After all, she was responsible for basically everything about it. She clutched her phone tighter. But then she took a deep breath, made her fingers relax. Panicking over last-minute details wouldn't do her any good. She could do this. It *would* all work out.

And who knew? If she and Jake actually found out 355's identity, and the lost pearls, then it'd boost admission sales, and bring in some much-needed investor funding for the museum, too.

She shoved her hands in her pockets and exhaled slowly as her mind drifted back over the day's events. Her heart thudded as she recalled the way Jake had looked at her over his drink this afternoon. Or how he'd seemed so happy and relaxed in her company.

Her phone vibrated. Jake?

She pulled it out—Melissa. "Hi there, I'm just heading back up to my place."

"Uh-huh... with Jake?"

Vanessa gave an involuntary giggle. "No-o." She sidestepped a man in a suit who'd stopped to buy a magazine from a newsstand.

"You sure about that?" Melissa teased. Without waiting for an answer, she continued. "So. How'd it go today?"

"Well, Jake and I haven't figured out who 355 is yet but we're definitely getting closer. I can feel it."

"I know what that tone of voice means," Melissa said. "You like him."

Vanessa blushed. "We're just...friendly colleagues. Working on this together."

"Mmm-hmm. I know that's what you like to tell yourself."

Vanessa resisted the urge to roll her eyes. "Melissa, you know my track record with men. He needs to stay in the friends camp."

But Vanessa could hear the lack of

conviction in her own words. Her pulse thudded. She did like him and—She sighed. "You're right." She bit her lip. "I'm just afraid to admit it. The thing is, I don't know if he likes me too, or if his friendly, playful personality is just how he treats everyone, and so he thinks we're just...colleagues. Besides that, there's the whole fact that he's going to be gone when this episode wraps."

"So why don't you ask him?"

Vanessa's eyes widened. "I can't just up and ask him that." She waited with a cluster of people at a street corner for the light to change.

"Why not? It's the 21st century." A motorcycle revved its engine, and nearly drowned out Melissa's words.

Vanessa raised her voice. "Because that could ruin what we do have." The remark earned her an amused look from the gray-haired woman beside her, who had a perfect perm and toted a rolling suitcase.

As the light turned green, the motorcycle roared off in a cloud of exhaust.

Vanessa sighed. "I don't want to go tiptoeing around him after I embarrass myself by asking. It's better to just keep things under control, under the carpet. Besides, like I said, he likes to joke around, have fun, kid people. So why should I think he's treating me any differently than any other woman he knows?" She hesitated. "I mean, after the way Eric treated me, how can I trust myself to be a good judge of a man's character?"

"Awww. I think you've just had a few scars on your heart that might be getting in the way..." Melissa's voice was gentle. "I wish I could give you a hug right now."

"Thanks."

After a pause, Melissa said, "But if you're wondering what Jake's thinking, you should just ask him. Because I mean, not to be blunt, but what's the point if you don't?"

"Uh, the point is, I don't risk getting hurt," Vanessa crossed the street. Not too much farther to her place.

"You can't just sit around and do nothing," Melissa pointed out.

"That's your modus operandi, not mine."

"True, but why not give it a shot? You never know."

Vanessa tucked a loose strand of hair

behind her ear as she rummaged in her purse for her keys. "Listen, I just..." She took a breath. "It wouldn't be professional. Can we talk about something else now, please?"

Her friend laughed. "All right, all right."

They continued to chat as Vanessa went into the building and let herself back into her apartment.

But after she hung up and put her phone down on her coffee table, she couldn't help but remember the way that Jake had held her gaze as they'd talked on her couch. Or the feel of his skin beneath her fingertips as he'd told her the story behind his bracelet. The look of earnest openness in his blue-green gaze, and the—

She shook her head. All this daydreaming wasn't doing her any good. It would only create heartbreak in the end. When the episode wrapped. When he had to fly off to some far-flung destination.

But her heart didn't listen. Maybe Melissa was right? What would it hurt if she asked him straight out? Found out his true feelings?

Her breath caught. What if... a slow

smile spread across her lips. What if she asked him to be her plus one at the gala? She needed a date for it anyway. So she'd gauge his reaction to her query. Then she'd know, once and for all.

She took a breath. Now that she'd gotten that straightened out, she needed to focus on the letter at the library.

Hmm. Making the sympathetic stain was pretty straightforward. But that's where the easy part ended.

She needed to apply the stain to the letter. Preferably, in a controlled environment.

But in order to make that happen, she'd have to talk to someone with authority at the archives division of the library, who could give permission for her and Jake to look at the letter again and apply the stain to it.

She tapped her phone against her chin.

She needed—of course. She'd start at the beginning. Kali had been in the museum world a long time, after all, and had all sorts of connections.

She looked down at her phone screen and winced. Kali had so much going on at the moment, she hated to bother the other woman. Then again, this interesting history-related distraction might cheer up her boss a little.

She dialed.

VANESSA STIFLED A yawn as she headed back over to the main library branch early Friday morning. The conversation with Kali about the letter had gone well, and she'd been up pretty late the night before to make sure she'd had everything correct as she'd made the sympathetic stain formula.

As she approached the stone lions and saw Jake, her pulse jumped. He met her gaze and gave her a warm smile.

She returned it but just then, her phone rang. She tore her gaze from his and checked her phone screen. Oh. The head of New York Public Library's manuscripts and archives division. "Hello? Vanessa speaking."

"Vanessa, it's Renee. We spoke yesterday. Just calling to confirm the schedule I'd outlined with you: since your request is so specialized and the library's not yet open to the public today, I'll be at the main doors there in about five minutes to let you in. Everything's been set up for you."

"Right. Sounds good. I've just arrived, so things are on target. Thank you."

She slid her gaze to Jake again.

He leaned against the base of one of the lion statues and scrolled through his phone. The sleeves of his slate blue button-down were rolled up to his elbows. Steam rose from a takeout tray of coffees balanced on the ledge beside him. The film crew milled around nearby.

She ended the call and put the phone back into her purse.

Jake glanced up. "Hey there. Didn't want to interrupt your call earlier but..." He put away his phone and reached for the takeout tray. "It's pretty early, so I brought you this."

Her heart fluttered as he handed her a latte. "Oh, thank you. Think I need this." She took a sip—mmm, just the right amount of sweetening. "I feel like I'm taking advantage." She laughed. "You keep buying me drinks."

"Vanessa." Jake put a hand on her arm and squeezed. His gaze lingered on her face. "The last thing you need to do is worry—I got you a latte because I *wanted* to."

Butterflies swooped through her stomach at his expression. She didn't know what to say, so she didn't reply; instead, she just nodded, and gestured for him to go first as they continued to the entrance.

"Was that call good news?"

"Yes," Vanessa replied as they headed toward the door. "The letter will be out and ready for us. They've prepped everything for us to look at it again."

"Great. I have some good news myself. I found a possible lead here at the library yesterday that you might be interested in," Jake said.

"What's that?" Vanessa said as she adjusted the strap of her bag.

"You'd said you hadn't known the name of the merchant's shop at this address. Well," he paused, "on this old map they had, I found the name of the merchant. He—" But just then, a dark-haired woman appeared.

"Hello, Vanessa, Jake. I'm Renee. It's nice to meet you both," she said as she unlocked the door and held it for them,

HIDDEN TREASURE OF THE HEART

and the film crew. "Come on in."

Vanessa's pulse spiked as she stepped across the threshold. The answers they needed could be right here, in that letter.

As they headed up the stairs and into Room 328, Vanessa slipped on her gloves and slid Jake a glance. She walked over to the letter, which had been laid out on a table.

He was in conversation with a few of his crew members, and looked completely in his element. Vanessa's gaze lingered on him as she recalled Melissa's words.

But no. Vanessa's chest tightened. She couldn't just...outright ask him. She bit her lip. What was she thinking? She wasn't bold like that. There was a reason she preferred the sidelines to the spotlight.

Her heart thudded.

But Jake would leave eventually. He had to. Right? He looked across the room at her and began to move toward her. She made herself look back down at the letter. She didn't need to complicate her life, or tangle up her heart, in something like this.

She got out the beaker and other supplies she'd brought, and arranged them. Jake came up to the table, and stood nearby. She picked up the mixture that contained the sympathetic stain, which was in a small glass beaker next to the letter.

"You ready?" Jake murmured, his lips near her ear.

Tingles shot down the back of Vanessa's neck at the warm caress of his breath against her skin. "Mmm-hmm," she managed.

She picked up a cotton swab and forced her attention to the task at hand as she carefully dunked it into the liquid.

"So how does this work, exactly?" As Jake stood nearby, she felt his body heat like a physical touch.

"Well, from what I've read, the stain acts as a re-agent." She applied the cotton swab to the antique paper and began to move it across the page in a systematic motion. "So wherever the invisible ink has been used, this counteracts that and, with the application of heat, it should make the message appear." She bit her lip and glanced at him. "If there even is a secret message."

He nodded. "What can I do to help?"

She jerked her chin in the direction of

the small flashlight she'd placed nearby. "Can you pick that up, please, and then just hold onto it for a sec?"

"Sure. So was heat always used?" Jake reached for the flashlight she'd set on the table and clicked it on.

"As far as I know, either heat or a chemical called sodium carbonate is needed to reveal the words, so I figured a flashlight bulb would do the trick."

"Ah. Okay, cool."

For a second, as Vanessa's eyes drifted back down to the handwriting in front of her, she imagined the woman writing the letter, in that blue moire gown, perhaps, sitting by a window at her writing desk, quill pen in hand, her heart filled with the hope of new love—

"You look a million miles away," Jake murmured.

"Wha—? Oh," Vanessa startled. "I was just wondering about 355. What did she look like? Was she happy? Did she have any brothers or sisters? You know, something that gives us a fuller picture of her life."

"Well," Jake said, "That's part of the mystery we're trying to unravel, here."

Vanessa couldn't help a sigh as she got to the bottom of the document. "We might never know the whole story."

"But we're beginning to build a more complete picture," Jake reminded her.

"Good point. And maybe this will give us another piece of the puzzle to add to the exhibit," Vanessa said. "Can you bring the flashlight closer?"

Jake did as she asked.

She held the page near enough the flashlight that the warmth would affect the antique paper.

Nothing happened.

Jake's brow furrowed. "What's supposed to happen?"

"Well, normally the message would appear when the—"

"Look at that!" Jake pointed to the third paragraph of the letter.

Vanessa's heart leapt. Faint writing had appeared in the blank space between the third and fourth paragraph.

Jake stood so close their shoulders brushed. "We did it," he whispered as he met her gaze. From this close, she could see shades of deeper indigo and emerald in his blue-green eyes. A slow smile spread across his lips.

Vanessa's gaze lingered on his mouth. They were so close...Her heart squeezed. His sandalwood scent drifted to her. What would happen if she—No. Her eyes darted to the cameras. What was she thinking? She couldn't think like this.

"We did." She made herself look at the writing. "So what does it say?"

Jake's brow furrowed. "It looks like some sort of... recipe?"

She put down the letter and then ran a gloved fingertip across the revealed words. "But a recipe for what?"

"Some sort of drink..." Jake scanned the lines.

She read over his shoulder. "Huh. It's a recipe for drinking chocolate." Vanessa began to pace. "So what does this mean?"

"Maybe we're supposed to make it, drink it and find out." Jake chuckled.

"As much as I love a good hot chocolate..." Vanessa looked at the recipe. She paced faster. "Back in the 18th century, Colonists who were opposed to the tea tax began to drink chocolate instead."

"Okay," Jake said as he studied the letter. "But why would that be such a big secret?" He ran a hand through his hair and his jaw tightened.

Vanessa shook her head. "I'm not really sure. It shouldn't be. I mean, people all over the Colonies did it."

"Then why bother to conceal that?" Jake's brows drew together. "Especially in something like a love letter." He tapped his foot. "This is getting more drawn out and complicated than I thought it would be."

"Ugh, I know." Vanessa rubbed her forehead. "It doesn't make any sense."

Several minutes passed in silence. Jake drummed his fingers on his thigh.

"There has to be something that we're missing here. But what?"

Jake groaned. "I have no idea."

Vanessa kept pacing. The silence stretched.

Jake passed a hand across his face, his tone weary. "The first riddle point us to Rivington's coffeehouse..."

Vanessa stopped pacing suddenly.

"Yes." She spun on her heel to face him. "And," she continued as her eyes widened, "this second piece of the puzzle here refers to something people could drink."

Jake rubbed the back of his neck. "Okay..."

"What if we put those two things together?"

The corner of Jake's mouth lifted and the sparkle returned to his eyes as he looked at her. "Impressive."

Vanessa grinned at him. Her pulse spiked as he held her gaze. It was so much fun to unravel these clues, to explore an avenue of history that very few people had, and to do all that...together. Her breath caught as he continued to look at her.

"So." Jake blinked and pulled his phone out of his pocket. "Let's see what else we can dig up on Rivington."

Jake typed in *drinking chocolate* and *James Rivington*. "Ah-ha." He began to read aloud.

> *During his time as owner of Rivington's Coffeehouse and as the publisher of* The Royal Gazette, *his popular establishment thrived. It developed a reputation as not only a gossip hotspot but also for excellent drinks.*

Jake paused and angled the phone so Vanessa could see. She leaned in toward him to read the second paragraph over his shoulder.

Rivington's brewed strong coffee; it also became known for serving drinking chocolate using bittersweet chocolate. In fact, it has been documented that patrons who liked to indicate their political leanings, would order chocolate instead of coffee as their beverage of choice.

"So where does that lead us—back to Rivington's?"

Vanessa fiddled with a strand of her hair. "That's a dead end." She narrowed her eyes in thought. "And no one found anything besides the diary there, did they?"

"No." Jake ruffled his hair. Vanessa watched the motion and couldn't help but imagine what it might feel like under her fingertips.

"But...?" Vanessa caught the look in his eye.

"Remember that first line of the riddle?"

Vanessa nodded. *"First taste of love is bittersweet."*

"They used bittersweet chocolate to make the recipe," Jake said, "And we have a recipe here."

"Right. So maybe this is about more than the chocolate recipe itself," Vanessa said.

"What do you mean?"

"I think we're confusing the forest and the trees. They *made* the drink at Rivington's, yes... but what do you make hot chocolate in?"

"Boil water in a kettle. Same as what you make tea in." Jake replied.

Instead of saying anything, Vanessa pulled out her phone, made a few keystrokes and then turned the phone so Jake could see too.

"What's that?"

"It's a sterling silver pot from the 1700s, designed specifically for making drinking chocolate. They didn't have instant cocoa back then, so you had to mix together the milk, sugar, spices and grated chocolate yourself." She pointed to the screen. "See how the lid has a hole in the middle? That's for the paddle to fit through, and you agitated the handle to froth the contents. Then you'd end up with hot chocolate."

"Interesting. So you're suggesting we need to find a chocolate pot?"

"But not just any chocolate pot. We need the same one that Nathaniel and 355 used."

JAKE WHISTLED. "THIS'LL be like looking for a needle in a haystack—" A slow grin spread across his face "—the kind of challenge I love best."

"Just like that time you went off to Zanzibar to look for King Solomon's lost mines, huh?"

"Wait..." Jake shoved one hand in his pocket and ducked his chin ever so slightly as he regarded her. "You saw that episode?"

"It's my favorite one. So good." Her eyes lit up. "That free-diving scene where you..." Vanessa's cheeks flushed. "Uh, I mean." She cleared her throat, brought her gaze back to his and finished her sentence with a simple, "Yes, I did."

A buzz jolted through him at her words. People had complimented his show, said they were fans, before, of course. At conventions. At speaking events.

But somehow—his breath caught as his gaze lingered on Vanessa—having *her* say it felt like the very first time he'd ever heard it.

"Thank you," he said quietly as he looked into her eyes.

She smiled she held his gaze. "You're welcome."

There was a beat of silence. Oops. They were still filming. He'd better say something professional-sounding.

"So, before we got onto the topic of this letter, I'd mentioned a bit of good news."

"Right." Vanessa tucked a strand of hair behind her ear. "Something about a merchant."

"Your museum was a tea merchant's shop named Mason's Teas & Fine Imports."

"That's amazing." Vanessa grinned. "And the time period matched?"

Jake nodded. "Could mean 355's last name was Mason."

"It could..." Vanessa tilted her head.

"We'll have to do some research. It's just conjuncture at this point, since we don't have any solid evidence to back it up."

"No, we don't. But," he gestured toward the letter, "maybe this'll give us a clue about that while we're working on the chocolate pot angle. Any suggestions on where to look next?'

Vanessa tapped her forefinger against her chin. "I think we've done all we can here, so let's head back to the museum. If I remember correctly, the Museum of the American Revolution in Philadelphia has a whole exhibit on sterling silver used during the war." She picked up her bag. "We'll start with a call to them."

Vanessa and Jake thanked Renee and headed out of the library, the crew not far behind. Once they all got back to the museum, Vanessa made a beeline for the phone on her desk.

But a few minutes later, when she'd hung up, she turned to Jake. "The curator I know there said that they didn't have any chocolate pots at the moment." Her shoulders drooped.

Jake shook his head. "Maybe if we brainstorm every possible angle?"

But even after they did that, they were no closer to an answer.

"Hmm. Okay." Jake clenched his jaw and resisted the urge to look at his calendar app with that looming deadline. "Maybe we need to narrow things down a bit more?" He crossed his arms and narrowed his eyes. They had to figure this out. "What if we confine our search to New York City?"

"Still a pretty big area," Vanessa mused.

Jack scraped a hand across his stubble. "If we call all the museums within the New York metro area, we'll bound to come up with something—I hope."

They spent the next hour making calls and scrolling through museum websites.

"Still nothing." Vanessa sighed. "Needle in a haystack might be right."

Jake jiggled his foot. "Let's just keep—"

Suddenly, Vanessa's desk phone rang. She picked up the receiver. "Hello? Vanessa speaking."

Jake watched Vanessa cradle the phone against her shoulder as she picked up a pen and scribbled something down on a piece of paper. "Right. Okay. Thanks." She hung up, her eyes bright as she looked at Jake.

Hope flared in his chest.

"That was my Philadelphia contact. She said she knows someone I can talk to at the Met."

Finally, a breakthrough. "Awesome."

Jake's pulse spiked as he held her gaze. She loved this as much as he did, didn't she? His stomach tightened. The gleam in her eye told him that yes, she definitely did.

His breath hitched. What would happen if he asked her to go with him after shooting this episode? Asked her to take that next adventure with him, set off to parts unknown...together? Heat filled him as she watched him. He had a feeling she just might say yes.

"Hey, Jake," Bryce said from a few feet away. Jake tore his gaze away from Vanessa's.

She took a hasty step around the desk and began to shuffle through papers.

Jake chose to ignore the ping of disappointment in his chest at her move. "What's up?" He turned to Bryce.

"I'm just gonna fix some coffee. You guys want any?"

"I'm good." He glanced at Vanessa, who

shook her head.

Bryce started to turn away.

"But you knock any hidden treasure out of the wall in there, man, you'll give me a cut, right?" Jake called after Bryce as he and a couple more on the team headed into the break room.

"Guess we could take a bit of a break, too." Jake shifted his attention back to Vanessa. "How's the exhibit coming along?"

Vanessa stopped her paper shuffling. "Good, actually. I've gotten the exhibit description all written up. Now I'm working on numbering the artifacts and drawings, and some other stuff that'll actually be on display for people to see."

"Oh cool. Glad it's going well." Jake said in a warm tone. "What about the gala?"

"Well, the tickets have all sold. And there seems to be a decent amount of interest in the silent auction, which takes place at the gala."

"Great to hear."

"But," she twirled a strand of hair around her finger, "I've been thinking..." She paused. "If this all leads somewhere..."

Jake held his breath.

"... it'd be fun to do a whole exhibit focused just on Agent 355. Even add in the earrings my grandmother gave me."

"That'd be fantastic."

"Thanks. I—"

"Jake!" Bryce called from the break room, "I think you should get in here."

JAKE AND VANESSA exchanged a look on the threshold of the break room as Bryce held up some old-looking papers.

"I'm having deja vu all over again." Jake winked at Vanessa as she glanced from Jake to Bryce, and back to Jake.

"More pages?" She took a step toward Bryce.

"Looks like it," he said.

"I thought we got everything out of there," Jake murmured.

"Guess not quite." Bryce shrugged. "Another stone loosened somehow. In fact there's still *more* loose mortar here." He jerked a thumb behind him. "But I've been at too many locations with you not to expect the unexpected."

Jake laughed. "True."

"Don't move," Vanessa replied. "I'll be right back."

A moment later, Vanessa came back into the room with her gloves. She assessed the antique papers then looked up at Jake, her eyes bright. "They're more diary entries."

"From 355?"

Vanessa nodded and angled the paper so Jake could read it too.

11 June 1780

Though it pains me greatly to record this, I must have somewhere to relieve my burdened heart. Father has, this night, formally given his permission for Lord C— m to court me.

I fear his attentions are rather…ardent, and that marriage is on his mind. But I take some comfort in bringing Nathaniel's face, as well as the Cause, to mind even as I make polite conversation with Lord C— m.

He tells me of his achievements and his position as Royal Navy commander. Indeed, tonight he seemed to talk of nothing else. Most fortunate. He must assume it impresses me. No doubt the quantity of sherry he consumed, coupled with his incorrect assumptions about his present company, effected his lack of caution.

Little does he know how this plays into the favor of the Patriots, for he let slip that the British know of the French fleet set to land at Newport. I am sure 711 will make good use of this.

"711?" Jake slid a glance to Vanessa.

"General Washington's code number designation."

"Oh, right. I didn't *think* she was referring to Slurpees in that sentence, but I just wanted to make sure."

Vanessa swatted Jake's arm.

"So she's openly admitting here," Jake said, "that she's using this guy to pass information on to Washington and the Patriots."

"Right," Vanessa said. "And it looks like her father approved of the match, since he was the one to introduce them."

"Probably wanted to make sure his daughter married a nice Loyalist. But what's this about the British finding out a French fleet was landing at Newport?"

"I don't know every detail of every Revolutionary battle, so let's see here." Vanessa turned to her phone's search engine.

"Okay. According to this online article, after the Colonists got France on their side, a French fleet was sent to Newport, Rhode Island to drop off troops there. But because the British occupied New York, they had control of Long Island Sound."

"And Newport's above Long Island," Bryce added.

"Yep," Vanessa said. "After the British found out about the French fleet, they planned to intercept it before the French troops could land."

"But it looks like 355 tipped Washington off to that fact," Jake said.

"Exactly." Vanessa grinned. "Thanks to this Lord C guy."

"You know," Jake said, "I wonder if we looked him up, he might point us to more clues about 355's identity?"

"Good idea. Let's make a note of that." Jake said, as he pulled up the sticky notes app on his phone. He turned back to the letter. "But why didn't she just write out this Lord C's name?"

"Would've been convenient for us, wouldn't it? But that was a pretty common practice back then. Usually happened in letters; in fact, in some of Washington's correspondence, he uses the abbreviation C—r to mean Culper."

"Huh."

"And from time to time you see this type of abbreviation in journals and such. If the person knew who they were referring to, they didn't bother writing in the full name sometimes."

"Makes sense. What's on the other page?"

4 July 1780

Though I told Father I met with Sally at Rivington's, I confess I met Nathaniel instead, as he works there from time to time. And, oh, he has introduced me to the most divine of delicious treats — drinking chocolate. I have never before tasted anything so rich and heady. Unless, of course, one counts the taste of her true love's kiss. But a lady does not speak of such things...

He requested the beverage specially then whispered in my ear of its secret meaning among those of the Cause. Rivington even uses a specific chocolate pot for the purpose.

I know that I shall always, from this day forward, be unable to partake of that beverage without also thinking of him.

'Tis preferable to thinking of Lord C— m, though he has done his best to infringe upon my thoughts. At our most recent meeting, he boasted of his latest capture: Cignet. I'm told the French frigate now sits in New York harbor awaiting a refit.' 'Twill be renamed the Swan and flies the British colors.

I had half a mind to inquire as to the whereabouts of my worsted wool amongst its cargo, but I imagine the Royal Navy has made good use of my material.

He did regale me, too, with the wonders of the ship's hold, includ-

ing a mahogany chest, which contained a cache of the largest pearls he'd ever seen. But when I pressed him, he remarked upon my love of such baubles, then claimed to know not if the cache still resides there.

Those pearls were intended for 711, to provide funds to bolster the Cause.

I have made it known to 721 that I shall stop at nothing to obtain as much information as I can as to the current whereabouts of the cache, and do my part to retrieve it.

Jake met Vanessa's gaze. "Now we have proof 355 was definitely involved with the pearls," he said.

"And it looks like she never got the material to make the flag," Vanessa said.

"Which is how she must've decided to use her own cloak," Jake added.

Vanessa nodded then pointed to the letter. "And here, she talks about a specific chocolate pot at Rivington's. We were right." She scanned the lines again. "Do you think she used that specific one to somehow to pass a message on to Washington or other Culper members about the pearls?"

"Only one way to answer that."

Mid-morning Saturday, as Jake's rented Land Rover headed along Route 25A out east toward Setauket, Long Island, Vanessa watched the sunlight as it filtered through the trees, glad to focus on the open space outside the vehicle.

But she couldn't help admiring that same light glint off Jake's wavy brown hair and highlight the gold undertones as he drove. Her heart gave a double-beat. That teal blue shirt was a good color on him.

She tucked a strand of her hair behind her ear and pulled her eyes back to the road ahead, as she tried to ignore just how close together they were sitting.

Vanessa fidgeted with her seatbelt strap for a moment before she took her phone out and absently flicked through the apps. She hoped Jake didn't notice her nervousness. Then again, it wasn't every day she was alone in a vehicle for two hours with her celebrity crush. She hid a grin.

Jake pushed his aviator sunglasses up and then downshifted as they slowed for an intersection.

"Huh, I hadn't realized that," Jake murmured.

"What's that?" Vanessa looked up from her phone.

He indicated a small brown highway sign. "See that white carriage silhouette?"

"Oh yeah, it says Washington's Spy Trail. I didn't realize this road had a nickname. Makes sense, though. Culper members must've used this route to travel back and forth between the city and Setauket."

Just then, Vanessa's phone dinged. She checked the calendar notification. *Final seating arrangements meeting @ 4 p.m. today.* Right. She'd almost forgotten.

"This is a nice change of scene from the city," Vanessa commented.

"It is, but I might be a tad bias. I'm actually from the East Coast myself."

"New York state?"

"Nope. A tiny town up in Maine," Jake said.

"Oh yeah? I haven't been much past the L.L. Bean store in Freeport, out that way."

"I get all my camping gear there," Jake said.

They drove awhile in companionable silence as Vanessa watched the trees and houses roll by.

Finally, Jake said, "We're getting near Setauket. Where did your contact at the Met tell you this woman's house was, again?" Jake adjusted his grip on the leather-wrapped steering wheel. He glanced at Vanessa then at the in-dash GPS. "I swear, this thing has a mind of its own. I think it's probably broken."

Vanessa double-checked her phone then read the address to Jake before she craned her neck to look around. "So my contact, Cindy, said Rhonda Miller's was on the right, oh, just off the highway here."

Jake slowed and signaled.

"Wait, maybe it's the next right? Uh..." She reread the address. "No, no, it's here. I think."

Jake made a right onto the quieter street Vanessa indicated. "Okay."

"...And then there'll be a red mailbox on the opposite side of the street—" she sat back "—which I don't see anywhere."

She gave a frustrated sigh and put her hands in the lap of her khaki capris. "I'm hopeless with directions. I get so turned around out here."

"And this thing keeps telling me to make a U turn." Jake chuckled. "Technology. Why doesn't it work right when you need it?" He tightened his grip on the wheel. "But we'll find it."

Vanessa's gaze drifted to Jake's hands. How many places had he navigated from the driver's seat of an SUV? Nepal...Ghana...What if Jake reached across the console and put his hand on her knee, his palm warm, his fingers strong, sure—

No. She tore her mind away from the daydream and fiddled with the hem of her yellow T-shirt. He was leaving. She couldn't do this to herself. "Let's hope. It's our only good lead," Vanessa replied. "Cindy mentioned the Met's installation of Revolutionary War silver was donated by Rhonda Miller's husband. He collected chocolate pots, and that was where they'd gotten their original donation."

Vanessa looked out the window. "Hmm, I still don't see the right house." She checked the address again. "Unless it *was* supposed to be that next street..."

They drove a ways farther, around a slight bend in the road. As they rounded it, Jake lifted a finger off the wheel and pointed. "I see a red mailbox up ahead. Think this is the house, across the street here."

Two huge oak trees stood on either side of a two storey Federal-style home painted a light blue. It had bright white trim and a shiny brass knocker in the middle of a red front door.

Vanessa peered through the windshield as the vehicle came to a stop a few moments later by one of the large oaks.

Jake cut the engine. She caught a whiff of his sandalwood cologne as he unbuckled his seatbelt.

Vanessa wound a strand of her hair around her finger and said with a laugh. "Sorry about that. I'm not the best navigator."

Instead of replying, Jake fished something out of one of the small zippered pockets on the sleeve of his safari shirt.

She noticed the way the cotton stretched across his chest when he held out the item to her in his open palm. A compass.

Her heartbeat sped up when he met her gaze as the needle pointed to N.

"No worries. We're not lost." Then he winked as he reached for his door handle and said, "Let's do this."

HIDDEN TREASURE OF THE HEART

She fumbled for her own door handle, then stepped out and shut the door.

"Hello there," a female voice called.

A woman with thick black hair woven into a French braid came around the side of the house.

She looked to be in her mid-sixties, and she wore a pair of sturdy bright yellow gardening gloves. She carried a set of pruning sheers in one hand, and pushed back the brim of her straw hat with the other, before she waved at them.

"Hi there." Jake called back and strode over to greet her. Just then, Bryce and the crew pulled up in the equipment van behind Jake's Land Rover. They parked, quickly got out and followed Jake.

As Jake shook hands, Vanessa took in the rest of the scenery. More large oak and maple trees surrounded the back of the property, and the house was situated on a large sloping lot.

So near New York but so peaceful out here, too. Vanessa took a deep breath of the fresh air and stretched. Her fingertips brushed the rough bark of one of the oak trees they'd parked near, and she tilted her head to look at it.

Must be three hundred years old, at least. It was absolutely huge. She craned her neck to look farther up the leafy green canopy.

As she did, she noticed a sort of indentation in the bark just above her eye level and frowned. Was something carved into the wood?

She took a step closer. Yes. It looked like...She cocked her head and brushed her fingers across it. Initials, with...was that a heart around it?

She slowly traced the slightly crooked heart shape, and the initials inside.

"H.M. + N.W.," she murmured under her breath. "Huh."

But she was getting sidetracked. She stepped around the tree. She'd better stop lollygagging and get over to the house.

She saw Jake and company standing near the front steps, talking to Rhonda. Looked like he was explaining a few filming details to her.

Jake glanced over at Vanessa as she approached. "Didn't get lost, did you?" His eyes sparkled.

"Not this time."

"Vanessa, this is Rhonda Miller." Jake

indicated the older woman.

"Nice to meet you, Vanessa. You must be who Cindy mentioned."

"Yes, I work for the Women of the American Revolution Museum in the city." Vanessa smiled.

"Well, let's not stand around on the steps. I have far more comfortable places inside. Come in." Rhonda opened the door and walked into the front hall.

A little while later, they'd all assembled in the living room, which had a picture window and a view of the side yard. Black-eyed Susans and butterfly milkweed bloomed in neat rows around some weathered statuary and snowball bushes.

"Your yard is lovely," Vanessa commented. She sat near Jake on the long low white couch.

"Oh, thank you," Rhonda said from a matching armchair opposite. "My late husband always used to say for every flower I planted, he'd get to collect another piece of Revolutionary silver."

Jake leaned forward and Vanessa felt the couch cushions move ever so slightly under her as he did.

"Speaking of," Jake said, "how did your

husband get into that? You'd mentioned he had a few chocolate pots?"

Rhonda laughed. "Several, yes. He donated a lot of his silver collection to the Museum of the American Revolution, but he passed away suddenly last year. So he never got a chance to do anything with his chocolate pots." She looked back and forth between Vanessa and Jake. "But I understand you two might want to take a look at them?"

"Yes, please." Vanessa shared a glance with Jake.

"It just might change history if they do," Bryce chimed in.

"Well," Rhonda said, as she got to her feet, "who am I to get in the way of that? It's just down here."

They followed her as she walked to a door at the end of the hall. She took a key from her pocket and fit it into a substantial-looking lock. The door swung open and she stepped inside.

The crew followed, and the lighting guy scurried past Rhonda to arrange reflectors.

Once things had been fully set up, Jake and Vanessa walked into the room.

Jake let out a long, low whistle as he looked around the room. "You've got to be kidding me. This is incredible."

Rhonda laughed. "What can I say?"

Every flat surface was covered with some sort of chocolate pot.

"They're everywhere." Vanessa's eyes widened. "You could start your own museum, you have so many."

"I could," Rhonda folded her arms across her chest. "Take as long as you like. And if you have any questions, I'm happy to try and answer them. Though I can't guarantee I'll know what you might want to find out."

Jake chuckled in disbelief and shook his head as Vanessa came over to him. "I feel like I'm in *Indiana Jones and the Last Crusade*."

"At least there aren't some Nazis lurking."

"And I'm pretty sure I'm not going to die if I don't pick the right one." Jake ran a finger down the spout of the nearest pot. He pressed his lips together for a moment. "But the show's future is riding on this. So let's get to work."

After a second, he added, "So how are

we going to figure out which one Nathaniel and 355 used?"

"That's an excellent question..." Vanessa paused and thought a moment. "Let's keep a watch for details specific to the 18th century."

"A good place to start."

But three hours later, they'd barely made a dent in the collection. "All these different eras are mixed together. We need some way to narrow things down even more," Vanessa muttered to herself and tapped her finger against her bottom lip.

She darted a glance toward then away from the cameras. Best to keep pretending she wasn't being filmed.

Jake closed his eyes a moment and a frown line appeared between his brows. He rubbed his shoulders and slowly exhaled.

Rhonda stuck her head back into the room. "How's it going?"

Vanessa turned to Rhonda. "Did your husband have some sort of...cataloging system for all of this?"

The older woman shook her head. "I actually really don't know. I never specifically asked him. And between you and I, honestly I wouldn't know one chocolate pot from another."

Jake had just set down an elaborately carved chocolate pot with an ivory handle when Rhonda spoke again. "But I do know that my husband's most recent acquisitions are those pots over in that far corner." She gestured. "He'd acquired them just before he passed. I remember he made a comment, something about them being specially made in the Colonies."

Jake and Vanessa exchanged a look and headed over to the far corner.

Vanessa picked up the first pot and examined it. "Looks pretty fancy. Then again, they're all starting to look alike."

"I know exactly what you mean." Jake gave a theatrical groan.

"This really could be a needle in a haystack." Vanessa massaged her temples. "Maybe Nathaniel meeting with Agent 355 at Rivington's has nothing to do with any of this." She waved a hand to indicate the room.

Jake put a hand on her shoulder. "Eventually, we'll work our way through the whole collection," he said, a determined set to his jaw. "I'd think there has to be *some* indication of something."

The man never quit, did he? Vanessa's heart swelled. His optimistic determination was endearing—something else about him, she realized with a jolt, that she'd really come to appreciate. "Right." Vanessa gave a firm nod as she picked up another pot and examined it.

"Sorry," Rhonda said. "but did you say Nathaniel?"

Vanessa nodded then explained what they were doing and what they'd already uncovered.

"A man by the name of Nathaniel Wheeler was the grandson of the very first owner of this place. In fact, Nathaniel moved into this house right around the time that the Revolution started. I actually donated a few papers I'd found of his to a museum in Morristown, New Jersey."

Vanessa propped a hand on her hip. "His initials would be N.W., wouldn't they?"

Rhonda nodded.

A speculative look came into Vanessa's eyes and she glanced at Jake. "I think we'll want to see that big oak out front."

Jake put down the pot he held and they

all followed Rhonda out the front door.

Rhonda walked over to the huge oak that Vanessa had seen when she'd arrived.

"This tree," Rhonda said, "has been here since about 1760. Apparently it was planted by the first family who lived here."

"Wow." Jake placed a palm on the tree.

"So when you said Nathaniel," Rhonda continued, "well," she indicated the initials carved into the trunk. "This carving has been here since the Revolution. It's actually what sold me on the property."

"Why's that?" Vanessa asked.

"Because the story I always heard was that his lover..." she tapped the H.M. initials, "was supposed to be Agent 355."

JAKE SAW VANESSA pull up the notes app on her phone. Must be for her exhibit research.

"From the preliminary research I've done," Vanessa said, "I haven't been able to find any connection between that tea merchant's name and 355. Rhonda, do you know if the M in these initials stands for the last name Mason?" Her fingers flew across the screen.

"Unfortunately, I don't know what either initial stands for. No one I've talked to over the years seems to, either."

"Oh." Vanessa made a few final notations then lowered her phone.

"But isn't that romantic? Their initials are still here after more than 200 years." Rhonda patted the tree trunk. "Reminds me of my own marriage."

Jake flexed his fingers against the rough bark of the oak. Wait a second. He looked up at the engraved trunk, then around the property. What if they'd been going about this in entirely the wrong way, and a clue was hidden outside? His heartbeat sped up.

He turned to Rhonda. "Do you have a spare shovel?"

"I'VE GOT A hit over here," Jake called to Bryce. The low, long beep of the metal detector made Jake's pulse race. If he was right...

Vanessa snatched up the shovel before Jake could move.

Jake grinned at her then pointed at the ground near the base of the oak. "Let's try right about here. As close as possible to the target." He swept the metal detector again over the grass, just to make sure. The long, low beep sounded again, in the exact same spot—right by his foot.

"Dig here?" Vanessa said, her focus intent, completely oblivious to Bryce filming not far away.

"Yep."

The shovel bit into the neatly manicured lawn. Jake knelt beside Vanessa and they carefully upended the chunk of sod, making sure not to displace any of the grass.

Jake reached into the pack Bryce had brought over earlier, and pulled out a hand-held detector.

"What's that?" Vanessa said as she put aside the shovel.

"Now that we've displaced the dirt, it'll pinpoint things more specifically."

"Handy," Vanessa commented as she took a trowel and glanced at Jake. He waved the hand-held device and it emitted a sharp sustained beep about three-quarters of the way down into the hole they'd dug.

"Right over here," Jake commented. "I can dig if you want."

"Not a chance," Vanessa tightened her grip on the trowel.

"Looks like you've discovered a new passion," Jake quipped as he held her gaze.

She looked at him from under her lashes. "I think I have." Vanessa slid the trowel into the earth and turned over a few scoops. Just dirt.

"How come nothing's coming up?" She sat back on her heels.

"The detector says there's something, so there's something. Just gotta be patient," Jake murmured. "Trust me, I've done this enough. Sometimes it's deeper than you think."

Vanessa nodded. Handed him the trowel. "I'll leave this in the hands of an expert, then."

"Oh, I see how this is working. Now you give it to me?" Jake teased.

Vanessa laughed.

A moment later, there was a clunk of metal hitting metal. Jake raised his eyes to Vanessa's. Her eyes widened. His heart pounded.

"The moment of truth," he said as Vanessa leaned forward to help him brush away the dirt. They worked for several minutes in silence, and the buzz of adrenaline coursed through Jake.

"Look at that," he murmured, as a long, cylindrical shape was revealed.

"That must be..." Vanessa cocked her head.

"Yep," he said between clenched teeth as he tugged it free, "it's a chocolate pot."

Chapter Seven

VANESSA TUCKED A strand of hair behind her ear as she glanced up from the chocolate pot toward Jake.

He had a streak of dirt on his cheek, his hair was windblown, and the sparkle in his eyes made butterflies swoop through her stomach.

"This must be it," she whispered as she moved closer and reached a hand out to touch the blackened silver.

Jake held up the pot. "Man. You can just feel the history here."

"Yes," Vanessa murmured, her voice low, soft. She met his gaze. He did appreciate history, didn't he? Her heart jumped. He totally got it. Completely. But she couldn't get carried away. They were filming this, for heaven's sake. She cleared her throat. "I, um, so, this is definitely the right pot then?"

"I'd say that's a 99.9 percent yes," Jake replied. "Rhonda verified this tree was here in the right time period. The carved initials N.W. match the name Nathaniel Wheeler. That letter from 355 is addressed to a Nathaniel, which coincides with what Rhonda told us about 355. Besides, a chocolate pot does seem like a pretty unusual choice to just bury randomly in your yard."

Vanessa nodded. "It's as close an explanation as we're likely to get."

"Since it's so tarnished, we know it's real silver. And it's heavy. What're your thoughts?" Jake said.

"I'm not sure. Can I see it?"

Jake handed the tarnished silver pot to her. She opened the hinged lid, which didn't sit correctly. One of the delicate hinges had broken, and the handle had come unattached from its fittings on the side of the pot.

She peered inside. "Nothing in here." She angled it so Jake could see.

"Mmm." He rubbed his jaw, which made another streak of dirt.

Vanessa giggled.

"What?" Jake said.

"Your face..."

He pretended to look horrified. "Am I melting?"

"You have a streak of dirt right...there." She pointed to her own chin.

He reached a hand up to his face. His brow furrowed.

"No, no, it's—Here." She reached out, brushed her fingers against his jaw. His stubble grazed her fingertips and the warmth of his skin made a thrill ripple through her.

She had to resist the urge to keep her hand there, memorize the shape of his face. Instead, she slowly brushed her thumb along his jawline where the dirt stuck, and it fell away.

She heard his breath catch as their eyes met, and the blood pounded in her ears. She forgot everything except the exact shade of his blue-green eyes in that moment, the way that his expression seemed to gauge and comprehend more than she could begin to understand. If she leaned in, put her hands on his broad shoulders, brought her lips to his—

Her stomach tightened. No. They were filming right this second. What was she even thinking? She dropped her hand. Brushed dirt vigorously off her capris. He was just here to shoot this episode. He'd be leaving in a matter of days.

He cleared his throat. After a beat of silence, he said, "Thanks," and pulled his gaze back to the chocolate pot. "Well, if nothing's in it, then we need to look *on* it. Why don't we take it back to the house, polish it up, see what we can see? I'll send a message to my boss's husband Todd and ask his opinion, since he does know about antique silver pieces."

"Good idea."

With Rhonda's permission, they set up an area on the wide farmhouse-style dining table in the kitchen and got to work.

Before long, the pot shone like new. Vanessa snapped some photos. "Might as well document this while we wait for Todd to get back to us," she commented to Jake, who nodded.

"Could be something the museum could add to its collection," she said to Rhonda.

"I'm sure I'd be happy to donate it. Your exhibit sounds very interesting."

"We'd need to get all the paperwork

arranged first, though."

"Of course." Rhonda waved a hand. "Not a problem." She took a step over to their work site. "What have you found?"

Vanessa picked up the pot to show Rhonda.

Jake rubbed the back of his neck. "We think that's the maker's mark—probably a European name—on the bottom." He pointed.

Enque 7/64

"Interesting. Well, good luck. I'll leave you two at it."

Jake's phone beeped as Vanessa set the pot back on the kitchen table.

Jake read the text. "So Todd said he's never heard of that maker, but he said it does look like it could possibly be French. Also said it's not consistent with the other kinds of silversmith's marks common in the Colonial era."

Vanessa frowned. "But what else could it be? There are no other distinguishing marks. Just a few dents and dings."

"Which is kind of odd, right?" Jake said.

Jake's phone pinged again. "Todd said

he's also asked his former boss at Rick's Olde Gold in Madison. He'll let us know when Rick gets back to him."

"Okay." Vanessa exhaled slowly. "it's funny, because normally sterling like this is at least stamped 925."

"Which indicates....?"

"The percent of silver in the piece," Vanessa said. "Ninety-two point five percent, to be exact."

"I thought you didn't know anything about silver," Jake teased.

"Oh," Vanessa waved a hand, "that's just basic knowledge."

"Basic for a genius like you." Jake raised a single eyebrow.

Vanessa laughed.

"So is the 7/64 a percentage or something too?" Jake said.

"Mmm, I don't think so." Vanessa pulled up the search engine on her phone. "A lot of times, if an artist, in this case, a silversmith, had been commissioned to create a series of similar works, the number of each piece would be stamped on the bottom."

"So the seven indicates it's the seventh of 64 pieces commissioned?" Jake said.

"That's my educated guess," Vanessa replied. Just then, her phone dinged. She checked her notifications. "Oh no. How could I've completely forgotten?" Her eyes widened and she glanced from her watch back up to Jake.

"What is it?" His brow furrowed.

"I need to get back into the city like, right now." She shoved her phone in her pocket. "I have that final meeting with the event coordinator to go over the seating arrangements for the gala."

She winced. "And I'm already late."

Jake put a hand on her arm. "Don't worry. I'll drive you."

AFTER JAKE PULLED the Land Rover to a stop in front of Vanessa's museum, he took a deep breath as she unbuckled her seatbelt.

"Thanks so much, Jake," Vanessa turned to him. "You didn't have to drive me all the way back to the museum."

Jake rubbed a palm against the smooth leather of the steering wheel. "You're welcome." He held her gaze. "I wanted to."

"Well..." She picked up her purse. "I need to run."

Jake's heart rate sped up. It was now or never. "Wait. Vanessa?"

She paused, her hand on the door handle as she gave him a questioning look.

He held his breath a moment before he said, "I bought two tickets to the gala—gotta support history." He cleared his throat. "But uh, would you want to go with me?"

A slow blush crept up Vanessa's cheeks, and for a moment, neither of them spoke. Jake's heart skipped a beat as the silence stretched. Was she thinking of ways to politely reject him?

He felt his palms begin to sweat.

"You're inviting me to my own event?" She raised her eyebrows.

"Hey, any excuse." Jake fidgeted with the stones on his bracelet. "But seriously." He leaned forward, rested one forearm on the console. "You need a plus one, right?"

Vanessa's cheeks heated but she found she couldn't look away from him. Why was she hesitating? He was right.

Vanessa laughed as her stomach flipped. "Then my answer is yes, I'll go with you."

"So I can wear my fedora and leather jacket, then?"

Vanessa's eyes widened. "It's black tie."

Jake chuckled. "You're so fun to tease."

She narrowed her eyes at him and poked a finger toward his chest. "It's on Thursday night, mister. Not long from now, so you'd better be ready."

VANESSA EXHALED LONG and slow in an effort to stop the pounding of her heart. But her pulse jumped anyway when she replayed that look in Jake's eyes as he asked her to the gala.

She chewed on the inside of her lip. She'd chickened out of her own decision to ask him; he'd beat her to it. But she was more than a little relieved he'd chosen to take the plunge instead. Butterflies swirled through her.

"—have 500 arranged, then, correct?" Kali said.

Oops. Focus. Vanessa brought her attention back to her computer screen and the video call with her boss. "...Uh, yes. That's correct. There are 500 tickets and all of them have been sold. We'll have to wait and see what the totals are once the event is over and the proceeds from the silent auction are counted, but according to my preliminary calculations, the ticket sales should cover half of what we need for this fiscal year."

"Right. Good. I trust the final meeting with the event coordinator went well?"

Vanessa nodded, and decided there was no point in mentioning she'd been late for it. "Everything's all set and ready to go. All I need to do now is show up."

"Good. I really wish I could go but I still don't know how things will turn out with this latest surgery." Vanessa saw the older woman rub her wedding band.

"Kali, I know you're stressed, but please try not to worry about everything here. I've got it under control. You just focus on your husband, okay?"

Kali exhaled slowly. "I appreciate that."

"You're welcome." Vanessa wished there was something else she could do to help out her boss. But having a successful gala event would be the best thing—for the museum, her boss, and her own job—at the moment.

Unless—a grin flitted across Vanessa's face—she and Jake actually figured out 355's identity and found the pearls. *That* would make Kali ecstatic, since it could save the museum—investor funding for a find that big would surely pour in.

Kali leaned forward. "You've gotten a plus one then, right?"

Vanessa fiddled with a strand of her hair as she nodded.

"Well," Kali sat back. "Everything's all set then. Good luck with it, and have fun."

"Thanks." Vanessa held up crossed fingers.

LATE THURSDAY AFTERNOON, the bell over the tiny dry cleaning shop tinkled as Vanessa exited. She threw the plastic garment bag over her arm, and smoothed her hand across the plastic. The sunlight shimmered across the iridescent silver threads in the midnight-blue taffeta.

She checked her watch. She'd made all the rest of the preparations, and the only thing left to do now was get ready. Her heart skipped a beat. The event started at seven o'clock.

She let herself back into her apartment and put the dress down on her bed. Then she texted Melissa. *Just got my dress. Can you come down?*

Be there in ten!

A little while later, a knock sounded at the door before Melissa let herself in. "Vanessa?" she called.

"In here," Vanessa stuck her head out of the bathroom as she put the finishing touches on her toenail polish. She always wore this blush pink color for luck at big events. And tonight was definitely not going to be the first exception to her little rule, not when a date with Jake Ford was in the balance.

She wiggled her toes as they air dried, then padded barefoot from the bathroom back into her bedroom. Melissa was already there with her large makeup case. "So I'm thinking a pale shimmery silver would set off the midnight blue nicely," her friend said as she arranged a set of brushes on the vanity table.

Vanessa nodded. "I totally trust your judgment. I'm hopeless with my own makeup application."

"Can't have you looking anything less than your best," Melissa replied as she pulled out the vanity stool and indicated Vanessa should sit.

Forty minutes later, Vanessa assessed her appearance in the mirror. "You're right. The silver eye shadow just really compliments this material." She had a light dusting of blush across her cheekbones, and Melissa had pinned up her dark hair into a smooth French twist. "You're a wizard with makeup."

Melissa shrugged. "Just a side hobby." She checked her watch. "You might want to put on the dress now. Jake should be here soon."

Vanessa's stomach fizzed at her words as she slipped into the low-backed gown.

"Perfect," Melissa gave her a thumbs up as she helped zip up the dress.

"Thanks so much, Melissa. You're the best." She gave her friend a hug.

Melissa wiggled her eyebrows at Vanessa. "You'd better tell me every detail of your evening with Mr. Jake Ford when you get back."

Vanessa raised her hand. "Scout's honor."

"Go on, then," Melissa said. "Enjoy your evening."

After Melissa left, Vanessa paced back and forth in her apartment's foyer by the intercom. She resisted the urge to chew her lip. Couldn't smear her lipstick. Not that it was something she usually wore. She was more of a low-maintenance kind of—

Buzz-buzz.

Jake.

Vanessa fumbled with her sling-back heels as she put them on then pressed the talk button. "I'm on my way down," she said.

There was a crackle of static.

"I—be wait—" Jake's voice came through the intercom in a hiss of static. The building manager hadn't yet got around to replacing the ancient wiring but Vanessa assumed Jake'd said he'd be waiting in the lobby.

Vanessa nearly dropped the keys as she left her apartment and locked it then realized she'd forgotten her wrap and her clutch. She shook her head at herself, darted in to retrieve them, and then re-locked the door.

She made her way down the stairs and rounded the corner to head into the lobby. Jake stood there in the foyer.

He wore a crisp white dress shirt underneath a black tuxedo jacket with a black bowtie, and his hair was carefully styled.

He looked up from his phone and met her gaze. As he put his phone in his jacket pocket, the hematite stones of his bracelet caught the light.

She smiled. You could put the man in a tux but you couldn't take away his love of adventure.

She opened the interior door.

"...Hi, Vanessa." Did he sound a little breathless?

She knew the feeling. Vanessa's smile widened even as her heart sped into triple time. "Hi, yourself," she replied.

"You look...amazing," he said quietly, as his gaze took her in. She did a little twirl.

"Thank you." She straightened her spine and gave him a slow appraisal. "And you look very dashing."

He made a slight bow and pretended to doff a top hat. "You are too kind, m'lady."

He straightened and extended an elbow. "Shall we?"

She looped her hand over his forearm in response, and they stepped out onto the street together.

"I gave the horses a night off, so this Land Rover will have to do," Jake said as he opened the passenger door for her. She got in and he shut the door.

She leaned across the console and opened the driver's door for him from the inside. He chuckled as he slid into the driver's seat. "Equal opportunity, eh?"

"Always," she told him.

Morristown, NJ

AS PURPLE TWILIGHT fell, Jake pulled the Land Rover into a parking spot on the grounds of the Morristown National Historic Park. He turned off the engine, and he and Vanessa got out.

Vanessa's silver heels clicked on the brick pavers as they made their way over to a white two-story clapboard Georgian-style home, surrounded by lush lawn and large trees.

"The Ford Mansion." Jake read the sign. "Definitely not a relative of mine—that I know of."

He caught the low hum of voices mingled with the sound of violins as they got closer to the party.

Strings of soft white outdoor lights were festooned around a wrought iron latticework, and a wooden parquet dance floor had been set up.

"Washington sure knows how to throw a party," Jake said, in the hope the comment would distract Vanessa's notice from the slight tremble in his tone. He swallowed. He hadn't been this nervous—or this dressed up—since senior prom.

He took a deep, steadying breath. He could do this. He *was* doing this. He'd faced volcanic eruptions, mudslides and long treks through steaming jungles filled with poisonous spiders. He wasn't going to cave now.

She'd said yes, so really, that was the important thing. He smiled as he watched her look around the outdoor space, an expression of slight awe on her face. A slight breeze came up and she pulled her silvery wrap a bit tighter around her shoulders as they approached the crowd.

"If you get cold, just let me know," he murmured near her ear as her signature scent of sweet pea drifted to him. He closed his eyes a moment to savor it. "I can give you my jacket."

She looked up at him, those big green eyes soft with appreciation and kindness. "Thank you," she murmured back.

He saw her take a breath and hesitate a moment before she took a step away from him. "I need to go say hello to a few museum people."

"Sure, no problem." He shoved his hands in his pockets and glanced around at the sea of strangers. "I'll just...be here."

He pushed away the brief thought that claimed she was leaving him here on purpose, just like Laura had. No, this wasn't like that.

This wasn't his engagement party, after all. He wasn't being made to look like an idiot. He shook off the thought. Laura had been an entirely different person.

Vanessa put a hand on his arm for a moment and he sucked in a breath at the soft touch of her warm fingers. "Won't be long."

He nodded and she walked off. He fiddled with the stones on his bracelet. Should he have asked Bryce and the crew to come along? He winced. There was only about a week and a half to get this episode finished, and in to Sara.

But no, this gala really had no direct connection to what they were looking for. He pushed away the guilt that tried to needle him. Everyone on the team had been working hard. It was better to have a bit of a break. Some time off helped everyone be more productive, in his experience at least. They'd make up the slack tomorrow.

Jake wandered through the guests. Definitely a lot of big money out tonight. He noted the sparkle of diamonds and the glint of gold on more than a few guests.

These grounds were pretty extensive. He wandered in the direction of the house. Hmm. Was this the museum Rhonda had talked about? If they could take a look at Nathaniel's original papers, that might be a huge help.

Looked like they'd opened it up for the party guests. That was a nice touch, not to mention convenient for him.

HIDDEN TREASURE OF THE HEART

"Excuse me," Jake said to the museum staff member who stood just inside the door. "A woman by the name of Rhonda Miller out on Long Island said she donated some Revolutionary War-era papers to a museum in Morristown. Is this the place where they are?"

The staff member thought a second. "Oh, you're talking about the Nathaniel Wheeler documents. Yes, we have them."

"Great."

"Unfortunately, they're not on display at the moment. But if you're interested in things like that, Washington's writing desk, along with some of his war correspondence, is on display in here," the staff member said. "People often find that fascinating. Especially with the Culper code book currently on temporary loan from the Library of Congress."

That's right. Vanessa had mentioned the code book was on display here. "Thanks. Which direction is that?"

VANESSA MANAGED TO excuse herself from the long-winded monolog that one of her acquaintances had just started up. She scanned the crowd but didn't see Jake anywhere. Where was he?

A momentary panic sidled up to her and whispered that he'd left her by herself because he wanted to only focused on his own personal gain, his own career. She shook off that thought. Jake wasn't her ex.

She glanced over at the house and saw the golden glow of light from the first floor. Looked like people were coming and going inside, too.

She headed for the house and tried to dislodge the feeling of guilt that surfaced again at his expression when she'd had to step away from him earlier this evening.

She bit her lip but then shrugged. He was a grown man, and could handle himself. She wasn't responsible for his reactions to her actions. It was her life, after all.

She slipped through the door and noticed the signage pointing to the display on Washington's war correspondence. Oh, so that's where they'd put the original Culper codebook, too. Hmm. Maybe Jake was doing a bit of research?

Her heels clicked on the hardwood as

she made her way to the room set up with Washington's correspondence. She saw a table with papers and maps strewn across it, and a set of leather-bound volumes stacked on one side. In the corner stood a Windsor chair with a tricorn hat cocked over one arm.

Jake had his back to her while he looked at a display near the doorway. A glass case to his far right held what looked like some sort of ledger book.

She came up to him and tapped him on the shoulder. "Excuse me, are you Jake Ford?"

He did a double take then chuckled. "Would you like an autograph?"

Vanessa's heart skipped a beat at the gleam in his eye. "What were you reading?"

"Oh," Jake gestured to the placard and then to the display, "What I've read so far is talking about Washington's writing desk here and how he used it during his time as general in the Revolution. He apparently wrote his correspondence to the Culper members on it."

Vanessa looked at the fold-front writing desk, which had a bottle of ink and a quill pen arranged on it, along with a china teacup and saucer. "Looks like burled maple. Gorgeous."

Jake rubbed his hand across his jaw. "They certainly don't make things like they used to, do they?"

"Definitely not."

"By the way," Jake said, "didn't get a chance to ask earlier, but have you got any more leads on the Mason name?"

Vanessa lifted her palms. "It's a bit muddy. I spent what felt like hours on several genealogy sites. Found an Isaac Mason from that time period but while his wife was listed as Elisabeth, they had no children. At least, none that any descendants had listed. Then when I tried cross-referencing, you know how many hits came back with the last name of Mason? A lot. It's gonna take way more time than I thought."

Jake's jaw tightened for a moment. "If it makes you feel better, my team and I haven't been able to find anything conclusive, either, and the clock's ticking." He drummed his fingers against his thigh. "But," he straightened the cuffs of his tuxedo jacket, "I'm hoping things will get clearer."

"You and me both." Vanessa held up crossed fingers.

They both turned their attention back to the display case. Vanessa found herself standing closer to Jake—so she could read the placard more clearly, of course.

"Do you see that?" She pointed to the bottom half of the sign.

"What? Where?" Jake's shoulder brushed hers.

"Right here." Vanessa tapped the placard a bit farther down. "It says something about Agent 355."

It's widely known that Paul Revere used the coded signal 'one if by land, two if by sea,' and tasked Thomas Newton with hanging a lantern in Boston's Old North Church to signal that the British were coming. What's much less well-known is that Agent 355, one of the members of Washington's Culper spy ring, also used this means of coded communication. Though in her case, it was through a pair of garnet earrings.

Vanessa held her breath as she continued to read.

That pair of garnet earrings have now disappeared into the mists of time. But in the summer of 1780, Agent 355 attended a ball held at the headquarters of the British military stronghold in New York City.

She purportedly wore that pair of earrings—for two reasons. The first, in order to warn a man named Nathaniel Wheeler, who worked adjunctly with the Culper ring, that a cache of pearls from France, shipped to the Colonies aboard the frigate Cignet, had ended up in the hands of the British.

[The cache, originally intended to be delivered to General Washington, was apparently awaiting transport by the British from New York to a more secure location in Newport, RI, once they headed off the French fleet set to land there. But the Culpers, who wanted to intercept the cache, didn't know how the British would transport the pearls to Rhode Island.]

For the second reason, it is described that 355 used a pre-arranged code: one tier on her garnet earrings if the British went by land, two tiers if the British went by sea.

At the ball, she wore two tiers on her garnet earrings, thus letting the Patriots know that the British would transport the pearl cache by sea.

—*original source from the papers of Nathaniel Wheeler, donated by Mrs. R. Miller*

"But the pearls never made it to Newport," Jake murmured.

Vanessa pulled out her phone. "If we look up the history of what *did* take place in Newport, that might tell us something." Her fingers tapped the screen. "Says here that Washington basically decided to bluff the British."

"Oh?"

"He drew up fake battle plans and got a messenger to deliver them. The messenger told the British the documents must've fallen out of a saddlebag, and that he'd found them by the side of the road. The fake documents indicated that the Patriots had planned an attack on New York City. That kept them occupied, so the French fleet could land safely with their troops in

Newport."

"Okay. We know that much anyway." The sound of violins warming up drifted into the room.

"And we also know how the earrings I have were involved."

"But that doesn't tell us what happened after the ball. Or where the pearls ended up."

Jake met Vanessa's gaze and grinned. "But if I have anything to do with it, we're going to find those pearls. First, though—" He extended his hand to Vanessa "—may I have this dance?"

JAKE LED VANESSA back out onto the lawn. His fingers, interlaced with hers, tightened briefly before he readjusted his grip to pull her into his arms on the parquet dance floor.

He laid one palm against the small of her back, and the heat from his hand seeped through the thin taffeta of her dress.

Tingles zipped up her spine. With such a low-cut back to her dress, if he moved his hand up just a fraction of an inch, his bare skin would be in contact with hers.

Vanessa held her breath as he held her gaze. They began to move in time to the soft violin music.

Her hand rested on his shoulder; she felt the play of muscle under her fingertips as they moved together.

She swayed towards him.

"I never would've guessed you knew how to dance," she blurted out.

He chuckled. "You assumed I've only had lessons in treating a snakebite or swinging a machete?"

She lifted a shoulder. "Something like that. You dance well."

"Thanks. So do you."

They lapsed into silence for several beats.

"You look lost in thought," Jake murmured, as he caught her eye amid the swirl of other couples on the floor. "Penny for them?"

"Oh, I..." Vanessa paused. "I was just thinking about travel."

"Yeah?" He pulled her a little closer, their bodies now only inches apart.

"I'd like to do a bit more of it. I've been

so focused on my career, which I love, that I haven't done much globetrotting. But you've been to..." She waved a hand.

"Too many places for a regular passport." Jake winked. "Whenever I renew it, I always get the bigger diplomatic one—extra pages."

"That's what's so great about your show. Viewers have a way to experience so many places they've never been, understand globally historic artifacts from a new perspective. At least, that's why I enjoy the series. You must've done so many things around the world." Vanessa paused and studied him. "This might sound cliché, but...why?"

As Jake took a deep breath, Vanessa felt his shoulders rise and fall. "I've done a lot of crazy things in my travels, for sure. When you're high on adrenaline, a tightrope walk across an active volcano or an ice climb down Everest seems like a cake walk. You forget the risks. The danger." He shook his head. Jake's gaze focused inward for a moment, and his expression shifted from playful to...something else Vanessa couldn't quite pinpoint. "I've always been a bit of a thrill seeker. My crew is basically the same way."

Vanessa laughed. "How can you not be, given your occupation?"

"True..." Jake's thumb absently stroked the back of her hand. A jolt zipped through her and her breath caught.

"Well," Jake said in a quiet voice, "I have seen a lot of things, done a lot." But the expression on his face seemed almost...sad?

He continued. "People look at what I do and see all the adventure, all the travel, all the exploration and think wow, that's great. And don't get me wrong, it is." He smiled, his teeth very white in the dim, soft lighting. "I love what I do and I wouldn't trade it for the world. But..." His thumb stropped stroking the back of her hand and Vanessa wished he hadn't.

He let out a slow breath, and she felt it slide past her cheek. "What people don't see are the long hours, the months and months away from friends and family." He paused, held her gaze. "So that part's pretty hard, actually."

He steered them around an older couple who had stopped in the middle of the floor. "I'm gone almost 200 days out of the year. I mean, that's what the position calls for. But it can take a toll." He looked away for a moment. Swallowed hard. "On me, on people around me." His voice grew husky. "On...those I care about."

"What do you mean?" Vanessa asked quietly.

"My last girlfriend—" He cleared his throat. Blinked a few times. "I mean, my last relationship ended badly because of the amount of travel I did for my last job..." He didn't quite meeting her gaze.

Vanessa's heart swelled. "I can see how it would be tricky to balance everything," she said softly. "Must be hard on your heart."

Vanessa spread her fingers wide against his shoulder, and moved her hand down to press against the flat of his chest. She could feel his warmth through the crisp cotton, and as his sandalwood scent drifted to her, she found herself blinking back sudden moisture in her eyes. "My last boyfriend gave more significance to his career than to our relationship."

She melted a little at the compassionate look in his eyes. "I kept thinking that somehow things would be different." She sighed. "I mean—" She broke off and gave a soft laugh. "I'm sure you don't want to know that much detail about me and my personal life."

"I think it's brave of you to share."

"Thank you," she whispered. "I appreciate your listening."

"Of course," he murmured near her ear, as the violin music swelled around them. "And thank you for listening to me. I don't usually share that much with someone I've just met, but you are..." His gaze lingered on her eyes, then slid to her mouth.

Her breath stuck in her throat and her pulse sped up as his long, strong fingers glided up her bare back—

Her eyelids fluttered closed as he leaned close, lowered his head and pressed his lips to hers. She moved her free hand around to the back of his neck and pulled him nearer.

Her heart swelled. Oh. She melted against him. As the warm softness of their kiss filled her senses, the slight roughness of his stubble grazed her cheek, and shot tingles through her. His hand came up to cup her face while he slid an arm around her waist, and tugged her closer still. She a gave a quiet sigh. She felt like a helium balloon released skyward.

But a sudden vibration from his jacket pocket made her startle.

Buzz-buzz.

Jake ignored it.

Good. Because for a second—just one—she was reminded of her ex. He always answered his phone, no matter what was going on around him. But then Jake's phone buzzed again.

Vanessa tensed. Wait a minute. What was she doing? She shouldn't be kissing him, no matter how attracted she felt. She was getting too attached. And that meant she couldn't see Jake's character clearly. And when that happened, she'd wind up making the same mistake with Jake that she'd made with Eric…

What were *they* doing? Maybe Jake did like her, but he was leaving once the episode wrapped. This wasn't a good idea for them to kiss. Let alone at a public event in the middle of a dance floor.

Buzz-buzz.

"Oh, uh, I'm sorry about that," Jake murmured as he pulled away ever so slightly, his arms still around her. "Must've forgotten to put it to silent."

BUT AS JAKE released her and slipped out his phone to check the screen, he saw something that looked like hurt disappointment in Vanessa's eyes. She took a step back.

The violins faded and a faster song was struck up by the quartet at the edge of the dance floor.

"That's all right," Vanessa said. But Jake could see it clearly wasn't, though he wasn't sure why.

He saw her eyes dart from his phone to his face. She lifted her chin. "I—we, um— that was..."

She smoothed down her hair and took a deep breath, her spine straight. "Inappropriate." She looked away and blinked rapidly.

Jake felt the joy he'd experienced moments before, in kissing her, vanish like invisible ink.

He shouldn't have been so rash and impulsive. When would he learn? He swore under his breath. "Listen, Vanessa, I—"

She held up a palm. "No need to explain. it's all right. Mistakes like this happen."

Jake winced. A mistake? Is that what she thought their kiss had been? He could've sworn what they'd shared only a minute before indicated the exact opposite.

His stomach plummeted. He couldn't help but remember Laura's face as she broke things off, in front of all their friends. Left him standing there all alone at their engagement party...

His heart tightened. He'd picked up on Laura's growing unhappiness that he was gone for long stints doing the show. She'd accused him of loving travel and freedom more than her. Ironic, considering she'd left him. But maybe she'd been right...

They were supposed to have gotten married. He clenched his jaw against the old hurt. Didn't his proposal prove he'd loved her enough? He'd felt guilty about his love of travel and freedom getting in the way and causing the long distance element of their relationship, and wanted to fix things. He'd been so enthusiastically sure she'd been the one.

So he'd told her he would quit at the Travel Channel, and proposed to her. But it hadn't fixed anything. Before he could quit, the show had been cancelled, and then she'd broken up with him.

Jake crossed his arms as he regarded Vanessa, so close, yet so far away. Maybe he didn't deserve love in his life. He made himself take a steadying breath, but the pain lingered. He'd done it again: acted over-enthusiastic, made a leap of faith, assumed she'd felt the same...But she hadn't.

A strange sort of sadness filled him. He obviously didn't deserve love—people he cared about always left. It was true—with his kind of lifestyle, he didn't deserve both freedom *and* love.

"Now," Vanessa said, her tone much more formal, "I didn't get a chance to look at the Culper codebook in that display. Did you?"

Jake clenched his fists and attempted to force his mind back to the task at hand. They needed to figure out the mystery of the pearls, and he needed to concentrate on getting one hell of an episode done and in, instead of on how Vanessa made him feel.

Jake took another breath. Maybe Vanessa had done him a favor, acting like this. At least he knew now that she wasn't, apparently, interested in him.

He gave a brief nod, even as he tried to stem the flow of disappointment that coursed through him. No. Just focus on the mission, he told himself. That's what mattered here. That's what's important.

"I didn't." His formal tone matched hers. "After you."

As Vanessa turned and walked back up to the house, Jake read the message on his phone.

I was going through some of the interview footage to prep for the initial cuts. But I can't seem to find the Townsend files. After I did the initial upload, you did transfer them to the editing suite, right?

Jake's brow furrowed and his gut tightened. He swore under his breath as he scrolled through his contacts and hit Bryce's number. Bryce picked up on the first ring.

"*Hey man,*" Bryce said. "*How's the party?*"

"Oh, it's fine."

"That good, huh?"

Jake tamped down irritation at the teasing tone in Bryce's voice. He didn't have time for this. He gave a mental sigh. No, he shouldn't take his frustrations out on his friend just because Vanessa had basically rejected him.

He pushed aside the hurt. They were only colleagues, after all. He shouldn't have allowed himself to expect anything more.

Jake gave a forced laugh. "Sure is. Got your text. I'm sure I transferred the files to the online editing suite earlier today."

"Okay, but I actually don't see them there."

A knot tightened in Jake's stomach. "They should be." That was the only copy of the interview footage they had from Therese Smith. She'd been hard enough to get ahold of in the first place.

If they had to reshoot....it could mean a serious delay in the production schedule. And with the deadline less than two weeks away now, they didn't have time for this kind of thing.

Jake swore under his breath again.

"I've double and triple-checked, Jake. There's nothing there."

Jake rubbed his forehead. "So what do you suggest?"

"I can call the editing suite's cloud service, see if they somehow misplaced something."

"Good idea. Let's get on that. We can't afford to lose any footage. But especially not *that* footage."

Jake hung up the call and slipped his phone back into his pocket. He surveyed the crowd as his heart squeezed. Had Vanessa changed her mind and left the party? His jaw tightened as he caught a flash of silvery-blue. No, there she was.

Looked like she'd headed back inside without him. Not that he blamed her. He sighed. He should've kept his distance to begin with.

A minute later, he stepped back into the exhibit room they'd been in earlier. Vanessa stood in front of a glass case with what looked like a ledger book that lay open on a pedestal.

Vanessa's gaze flicked over him, her expression cool.

"Hi," he said quietly, as he ignored the

ping of sadness in his heart. But the show must go on—no pun intended. He almost smiled at that thought. Things must not be in dire straights if he still had his sense of humor. Right?

"Find anything?"

"Not yet."

Jake stepped up to the case. "Hmm." He glanced at the case and at the book inside. As he took a step closer to examine the book more fully, his thigh bumped the case.

There was a whirring noise, and Jake took a hasty step back. "What was that?"

He and Vanessa looked at each other; then Jake looked around the room. "I hope they're not gonna throw us in jail for wreck—"

Vanessa clutched his arm suddenly as she pointed to the case. "Look."

Jake used the excuse to move closer to Vanessa. "What?"

"Whatever you jostled was a mechanism to flip the book's pages."

"That's a relief. I'm not sure how I'd explain this to my insurance company otherwise."

Jake looked down. "There's a button

here." He punched it with his finger. The page flipped backward. "It's a toggle switch."

He pressed it again and the page moved ahead. He was about to reverse the direction again with the original page showing, when Vanessa's fingers tightened on his arm. "Wait."

"What is it?"

Though she'd claimed their kiss was inappropriate, she still seemed comfortable enough around him to touch him. So maybe she'd simply meant the time and place of their kiss was a mistake? A small kernel of hope sprouted. He re-arranged the goofy grin on his face to something more serious and professional.

Vanessa pointed. "See? I never knew that before."

"Knew what?" Jake read the lines Vanessa indicated. "It looks like a bunch of letters have been scrambled up."

Vanessa shook her head. "Not scrambled, per se. Rearranged."

"Isn't that the same thing?"

Vanessa shot him a look. "It looks as if the Culpers used that..." She scanned the usage notes penned in one column of the ledger. "...on occasion at the very beginning, when they were first figuring out what sort of coding method to use."

She tapped a finger against her bottom lip. Jake couldn't help but watch the motion and remember how good she'd felt pressed up against him, her skin warm under his fingers...

He cleared his throat, tore his eyes away from her mouth and back to the page. "That would make sense. They didn't really know quite how to do the coding in the beginning, and from what my writers found while researching this episode, the masters of encryption at this point in history were the French. So the Patriots looked to them for an effective coding method. But I seem to recall that Benjamin Tallmadge experimented with different sorts of codes. Apparently, so did Washington."

Vanessa turned to Jake, an excited look in her eyes. Jake's heart skipped a beat.

"Do you know what this means?"

"Um, no."

"Okay." She took a breath. "Let me get this straight in my head. That chocolate pot we found was once in 355's possession.

She was a confirmed Culper ring member who would've known about, and been told, most likely, these first experimental codes, since she'd have to know how to use them."

"I'm with you so far," Jake said.

"Okay. So, what if," she took a step closer to Jake, "she used that same encoding method—

"—on the chocolate pot," Jake finished, as excitement fizzed in his chest.

Vanessa pulled out her phone. Scrolled back to the photo she'd taken of the chocolate pot they'd unearthed.

"We've been looking at this too literally," Jake murmured.

Vanessa nodded. "Too straightforward. What if that *Enque* isn't a maker's mark or name at all? What if..."

"It's a scrambled word." Jake felt his phone vibrate.

"An anagram." Vanessa said, as she looked back at the Culper code book. "Just like the Culper ring initially used."

"BUT AN ANAGRAM of what?" Vanessa

drummed her fingers on her thigh as she looked down at the antique book.

"Jake?"

She tried and failed not to notice how Jake had pulled out his phone and was looking more at it than at her or at the book itself.

A twinge of annoyance filled her. No response from the man.

"Jake."

"Hmmm?" But he still didn't look at her. He was concentrating hard on his phone, texting.

She tried and failed to push aside her growing frustration. She crossed her arms. This was a massive discovery. So *why* was he glued to his phone? Surely he realized by now just how significant this was to her? To them? To history?

But no. Apparently, he didn't. She shot him a frown, and her frustration sharpened to deeper annoyance. *Apparently,* he cared way more about whatever was distracting him rather than what he should be focused on, right now.

She made herself take some deep breaths. Maybe she was overreacting. Maybe he really did have some important emergency—

She darted a glance at his phone screen, which she could see since they were still standing quite close together.

He was on social media? Of all the times...Her heart clenched.

Yep. It looked like he was focused more on his online presence than this piece of history that was unfolding in front of them.

Typical.

A dart of anger surged through Vanessa. Why had she thought Jake would be different than Eric? She pursed her lips. She'd been fooling herself. She put her hands on her hips. She should've known he'd be just like her ex. All these acting types were the same—more concerned about their online image than anything else.

She tapped her foot. "Jake," she repeated.

The frown of concentration stayed on Jake's face even as he finally looked up at her. "Sorry about that. I—" He interrupted himself and put his phone away at Vanessa's glare. A flicker of annoyance passed across his expression, and his mouth turned down.

Vanessa felt a twinge of guilt, which she pushed aside as she tapped the case with a finger, harder than necessary. "The anagram. Any ideas on what you think it's of?"

Jake avoided eye contact. He shoved one hand in his pocket and rubbed his other hand across the back of his neck. "I'm not really sure... I mean, well, I guess it's a matter of eliminating the possibilities."

Vanessa nodded. "*Enque.* Well, that's five letters. So there's neqeu, euqen..."

Jake frowned up at the ceiling. "Uenqe..."

"Wait." She smacked her forehead. "It's so obvious... It's *queen.*"

"Given the context of monarchy and rebellion, that makes sense."

Vanessa hunched her shoulders. "But why not king? George III was on the throne."

"There must be something we're missing. But what?"

Vanessa tugged on a strand of her hair as she darted a glance at Jake. "Queen," she muttered under her breath. "It's singular. I'm guessing that's significant, and—"

Jake's phone rang. He grimaced. "I'm really sorry—gotta take this."

Vanessa inhaled, about to respond. But he was already stepping away from her, pulling his phone from his pocket.

"There's been a bit of a blow-up with the major media outlets about the show. It's—" His phone rang again. "I need to answer this. I'm sorry," he repeated.

To Vanessa's eye, though, he didn't look sorry at all, only relieved to be away from her. Vanessa's gut tightened as she opened her mouth.

But he answered the call before she could reply. She balled her hands into fists and narrowed her eyes at the ceiling.

"Sara, hi. Yeah, I did. No, it's not—I just saw." A pause. "Unfortunately, yes. *The Early Morning Show* somehow picked it up... From social media, I guess."

Vanessa clenched her fingers tighter. So this was how it was with him, huh? She tried to take a deep breath. But she couldn't push aside the fear that began to swirl through her. He cared more about the show's image and his own reputation than uncovering real history that could possibly change so many things.

Fearful certainty filled her. She'd been used again, gotten caught up in falling in love and hadn't been able to see the warning signs clearly: his self-centeredness, his neglect and failure to acknowledge her. Why'd she think she'd be any better judge of character now, than she had been with Eric?

"What? We can't have that happen. No. It's not." He turned away from Vanessa and raked a hand through his hair.

Her eyes stung. History was repeating itself. Her stomach dropped as Jake paced farther away from her. No, he *wasn't* any different than Eric. She'd been an idiot to give him a chance to prove otherwise.

Jake continued to talk, but she no longer heard his voice. Instead, she saw the night of her very first museum exhibition. Recalled the expression on Eric's face when she'd confronted him after her showing. Remembered their huge fight in the street.

She'd asked him why he hadn't shown up, and he'd said he'd gone to an audition for his 'sure-thing big role.'

She'd tried to get him to see how the showing was her 'big thing,' tried to explain how important this was for her.

But he hadn't listened, had he? Hadn't acknowledged her then. In fact, he'd never acknowledged her during their whole relationship, really. But she'd been stupid enough to think, to believe, after their big fight, that he still loved her, that he would get that role, so she'd forgiven him. Believed in him.

And then the next day, he'd dumped her. Said she was too obsessed with her work to be a good girlfriend. Told her he'd needed to focus on his career, and claimed that their relationship would only distract him, and get in the way.

Vanessa's heart squeezed even as she pressed a hand to her chest. Her work was such a part of who she was... But he'd never acknowledged it—or her. Her eyes burned. She looked at Jake again. He didn't meet her gaze.

"Right, okay. I'll let you know right away. Bye." Jake hung up the phone and turned to her, his expression shuttered. "Vanessa." He glanced at his watch. "I know that I was supposed to be here for the rest of the party but I need to leave now. I'm sorry."

Vanessa said nothing as her stomach dropped to the floor.

Annoyance flitted across Jake's expression. "The show is going through a bit of a crisis. I need to do damage control and—"

"Oh, I get it. I do." Her heart twisted as she struggled to keep the bitterness from her voice. "Your job is important—more important than mine."

Jake jammed his hands into his pockets and the expression on his face darkened. "Vanessa, I don't know what your problem is, but this show is important too. My career could be at stake and you're—"

"—trying to focus on what's really important."

"So now you're prioritizing your career over mine?"

"If we find the pearls, it'll save the museum." She put her hands on her hips. "And your show."

"But we haven't found the pearls. There'll be no show to save if I don't deal with this crisis first." Jake crossed his arms. "Like I already said, this show, and my career, *are* important. To me."

"Exactly," Vanessa retorted. "To *you*. But you're not—"

"Listening to you? That's right, I'm not. You're not the host, the producer or a network exec for this television series. You don't have anything to lose if my show implodes. Which gives you no right to stand there and dismiss it." Jake ground his teeth and shook his head. "You're just like my ex. She was never supportive of me either." He shoved his hands deeper into his pockets. "I thought—no—hoped, you were different than she was. Guess I was wrong."

Vanessa opened her mouth to argue.

"Save your breath." His brows lowered and he turned on his heel. "Because I'm done." He walked out.

Chapter Eight

VANESSA SHIVERED AS she stepped back out into the night, alone.

She pulled her wrap tighter around her shoulders. But it did little good against the chilly evening air turned damp with the lateness of the hour.

As she rubbed her arms to get rid of the goose bumps, all she could think of was the sound of Jake's voice, low and soft in her ear, as he'd offered her his jacket. Had it only been a few hours ago that they'd been so happily dancing and talking and...kissing... together?

She pressed her lips together to suppress the tremble of her chin. She would not cry. Not here, not now, and especially not over Jake Ford.

He was ridiculous. Her feelings for him were ridiculous too. She straightened her spine. She was better off without him.

As Vanessa walked across the lawn to speak with one of the museum board members about the silent auction bids, she pasted a smile on her face.

She strode over to the gray-haired woman who stood by the silent auction table.

"Vanessa." The other woman smiled. "This was such a lovely venue. What an excellent idea."

"I think everyone appreciated the relevance tonight, Roseanne. How did we do?"

The older woman waved a stack of papers at Vanessa. "I'll be sure to let you know bright and early tomorrow. Right now, it looks like you could use some sleep. I think everyone could."

After Vanessa spoke with the event coordinator, she checked the late night train schedule back to New York. The last train back to the city was in thirty minutes. She called a cab to take her to the nearest commuter station.

She averted her eyes from the parking spot where Jake's Land Rover no longer sat, and climbed into the waiting taxi.

Well after two o'clock in the morning, Vanessa made her way up from the subway station and let herself in to her apartment. Her fingers fumbled with the key and she couldn't help but remember the very first time Jake had crossed her threshold, how she'd been almost giddy with nerves and excitement.

She clenched her jaw. Tried to shove aside the memories, and the certainty that she'd totally screwed everything up.

She heaved a sigh as she undressed and changed into her pajamas. Fear and worry warred with guilt and shame inside her. What if Jake was right? What if she had completely dismissed his concerns over his career? She winced as Jake's accusation came back to her. Had she actually done to Jake what Eric had done to her?

She narrowed her eyes at her reflection as she brushed her teeth at the bathroom sink.

No.

She spit out the toothpaste. He was the one in the wrong. He was the one who'd acted just like her ex. He'd dismissed all the effort she'd put in her own career, and completely abandoned her in favor of his own.

Pain stabbed at her heart like tiny

knives. This was how all her relationships would end, wouldn't they? She was going to be single forever.

She twisted the facet on and rinsed her mouth. Maybe that was just fine. Yes. She nodded at herself in the mirror. It was so much easier that way. No drama. No pain. And no Jake Ford in her life to complicate everything.

She walked into her bedroom, climbed into bed and went to sleep.

SUNSHINE STREAMED THROUGH the blinds Friday morning. The brightness of the light told Vanessa she'd slept in way too long. Oh no. Her eyes flew open. She had to get to work.

But then it all came back. The gala. The anagram. Jake's face. His words. Her heart squeezed.

She shoved back the covers and her thoughts as she got ready for the day. She threw on a pair of slightly wrinkled capris and a turquoise top. She needed to put that man out of her mind. It'd do her no good to think about him or their argument or…

anything else about him, for that matter.

She would bet that he certainly wasn't wasting time thinking about her. Best to put all her time and energy into her work, into finding out the identity of Agent 355. She didn't need Jake Ford's help with that. She was perfectly capable of doing things on her own.

After she'd eaten breakfast and locked up her apartment, she headed over to the office.

She walked through office door, waved at the temp, then went straight to the break room to make herself a cup of strong, hot coffee.

Her gaze strayed to the hole in the wall. The masonry company had said they'd come next week to fix things. Her eyes lingered on the hollow cavity as she waited for the coffee maker.

Why had the journal pages been there when the journal itself wasn't? She walked over to the wall and brushed her fingers against the rough edges of the cracked mortar. White chalky powder came off on her fingertips. Huh. Must be more loose mortar, like Bryce had mentioned...

But what was that? She felt along the

inside edge of the newly exposed crack. It looked almost like—she fished a pair of tweezers out of the junk drawer by the coffee machine—yes, a page. *Another* one? Good grief. But this one was singed. Someone had wedged it deep into the crevice created by the loosened mortar.

She carefully extracted and studied the blackened and soot-stained third of a page. From the char pattern, it looked as if someone had tried to deliberately burn the page but the flames hadn't quite finished the job.

> that I told him 'twas safe to retrieve the cache. Indeed, I full believed it, for the British were distracted by 711's bluff of an attack on New York. I had thought, in the ensuring busyness of preparing for the supposed attack, that he would not be discovered aboard the Swan. That he would not have been captured.
>
> But oh, 'twas not so. I feel the fault is entirely mine. I should have gone myself, as I had intended, but, he declared 'twas a task he wished to perform. Who was I to stand in the way of such passion? What is the nature of love if not thus? If only I had known...
>
> Yet my own fears and losses are but small compared to the greater sacrifices we all must make in this War of Indepen

"What is not the nature of love but thus?"

HIDDEN TREASURE OF THE HEART

Vanessa whispered to herself as Jake's face flashed through her mind. *"If only I had known."* She swallowed hard.

For several long moments, Vanessa stared down at the page. Re-read the words. Finally, she turned and walked slowly back to her desk and sat.

She drummed her fingers on the desk as she waited for her laptop to boot up.

She looked again at the paper. No date. But it must have happened after the ball. In the attempt to get the pearls back from the British, 355's true love had been, apparently, discovered and captured.

But what about Agent 355 herself? Vanessa flicked back through her mental file on the woman, and on what Rhonda had said about those initials: H.M.

She cupped her chin in her hand. If she'd—

Her desk telephone rang. She jumped. What if Jake—She snatched up the receiver. "Hello, Women of the American Revolution Museum, Vanessa speaking.'

"Vanessa, hello. This is Roseanne White."

"...Roseanne, hi. I hope you were able to get caught up on sleep after the gala last night?"

"Fit as a fiddle," Roseanne chuckled. "Listen, I've had a chance to tally everything up."

Vanessa's heart pounded. The ticket sales had done well—they'd gotten almost half of their needed funding from that. Now with the additional proceeds from the silent auction, things should be looking good.

"That's great," Vanessa replied. "How did we do?"

The other woman paused. "After I went through everything, I counted a second time just to make sure."

"I sense a 'but' in there."

"I'm sorry, Vanessa, but the silent auction proceeds did not help meet the larger goal the museum said it would achieve. The auction proceeds covered maybe a fourth of the amount they needed to."

Vanessa chewed on a cuticle. "So now what? Can we fix this?"

Roseanne sighed. "There's nothing else to do, Vanessa. As you know, this gala was the last hope. Now that the funding goal hasn't been met, I'm afraid the board is going to have to make some hard decisions here pretty quickly."

"What does that mean, exactly?"

"We'll put it to a vote but really that's just a formality. The museum is going to have to close."

Vanessa's stomach dropped. If she could find the pearls, and figure out 355's identity... But that was a pretty faint hope right now, realistically speaking.

She rubbed her temples. And despite her claim earlier that morning to figure things out without Jake, she didn't have any fresh leads to go on.

She sighed. So there was really nothing else for it, was there? She'd have to call her boss and break the bad news.

WAY TOO EARLY Friday morning, Jake forced himself to focus on the tablet in front of him. He stifled a yawn. He took a swing of coffee and did his best to push away the memory of Vanessa's expression as they'd discovered those first diary entries in her office's break room.

He put the black-and-red mug down on the dressing room table, as if the mere act of doing so would help him put aside the pain of their confrontation last night at the gala.

He winced. It didn't work. His thought returned—yet again—to their heated words. He sighed. What had he been thinking? He shouldn't've let things get so out of hand. He—No. This wasn't his fault at all. He clenched his jaw. She was the one who'd jumped down his throat.

He'd only been doing his best to protect his show, his reputation. He hung his head. But maybe she'd been right?

No.

She wasn't right. He wasn't focused *only* on his career. That was a ridiculous accusation. He narrowed his eyes at his reflection in the dressing room mirror as the stylist applied gel to his hair.

He wasn't some sort of self-interested...self-centered actor. He clenched his teeth. She'd gotten it all wrong.

He was only trying to do right by the show, for his fans. People across the globe loved this show and if it went down the tubes, so would his dreams. Something he loved so much, that gave him so much joy.

And wasn't joy an essential service to

the public? He straightened up. Yes. It was. Because without joy, the world would be a pretty grim place. Therefore, he hadn't made a mistake in walking away from Vanessa.

She was the one who needed to apologize, to—Hang on, what was he thinking? He wasn't actually *wanting* to forgive her, was he? He huffed out a breath. No. He wasn't. He set his jaw.

The stylist made a few last-minute adjustments before she left.

He was just going to get on with his life. He was better off without Vanessa, if she was just going to jump to conclusions like that, and hurl accusations at him. He was better off single. Besides, it wasn't exactly easy to find a woman who wanted to put up with someone who was gone for 200 days out of the year. And Vanessa had a stable job she loved. So, the whole thing had been doomed from the start.

But his heart clenched anyway.

"Mr. Ford?" An assistant stuck his head in the half-open dressing room doorway. "You're on."

"Great, thanks," Jake replied. He took a deep breath. It was time to focus on things that he could control. And right now, that was doing his damnedest to get this show's reputation back on track.

He headed onto the talk show set.

"...In three..." the cameraman counted down, and for a moment, Jake wished it was Bryce behind the lens. That guy had been around on his crew for so long he was practically family. And a little family, a little familiarity was what he needed right now.

"...Two...."

He took a deep breath. He could do this. He'd done this so many times before. It'd be as easy as jumping off a waterfall, right?

"....And one."

VANESSA MASSAGED THE base of her skull, but it did nothing to ease the throb of a headache building there.

She forced herself to look back at the computer screen. But her eyes blurred and she sat back with a heavy sigh. Now what? The conversation with Kali hadn't gone well, to say the least.

So here she was, scrolling through endless legal documents to try and find some sort of loophole in order to save the museum. And what about her exhibit?

She put her head in her hands and closed her eyes. But she wasn't a lawyer. She pressed her palms against her closed eyelids. The museum didn't have a budget for one. And she didn't know any, either.

With effort, she opened her eyes and lifted her gaze back to the page she'd been looking at, but all the words swam together.

She stood up and shut the lid of her laptop. She needed some fresh air and some fresh perspective.

Maybe she'd take a long walk in Battery Park. Yes. Some fresh air would do her good. She stretched and yawned and then grabbed the keys off the back hook, waved at the temp, and headed out the door.

As the breeze off the water buffeted her hair, she tucked a strand behind her ear and pushed her hands into her capri pockets.

She turned her head to look out at the water, as she attempted to shut out the throng of people around her.

Beyond the iron railing that stretched the length of the path, the wind-tossed waves caught the sun and made them sparkle and shine.

Normally, she loved the hustle and bustle here this time of year—thrived on that energy—but right now, she needed some peace and quiet. Looking out at the water gave her that sensation, even if she couldn't escape land right now.

The yellow Staten Island ferry chugged by, and she thought back to the peace and stillness of Rhonda Miller's wooded lot. Maybe, if she could ever afford it, she would look at property in Long Island. She recalled the rough bark under her fingertips as she looked up at those initials.

If Nathaniel's family had owned that property before the Revolution, then maybe there would be something...anything...that might give her more information. Because maybe, just maybe, if she discovered 355's identity, found the pearls, that would change the board's mind?

"Tag, you're it!" A little kid yelled as he sprinted by, ahead of a girl in pigtails who raced after him, spilling popcorn kernels in her wake.

Vanessa pulled up the search engine on her phone.

But after typing in Nathaniel's name and the relevant dates on pretty much every genealogy and museum database she knew of, she'd drawn a blank. All her searching had only confirmed what scant information Rhonda had already shared.

She blew out a sigh. Maybe it was time to give up, let go of this whole ridiculous chase. The museum was going under. So what was the point? 355's identity, and the pearls, hadn't been discovered in 250 years. Why'd she ever think she'd have any luck herself?

She'd failed.

Overwhelm washed through her. She looked up at the seagulls calling to each other as they rode the currents above the choppy waves.

Despair nudged in beside overwhelm. What was she doing, anyway? She couldn't keep the museum going. She couldn't figure out 355's identity or locate the pearls...

Jake's face came to mind but she shoved it away. No. Just no. Tears sprang to her eyes.

...And she couldn't win in her love life, either.

VANESSA MEANDERED ALONG the battery for what seemed like hours. She loved to walk, and would do it at times for hours. In New York, that wasn't really a hardship or an issue. One time, she'd gone nearly twenty blocks in heels because the subway line she'd been on had unexpectedly stopped for someone who'd gotten sick.

That had been for the interview for her current job, in fact. Vanessa gave a half-hearted smile at the memory. Back when she was full of enthusiasm, passion, for the museum, for the ideas she knew she could bring.

But now what? She brushed away the tears but they continued to fall anyway.

Vanessa stared down at the hexagonal paving stones as she walked. A pink bubble gum wrapper blew by, and a homeless woman who leaned against a tree, rattled an orange paper coffee cup she held. Absently, Vanessa fished for some change at the bottom of her purse and tossed it in.

The woman, who didn't look that much older than Vanessa, saluted her.

Vanessa turned her eyes back to the water. She was nearing the end of the path. A guy in a blue polo shirt adjusted his grip on a fishing rod that rested on the iron railing; its line dangled into the water.

As she came to stand at the same railing, she realized—that homeless woman hadn't looked like she was sitting there feeling sorry for herself. No. She was at least making some sort of effort to help herself, even if it was only asking for change.

That's what Vanessa needed to do, too. Her lips twitched at the irony—change. She needed to change her mind, change her outlook. She needed to push ahead. She couldn't give up. She *shouldn't* give up. She had to keep going. She owed it to herself, to the museum, and to history itself.

She retraced her steps to the museum.

Back at her computer, Vanessa read through the financial agreements again. Hang on. How had she not noticed this clause before? She must have been too tired and defeated-feeling.

Vanessa leaned forward. *Special circumstances*, the clause stated. She read the paragraphs under her breath, a slow smile starting to spread across her face.

Hmmm. She tapped her finger against her bottom lip as she studied the screen and the words there.

If funding amounts were not met, the applicant could appeal the decision and ask to file a loan extension. Could this work?

She picked up the desk phone. Paused. Should she ask Kali about this beforehand? No. She shook her head. Kali had enough to deal with at the moment.

Vanessa wouldn't bother her with this. Better to wait until things had been approved.

She grinned as she put the handset to her ear and dialed the board chair.

Monday morning, Jake sat at the gray office desk in his hotel room and rubbed his temples, alternating between worrying about how on Earth they'd be able to get this episode in with less than a week to go, and remembering how everything with Vanessa had imploded.

He jumped up, paced to the window, and looked at the skyline without seeing it. So he turned on his heel and flopped back into the leather office chair by the desk. He leaned back and lacked his fingers behind his head.

Thank goodness that interview was over. He could only hope that it would have a positive impact on the ratings and on the Internet trolls. Too bad he couldn't influence his love life in the same way.

He sighed, spun the office swivel chair around in a circle then booted up his laptop. He drummed his fingers on the desk. He needed to figure out this whole footage thing with Bryce. He fired off a text. A moment later, the reply came.

The online editing suite's cloud service is prepping for some sort of maintenance update, and has things re-arranged, so I'm still looking.

Jake groaned. Were things going from bad to worse? He scrubbed a hand across his jawline. No. He couldn't afford to think like that. Not in this business. He hadn't gotten as far as he had by thinking negatively. He took a deep breath and exhaled slowly.

He couldn't do anything else about the footage situation at the moment, or the response to his interview, so his energies were better spent elsewhere.

Like figuring out anything else he could dig up about 355. Because wasn't that the whole point? Find the pearls, find out the identity of the most elusive of Washington's spies? He forced an image of Vanessa's face out of his mind.

Yes. It was.

A FEW HOURS later, Jake sat back and tried to ease the crimp in his neck. Those letters. Those diary entries. He scrolled back through the photos of them on his phone. There had to be something else...some other angle he hadn't thought of.

His thumb paused on the second diary entry, and 355's words about Lord C.

Hmm. The man had served in the Royal Navy, and commandeered that French frigate. Surely his full name would be somewhere...

Jake's pulse quickened. If he looked up Lord C, perhaps that would be the way to find out more about 355. She had mentioned the man as a suitor her father approved of. What if they'd gotten married? The marriage certificate would have to show both of their names.

If they'd gotten married, anyway. He'd try looking up a marriage license, too. He jotted down some notes.

But first, perhaps, the best place to start would be the man's military records.

Jake pulled up a military archives website and plugged in the approximate dates and what little he knew about the man.

He scanned the results. Hmm. Lots of things related to the British occupation of New York, certainly. Now the trick would be to figure out how to narrow down the hits.

What would Vanessa make of this? For a moment, his heart constricted. He found himself imagining her green eyes lit with excitement—that same expression she'd worn when they'd pulled that first diary entry from the wall...

But Jake shook it off. He couldn't waste his time speculating on things that were over and done with. And completely out of his control.

He kept scrolling. Naval records, troop movements, ship manifests. Hmm. What was this? He leaned forward. It looked like some sort of prisoner roster that listed patriots who were captured by the British Navy and incarcerated on prison ships in New York Harbor.

Oh, and it also looked like... He looked at the top of the list. A naval officer with the last name of Callingham had orchestrated the incarceration.

Jake frowned. That started with a c and ended with an m. But lord was a title, and wasn't there something with the British aristocracy where a person's name didn't match what their title was?

He did a quick search. Yep. Mmm. So this Callingham person probably wasn't who 355 had referred to. He needed Lord C's given name.

Oh. What if he cross-referenced the name of that French frigate that 355 had named, with this list and see what he could find out that way?

Worth a try.

"Pay dirt," he whispered to himself forty-five minutes later as he read the naval report. It looked like a man named Geoffrey Charles White, Lord Cunningham, had been the commanding officer when the French frigate Cignet had been captured by the British Navy. It was taken to New York Harbor where it sat in dry dock to await a refit, then was renamed the Swan. That fit perfectly with what 355 said. This Geoffrey person had to be the man she'd mentioned.

Now knowing that, he'd see what else he could find...

A bit later, he'd come up with just two documents, but very telling ones. His pulse thudded as he studied them.

Headquarters, New York   Aug. 31, 1780

Dear Admiral:

In response to your inquiry of a fortnight ago, Sir, I am pleased to inform you that Mr. Nathaniel Wheeler has at last made a full confession. His attempt to retrieve the pearl cache from the Swan has failed.

Though...encouraged...by various means, Wheeler continues to deny all knowledge of any other parties who might have been privy to his actions. While I suspect he is lying, his stalwart stance will do him no good.

For I have already signed his death warrant. He is to be hanged as a Traitor to the Crown at dawn three days hence, along with four of his fellow treasonists.

I can find but little pity for someone such as that who believes in such flagrant displays of civil disobedience.

I am, Sir,
Your humble servant, etc.,
Cmdr. Geoffrey White, Lord Cunningham, Esq.
To: Admrl Wm. James
Halifax hqrts

PostScript: As for your other query, you may be assured that I am indeed familiar with Halifax, and would be most interested in a transfer to those Headquarters should the opportunity arise.

Real nice guy. Jake shook his head. So this meant that Nathaniel Wheeler, 355's true love, had been executed by the man who 355's father decreed she marry?

His thought turned again to Vanessa. How would she take this revelation? What would she have said if she'd discovered this? Why was he wondering? What if he actually asked her?

He jerked upright. If he presented her

HIDDEN TREASURE OF THE HEART

with the information, then... what? He frowned. No. He shook his head. She'd made it very clear she didn't want to give him the time of day.

He turned to review the second document, a partial newspaper article from *The Royal Gazette*.

SEPTEMBER 3, 1780
 DISTURBANCE AT GALLOWS

AFTER BRITISH TROOPS GARRISONED IN THE AREA SEARCHED THE HOMES OF SEVERAL SUSPECTED PATRIOTS, FOUR EXECUTIONS TOOK PLACE THIS MORNING. DESPITE THE EARLY CHILL AND HEAVY RAINS, A LARGE CROWD HAD GATHERED TO WITNESS THE CAPITAL PUNISHMENT, AND A HUSH HAD FALLEN OVER THOSE PRESENT. UNTIL A WOMAN IN A TATTERED RED CLOAK, WHO HAD SOMEHOW PUSHED HER WAY TO THE FRONT OF THE LINE OF SPECTATORS, CALLED OUT JUST AS THE EXECUTIONER SLID THE HOOD OFF MR. NATHANIEL WHEELER'S HEAD.

BUT ALL HER PROTESTATIONS DID HER NO GOOD, FOR SHE WAS EXPELLED FROM THE SITE FOR MAKING A DISTURB—

The rest of the article had crumbled away, and there was nothing more to the digital scan.

Jake tugged his earlobe. So 355 had shown up at her lover's execution and tried to stop it. Made sense.

Jake shuddered. If he'd been in the same position, would he have done the very same thing? Did he have that much courage?

He reread the article. She had on a red cloak. "Huh," Jake murmured. This must've been right before she'd gone to Sally Townsend's. Didn't Therese say 355 had shown up at Sally's door in a ragged red cloak? Yes. Jake rubbed his jaw. Yes, she had, and the timeframe certainly fit.

His gaze lingered on the article. His throat tightened. Did 355 find any happiness with Lord Cunningham? Jake's lips compressed. Judging from his character in that letter, Jake found it hard to believe she could have.

He exhaled slowly. She'd been denied true happiness, risked imprisonment or maybe even execution herself, to cause a stir like that. And she still hadn't given up.

But what was he doing? His heart

pinched. Sitting here in the 21st century, feeling a bit sorry for himself about his show, his career and yes, he admitted it, his love life too.

The pinch in his chest grew as he gazed at the words on the screen. Who was *he* to just sit around doing nothing about his love life? He'd been an idiot to give up, just walk away from Vanessa, from his chance at actually having love.

Look at 355. She pretty much was guaranteed unhappiness and yet she still tried to fix things, still made an effort.

He sat up straighter. This was his chance—what he needed to do, too. No, he wasn't facing an executioner, speaking out against injustice and wrongdoing, but the least he could do was make an effort, to show some strength of character, to at least *try*—he shook his head. No, he wasn't going to *try*. He was going to *do*.

He stood up, shut the lid of his laptop, tucked it into his messenger bag, slung the bag over his shoulder and head out the door.

He needed to fix things with Vanessa. And perhaps this documentation, if she would listen to him, would provide the means to do that.

The only thing left to do was do it.

The hotel room door shut with a click. Jake made his way out onto the bustling sidewalk and hailed a cab.

Chapter Nine

MONDAY MID-MORNING, VANESSA took a deep, steadying breath and adjusted the skirt of her powder blue suit. She crossed her fingers. She'd worn this outfit while filming that initial interview with Jake, and the gala video, so maybe it would bring her a little much-needed luck for this appeal meeting with the museum board.

The elevator doors dinged open. Vanessa sighed with relief to be out of the cramped space. She strode across the polished marble lobby and up to the reception area. After she gave the woman her name, she took a seat in one of the red leather club chairs that faced the windows.

She might as well do something useful. Her mind drifted back to 355 as she tapped her finger against her chin.

Maybe she'd missed something when

she'd gone over 355's diary entries with Jake.

Her heart lurched. Jake. If only he was here...But she pushed the thought aside. He wasn't. She scrolled back through the entries. Sighed. No. Of course there was nothing else there that gave any indication of a name.

Hmm. What about Sally Townsend's diary? Vanessa's brow furrowed. But she didn't think she'd taken any photos of it, since they hadn't found anything relevant...

Vanessa scrolled farther. Nope. She was right—no photos of Sally's diary.

But oops. There was one she'd accidentally taken somehow in what looked like Jake's rented Land Rover.

A grin crept onto her face as she recalled his quip about giving the horses the night off. Or how he'd looked at her, all that warmth in his eyes as they'd danced at the gala. Or when he'd kis—No. This line of thinking wouldn't do her any good. She hastily scrolled past the Land Rover photo.

But the next one that popped up was the one she'd taken at Rhonda Miller's on Long Island. The chocolate pot: side, front, back. She'd taken a lot of pictures of it. Top—and, she scrolled a bit further—bottom. She looked at the word on the bottom again, and the numbers. The—She frowned and cocked her head.

She zoomed in on the picture. She hadn't noticed *that* before. It looked like a sort of curved...scratch? Hmmm. Probably just from all the wear and tear that the pot had gone through. There were several dents on the bottom, after all.

She shrugged and put down her phone. She should go over this presentation in her head one more time. She shoved the phone back into her purse and stood to get a cup of coffee from the side table just as one of board members came down the hallway.

"Roseanne," Vanessa said, as she snagged a mug. She extended a hand, which Roseanne shook, as Vanessa juggled her coffee cup to her other hand.

"Vanessa. Nice to see you. We're right down the hall here."

They entered the conference room together. Vanessa's heartbeat accelerated as she saw all six of the board members present.

She resisted the urge to chew on her

lip. This was her last shot, and she had to do her best. She finished her laptop setup and straightened her spine as she turned to face the board members. After she thanked everyone for agreeing to be there, she launched into her presentation.

AS VANESSA WRAPPED up her case, she fought off a sense of worry. Just because they hadn't all looked incredibly enthused the whole time didn't mean things were totally a lost cause. Right?

One of the board members raised his hand.

"Yes?" Vanessa said.

His expression was skeptical and Vanessa tried to ignore her sinking heart.

"You mentioned increasing attendance as one avenue for contributing to the loan payments, if this extension is granted. But I admit, I'm a bit...Well, I'm just going to ask if you could elaborate a bit, please?"

Four of the six other board members nodded and glanced at each other.

The man who'd spoken pursed his lips and steeped his fingers.

For a moment, she thought about mentioning the pearl cache, and 355's connection to it. But she hadn't found the pearls—or 355's identity.

No. She'd better wait. She'd barely gotten her own hope back. Best not to raise the hopes of anyone else without having something concrete first.

Confidence. She needed to project confidence. She straightened. Tried to sound as professional as possible.

"Well, I've been working on various scenarios. But to be specific, we believe that increasing our collaboration with local elementary schools would boost the numbers enough to make a difference," Vanessa replied.

"I see," said another member, who peered at her from over half-moon reading glasses, an uncertain look in her eyes as she glanced from Vanessa to the final slide of Vanessa's presentation.

"Does anyone else have any questions?" Vanessa forced her tone to be light.

Silence. More skeptical looks. More whispered exchanges.

"Vanessa," Roseanne said as she stood up and looked at her board members.

"Once we make our decision about this appeal, we'll let you know." She scanned the room.

"So that means…?" Vanessa asked.

Roseanne flipped through her agenda. "We'll let you know the results by 7 p.m. tonight."

VANESSA'S SHOULDERS HEAVED with a sigh of relief as the elevator doors closed. She leaned back against the cool mirrored wall and closed her eyes. It was out of her hands.

She'd done her best. Now all she could do was wait on their decision.

She resisted the urge to chew on a cuticle as the elevator rode down to the main level.

The doors dinged open. The early afternoon sun beamed through the tall plate glass of the building's windows as various employees milled around, either waiting for the elevators or chatting in small groups.

She pushed the revolving glass door and gave a nod and smile to the doorman as she stepped back out into the busy street.

She tried to get her thoughts back, but somehow they'd gotten scattered as she'd finished her presentation and then rode down the elevator.

She rolled her shoulders and took a breath before she hiked her purse up her shoulder and walked the half block to the nearest subway stop.

As she went down the first set of stairs, she nearly slipped on a spilled mint chocolate chip ice cream cone with several napkins fluttering around the green stickiness.

She muttered under her breath and sidestepped the mess as continued on her descent to the subway platform. But a couple of the ice cream cone's napkins caught the stairwell draft and fluttered past her line of sight. The bright yellow and blue logo, along with the words, *Lucky's Ice Cream*, caught her eye.

The logo showed a cartoon horse that stood in the middle of a bright yellow horseshoe and ate an ice cream cone.

Vanessa's lips quirked. She hadn't heard of that particular shop but she loved ice cream and—

What? Wait a minute. She came to a full stop the last few feet before the turnstile, which earned her annoyed glances from three people behind her.

"Hey," one of them called, "you going through, or what?"

She flashed an apologetic look at the other commuters as she fished out her Metrocard, and her fingers tightened around the small piece of plastic as she swiped it. That horseshoe... Horses wore horseshoes.

Her head jerked up. She scrambled for her phone as she went out the other side of the turnstile and walked to the platform.

A whoosh of air told her the train had arrived, but she didn't look up as she scrolled quickly back through her images.

Now where was it again? There were the pictures of the letters, the diary. Jake's Land Rover... Her heart squeezed.

Oh, here it was. The bottom of the chocolate pot.

The subway car's doors swooshed open and people disembarked.

She clutched her phone to her chest at the crush of commuters rushed in various directions. The waiting group of people squeezed on board.

Once she'd snagged a hand strap, she turned her attention back to her phone. She squinted at the curved scratch on the bottom of the chocolate pot.

She swallowed. What if it wasn't a scratch at all? Could it have been done deliberately as some sort of sign or symbol?

She zoomed in on the photo. Turned her head this way and that. Hmm. Yes...it did look, now that she examined it more closely, like it *was* deliberately done in a horseshoe shape.

355 had mentioned horses in her correspondence. Why hadn't she thought of that before? Probably because she'd been too busy noticing Jake and getting carried away by the excitement of their find to think much about it.

Her phone pinged. A new notification from Melissa, who'd reposted a message directly from the Globetrotter Network's feed: *Don't miss this exclusive interview with Jake Ford, aired on* The Early Morning Show. Vanessa's finger hovered over the play button.

Her heart skipped a beat. Jake. A surge of longing swirled through her. What had she done?

She stared at the play button above the frozen image of Jake's face as he sat in the studio. She might've made a huge mistake.

Her finger hovered above the screen.

She recalled his angry expression at the gala and winced. She might've let her fears get the better of her, and leapt to conclusions that were....her shoulders hunched as she admitted it to herself...incorrect.

She'd been so sure of herself, painted Jake with the same brush as her ex. But, she inhaled carefully, maybe he wasn't like her ex. What if he *wasn't*?

She held her breath as she pressed play. After the five-minute clip ended, she studied the still of his face.

Maybe she was letting her pride get in the way of something good and right. Maybe she'd been more than a little unfair to him—*of course* he was going to be worried about his career. She gave a bigger sigh. She'd judged him quite harshly.

She'd just gotten triggered by his actions. She'd become confused in her head about who Jake really was, thinking that he was acting from the same self-centered place as Eric.

But he hadn't been, had he? She remembered the compassionate look in his eyes as they'd talked on the dance floor. The sound of his voice as he'd whispered her name right before he'd kissed her, how he'd really *listened* to her that day in the library. The curiosity in his gaze when they'd unearthed that first journal entry together.

Vanessa recalled the glee on his face as they'd discovered the chocolate pot. Him sharing so openly that day in her apartment...

She shook her head. Jake wasn't anything like Eric. She'd mistaken her fears for reality, and let her triggers cloud her judgment of the situation. She tucked her phone away. So what was she going to do about it?

She needed to apologize for all those things she'd said. But was it too late? She winced. He'd looked really hurt and upset when he'd walked away.

Would he even be willing to listen to her?

She straightened her shoulders. No way

around it. It didn't matter what he did or didn't do or say. *She* needed to do the right thing, be the one to apologize. And then maybe he'd let her tell him her revelation about the symbol on the chocolate pot.

After all, they might now have another shot at finding the pearls and figuring out 355's identity, which just might sway the board's decision in the museum's favor.

The subway's automated voice announced Vanessa's stop and she threaded her way around people to the open subway doors.

Her heart felt lighter as she walked upstairs, as if she were moving up to a place where she wasn't condemned forever for her past mistakes, and could start fresh.

She headed for her apartment a few blocks away. After the usual rattle and jiggle of the outer door, she went inside to her apartment. She let herself in, kicked off her shoes and put her purse on its hook by the door.

The question was, what was the best way to apologize? Maybe a little drama, a little flair, to get his attention, show him she meant it. Hmm. She fished her phone from her purse and brought up Jake's contact information.

She chewed on a cuticle. Maybe if she—

Buzz-buzz.

Vanessa spun around and groaned. Did the downstairs neighbors lose their keys again? She put her phone down. She'd better let them in.

She pressed the intercom. "Yes?"

The crackle and pop of the ancient mechanism came to life. When was the landlord going to fix it? "Hey—uh—t a pizza deliv—for 14B."

Vanessa frowned at the disjointed, static-y voice. "I didn't order a pizza."

"Y—sure abou—tha—?—ineapple-chicken—t's gettin—cold."

Vanessa's brow furrowed. Obviously the pizza delivery guy had gotten confused.

"I—" Vanessa interrupted herself. Wait a minute...

Suddenly she began to laugh as butterflies swept through her stomach. "Jake." She pressed the door open button. "Come on up."

A knock sounded at her apartment

door a minute later. When she opened it, her heart jumped, and she ducked her chin. "I, um, thought you were pulling my leg."

Jake tucked his aviator sunglasses into his shirt pocket. "Would I do something like that? Wait, don't answer that. Are you hungry?"

Vanessa looked down as Jake held out a pizza delivery box. The aroma of pineapple and chicken drifted to her.

"I came to delivery an apology pizza," he said.

Just then, she heard another voice from around the corner say, "That's our cue." Nadine and the lighting guy appeared, sans cameras. Instead, they held a hand-painted banner between them that read: *I'm sorry, Vanessa.*

Vanessa's hand flew to her mouth and a half-gasp, half-laugh escaped her. She whipped her gaze back to Jake's face. He looked—her heart skipped a beat—so earnest. And, well, apologetic.

"I'm sorry, Vanessa," he said, before she could say anything. "I couldn't see beyond my own past, into...the present." He continued to hold her gaze. "My ex—" he shook his head, "basically up and left..."

he winced "...after I proposed to her. She wasn't supportive, really, of my career choices and so when you said what you did, it hurt."

Vanessa crossed the threshold and put a hand on his shoulder. "I'm sorry to hear that, Jake. And I'm sorry for basically starting the fight at the gala." She took a breath. "The thing was, well, with you being on your phone like that, and then saying to me you needed to deal with the show and your career, honestly, I thought you were telling me that what was important to me didn't really matter, just like my ex did. But when I saw your interview, I realized..."

"He and I weren't cut from the same pizza dough?"

"Something like that." Vanessa's stomach rumbled.

Jake raised his eyebrows. "Maybe now's the time to prove it?"

"I think you're right. Besides, I haven't eaten lunch yet."

"Good," Jake said. "That park across the street looks like a perfect spot."

"Great." Vanessa grinned. "Uh, but I should change out of my suit. I'll be right back."

Vanessa dashed to her bedroom and put on jeans and a T-shirt. Her eyes strayed to the jewelry box and the garnet earrings. On a sudden impulse, she slipped the earrings into her pocket, then headed out to the front door, locked it and went downstairs with Jake.

JAKE SET THE pizza box and a copious amount of napkins down onto a picnic bench nestled under a maple tree. Dappled later afternoon sunlight filtered through the green leaves and speckled their surroundings.

Jake's heart jumped as he looked at Vanessa. She'd accepted his apology—and apologized to him—but he hadn't shared everything in his heart with her... Hadn't told her the extent of his feelings. Was now the right time?

His mind flicked back to their dance, how she'd responded when he'd kissed her. Surely that had meant something?

He tried to shake off the self-doubt but it didn't work. What if he did tell her how he felt, and she rejected him again? He didn't know if he could take it a second time.

He brushed away those thoughts. Now wasn't the time to worry about that. He and Vanessa were a team again. Maybe now they could solve this mystery. His phone beeped—Bryce. *Be there in five. Haven't been able to get ahold of a tech at the cloud service. They've shut down access for some sort of maintenance. According to their FAQ, customer service will become available sometime later tonight.*

Jake's jaw clenched as he fought to push aside panic. He took a deep breath. There was nothing he could do. Best to focus on the task at hand. Jake smiled at Vanessa and opened the pizza box lid for her.

"Mmm, this looks delicious," Vanessa said as she took a slice.

"They say," Jake said as he took his own slice, "that the water is what makes New York bagels so good. So maybe that's why New York pizza's so good too." He took a bite.

Vanessa looked thoughtful as she finished her slice. "Huh. Maybe you're right."

Jake reached for a second slice. "I

found out who that Lord C guy was."

Vanessa put her palms flat on the table and leaned forward, her eyes wide. Jake nodded at her unanswered question.

Just then, Bryce and the rest of the crew came into the park and set up.

Jake explained to Vanessa how he'd found out Lord C's name was actually Geoffrey Charles White, Lord Cunningham. He also showed her the man's letter about Nathaniel's capture, and the partial newspaper article about Nathaniel's execution, and 355's failed attempt to save him.

"It's so sad," Vanessa said. "In another diary entry I found in the break room, 355 said she blamed herself for his capture, and had intended to get the pearls herself."

"Wow. You're right—very sad," Jake said.

After a pause, he continued. "So that must mean, since Nathaniel wasn't able to retrieve the pearls, they were still aboard the ship then."

"Must be," Vanessa said.

Then she shared the news about the horseshoe marking with him when she pulled up the picture of the chocolate pot on her phone.

"But the thing I don't get is," Vanessa said as she set down her phone on the table, "what does a horseshoe have to do with that other marking on the bottom?"

"I'm not really sure. I mean, we know 'queen' but other than that, we don't really have anything else to go on." He sat back and rubbed his jaw.

Vanessa crossed her arms. "It's possible," she cocked her head, "that because the horseshoe is symbol of good luck, whoever smithed the chocolate pot decided to add that in."

"But it doesn't look like a professional job," Jake said as he studied the photo. "It looks more like someone took a sharp knife and crudely scratched the surface."

"That's a good point." She reached for another slice of pizza and took a bite. She chewed slowly, her eyes narrowed in thought.

Jake took a third slice of pizza.

Vanessa suddenly sat upright, her expression animated. "Hang on. Do you remember that letter 355 wrote to Sally Townsend?"

Jake nodded. "The one we saw at her

descendant's house?"

"Yep. In it, 355 mentions something about how it was 'delightful' to go riding with her friend."

Jake nodded slowly. "That's right. I'd forgotten all about that. Actually," he paused, "now that I think about it, she did mention something about horseback riding in that first diary entry we found, too. So you think this symbol could have something to do with 355's horse?"

"I think 355 liked horses, and she put that symbol here to point us to the next clue."

"THE NEXT CLUE?" Jake echoed as he sat back and wiped his mouth on the napkin and shut the pizza box. Excitement flared in his gaze and Vanessa couldn't help the surge of excitement that zipped down her spine at the look.

He'd worn almost that same expression on the dance floor...Their kiss rose in her mind. But the camera was firmly on her, so she pushed that thought aside. Instead, she nodded, businesslike, and pulled up the photo again. "I've also been thinking about what these numbers might mean."

Jake angled his head to look at the photo. "You mean the 7/64 thing?"

"Yes."

"I can help with that, actually." Jake hesitated before he continued. "Todd had gotten back to me but I hadn't said anything to you because that was after...um....Anyway, according to Todd's chat with his former boss, Rick, the 7/64 actually didn't refer to a certain smithing run."

"It didn't?" Vanessa rubbed the bridge of her nose.

"No." Jake shook his head and put his phone down.

"This is...." Vanessa started.

"...a challenge?" Jake nudged her.

"You could say that." Vanessa looked at him. "But still," she said. "We're going to figure this out." She pursed her lips. "If it's not a number designating a certain run of chocolate pots, then we need to narrow down the possibilities of what other sorts of things it could represent."

Jake nodded. "That's what the Internet is for."

Vanessa drummed her fingers on the picnic table. "Numbers. So we know now that it's not a sterling silver designation, either."

"Nope," Jake said as he scrolled through his phone.

"Numbers, numbers," Vanessa muttered to herself. "Math was never my strong suit. But I mean, the 7/64 does look like a possible division symbol. Do you think dividing them would do anything?"

Jake pulled up the calculator app on his phone. "Can't divide 7 into 64, or vice versa. Won't work. You get some weird decimal number."

He frowned. "I suppose it could be a fraction. Seven sixty-fourths."

Vanessa shook her head. "That's too... vague. Besides, the Culpers didn't use mathematical symbols to pass coded messages."

"That we know of," Jake added.

"Right..." Vanessa put a finger to her chin. "But they did use numbers as replacements for people, places and things," she said slowly.

Jake leaned toward Vanessa and, again, she caught a whiff of his sandalwood scent.

No, she couldn't afford to get distracted here. She had to focus. But her mind drifted back to the dance floor anyway. How his arms felt around her, his fingers on her bare back, the warm press of his—

"That's it," Jake exclaimed.

Vanessa blinked. "What?" A blush spread across her cheeks when he gave her a questioning look.

"The numbers. Remember how we were looking at that code book in Washington's headquarters?"

Vanessa nodded. "The code book was the key, where all the words represented by numbers were listed."

"What if we take out the / symbol?"

Her eyes narrowed in thought. "We're left with 764."

"Which stands for...?" Jake said.

"I don't know, I don't have the whole thing memorized," Vanessa said with a laugh.

"I snapped some photos of it. Let me just get to the one that has the 700s listed."

He held up his phone and tilted it sideways so the image enlarged to its maximum capacity. He pointed to 764 in the column of numbers. "Inn," he said.

"That's what it means."

Vanessa's eyes narrowed and she drummed her fingers on the table again. "So we have a sort of specific location. Would it be logical to assume they mean one in New York?"

"Probably so. There would've been a lot of inns at the time, though," Jake murmured.

"So the trick is figuring out which one she meant." Vanessa scanned the list again and then she turned back to the photo of the chocolate pot she'd shown Jake earlier.

"Maybe the number doesn't tell us the specific inn."

"Okay. What're your thoughts?"

Vanessa leaned forward. "It's already spelled out. Literally."

"Oh. You mean it's called the Queen Inn?"

Vanessa nodded. "If I do a search for that, it should..." Her fingers flew across the phone screen. "No results," she said.

"What if you try horse shoe?"

"Nothing either." Vanessa sighed.

"If it's any consolation, you really had me going there for a second."

Vanessa laughed. Jake put his phone

away, and his arm brushed her hand. Her skin tingled. They sat so close... But she pulled her attention back to the task at hand.

"It has to have some connection," she murmured under her breath.

"What if it literally meant a queen?" Jake said.

"No, I don't think so. But there's some connection between the two things. Queen. Inn. There has to be...Oh!" Vanessa sat up a little straighter. "I think I figured it out."

"What?" Jake said. "Where?"

"Queen isn't the *name* of the inn," Vanessa said. "It's referring to the location."

"You've lost me."

Vanessa pulled up a map of Lower Manhattan. "The oldest parts of this area," she said as she pointed to the screen, "are here. And," she zoomed in on one of the streets that intersected Wall Street. "Look at this name."

"Pearl Street?"

"Remember I said it was named Queen Street during the Revolution?"

Jake nodded.

She grinned as she felt her pulse jump, "Greene's Inn, a colonial building, was—still is, actually—located there. It was one of the only inns in the area at the time."

"Then what are we waiting for? Let's go."

Chapter Ten

LATE AFTERNOON SHADOWS lengthened into evening as Vanessa walked beside Jake along Pearl Street. They passed an outdoor dining area, and the chatter of diners, mixed with the rush of traffic, drifted to her.

She pushed aside the knot of nerves. The board's decision was out of her hands. The best thing she could do now was get to the bottom of this trail of clues, which would hopefully give her another way to save the museum...

"Here we are," Vanessa made an expansive gesture toward the 18th century building in front of them.

"You can really tell it's been here awhile," Jake said. "Definitely different from that brick and glass skyscraper behind us."

The white clapboard inn had a row of

six-by-six windows done in green trim, with matching green shutters. A flag hung above the entrance. As Vanessa approached the door, painted the same color, she saw several bronze historic plaques mounted on the side of the building.

Someone had locked a blue mountain bike to the iron banister beside the front steps. "It's not too far up, actually, from the tavern where Washington gave his farewell address to his troops after the war ended in 1783."

She walked up the steps. Through the wavy glass window pane, Vanessa noticed diners sat in high-back Windsor chairs at round tables with pewter candlesticks. "They serve traditional Colonial food here. Supposed to be some of the best in Manhattan."

"I'll have to try it sometime," Jake said.

They stepped through the door into a long, narrow hallway. On the left was an open space that housed the large dining area, which, Vanessa noted, had a large fieldstone fireplace, pale green walls, and wide plank flooring darkened with age.

Straight in front of them was a set of narrow and steep wooden steps. On the right, just in Vanessa's line of sight, was another room. She craned her neck. Looked like the bar area, along with a hall that probably lead to the kitchens.

"So let's keep our eyes open for any horse or horseshoe symbols around," Vanessa said.

Just then, the maître-d' approached. "Would you care to look at some menus?"

"Thanks," Jake said. "The food smells really good. But actually, we're here in the city shooting a television show. I made a call to Carrie, the manager, not long ago about permission to look around. Name's Jake Ford. She should be expecting us."

"Oh, okay. Just a second. Let me get her."

A minute later, a tall woman joined the small group of Jake, Vanessa and TV crew in the hall.

"Hi guys," she said. "Nice to meet you all. I'm Carrie."

"Likewise. I'm Jake." He shook her hand and then introduced everyone else. "You ready to get started?"

Carrie nodded and began to walk down the hallway as the group followed. "After we chatted, Jake, I went through what I know about the history of the building and the items in our small collection of artifacts."

"Great. This place has been here awhile, yeah?" Jake said.

"Since 1725. It's New York City's oldest continuously run inn. George Washington slept here." She laughed. "So many places say that, but we have proof. There's actually a small museum in one of the wings of the building here. But it's closed for renovations and maintenance at the moment."

"I'd love to take a look when it's done," Vanessa commented.

Carrie nodded. "Since this place has been here so long, we have quite a few interesting items. I'm sorry to say, though, we have nothing relating to what you'd mentioned in your brief, Jake."

Vanessa exchanged a look with Jake.

"Maybe the best thing to do would be give you a tour of the building," Carrie said.

As Jake and Vanessa walked through the building, the wooden floorboards creaked under their feet. "I don't seen any symbols yet," she said.

"Me either," Jake replied. "But let's both keep our eyes peeled."

After they'd explored what seemed to Vanessa to be every inch of the space, though, they'd come up with nothing.

"Since this place was an inn, it must've had a stables." Vanessa turned to Carrie.

"It did have a stable out back, yes. Still there. It's not open to the public, since it's used mostly for storage. But I can show you if you want. We haven't really touched it. Just made sure it has a good roof on it. No one goes in there much"

"My kind of place," Jake said. "Lead on."

Carrie led them down the hallway that passed the bar and the kitchen. At the far end, on the right hand side, was a wooden door with a porcelain knob.

"This will take us right out back," Carrie said. She took an ancient-looking key from her key ring, unlocked the door and pushed it open.

A WHOOSH OF cool air fanned Jake's face as they stepped into the dim interior of the former stables. His pulse spiked. What would they find in here?

He exchanged a grin with Vanessa as they followed Carrie down the narrow aisle between stalls.

"As you can see," she said, "it's pretty much all storage." She waved a hand. On both sides, the stalls were filled. Tables were piled neatly on top of each other beside stacks of chairs. Boxes and crates and even a few barrels stood in other stalls.

Carrie said. "All the stalls were here, and then," she turned a corner. "The tack room's in here. Grooms' quarters were upstairs."

"It's a little bit cramped in here. Watch yourselves." Carrie stepped into the small space and flicked on an ancient light switch.

Jake chuckled. "This isn't exactly ideal shooting. But you've handled worse, hey, Bryce?"

Jake clapped the cameraman on the shoulder. Bryce flashed him a thumbs-up as he headed to a pile of wooden crates in the farthest corner of the room opposite Jake and Vanessa so he could get the widest shot possible.

"So," Carrie gestured. "As you can see, there's not really much to see."

"Mmm," Jake rubbed his jaw. "This place itself is pretty cool, though. I mean, look at this. All these stones are hand-laid, and," he brushed his fingertips along the wall nearby, "you can see all the trowel marks here from where they applied the mortar." He shook his head.

Vanessa came over to him. "You really get a sense of the history of a place like this."

She couldn't help grinning at Jake's enthusiasm. He loved history as much as she did, that was for sure.

"Bryce," Jake called over his shoulder, "Maybe you should get a shot of the stonework over here."

Vanessa saw Bryce take a step sideways to get a better angle for his camera. He paused to move a few wooden crates out of his way. But as he straightened again and picked up the camera, his foot slipped on the uneven stonework on the floor and he lost his balance.

The heavy camera didn't help, and they all watched, eyes wide, as Bryce crashed backwards onto the floor.

A second later, they all heard a splintering sound as old, rotted wood gave way and Bryce disappeared from sight.

"BRYCE!" JAKE YELLED, as he sprinted across the space to the spot where the cameraman had vanished.

A hole now gaped in the floor. Vanessa noticed Bryce had fallen through what must have been an old wooden trap door.

"Bryce," Jake called again, "Are you all right, man?"

A muffled "I'm okay," came from below as Jake peered into the hole. "Think I saved the camera, too."

The manager rushed over, her hand pressed to her chest. "No one had any idea this was here! I'm so sorry about this."

Jake knelt down on the stone floor, about to extend a hand into the dark. But before he could, Bryce's arm, soon followed by his head and the rest of him, along with the rather beat-up looking camera, appeared.

Bryce dusted himself off. "I'll get reshuffled with the equipment."

"If you're sure you're okay." Jake clapped Bryce on the shoulder. "You certainly seem to be drawing all the short straws on this trip, aren't you?"

"Just a few cuts and scrapes. I'll be fine. That's why I have health insurance. But I'd say I had a lucky break." Bryce held up a horseshoe with square-headed nails sticking out of it. "Was underneath one of those old wooden crates I moved to get a better angle for the shot. Must've been nailed onto the trap door's frame originally."

"Like how people would hang horseshoes over doorways for luck," Vanessa said.

"Except," Jake said, "how do we know that one's not just some random leftover? This was the stables after all."

"Can I see it?" Vanessa said. Bryce handed it to her.

She examine the rusted iron horseshoe. Flipped it over in her palm and frowned. "I don't see anything unusual about it. Could just be—Oh," she brushed away the flaked pieces of rust at the top. "That's a 5 stamped there on the edge."

"And look," Jake counted the nails.

"There are three on one side, and five on the other. Which equals 355." A big grin spread across his face. "Secret trap door that just happens to have a horseshoe deliberately placed nearby, with 355 clearly indicated. What do you say the chances are that's our symbol?"

"Only one way to find out," Vanessa said, as she came to a stop beside Jake and peered into the dark cavity. "What is this place?"

"I'm not really sure..." Jake said before he crossed to the equipment bag Bryce had brought along. He pulled out a pair of headlamps from one of the pockets, came back to the opening and flashed one of the lights around. "Some sort of cellar? Looks like there's stone steps." He turned to Bryce. "You're lucky you didn't split your head open. I think it's better if you guys stay up here at least for the moment and get what shots you can on solid footing," Jake said.

"Got it," Bryce said.

Jake handed Vanessa a headlamp and showed her how to slip it on before he put on his own. Then he extended a hand. "Shall we?"

They descended together.

Their light beams illuminated only a small section of the steps. Vanessa trailed her fingers along the dank wall to help keep her balance and her courage.

There was a sudden rumble, and a shower of dirt rained down. "What was that?" Vanessa's eyes widened.

"Subway, I'd guess," Jake said as their feet touched bottom—a hard-packed dirt floor. Vanessa heard Bryce and the rest of the crew move around above them.

She swallowed hard. This wasn't exactly a roomy space. "Jake, uh, just to let you know, small spaces like this can sometimes make me nervous."

Jake's brows drew together and he titled his head. "Are you okay right now?"

She took a deep breath through her nose and then exhaled slowly through her mouth as she let her attention focus on her breath. Calm filled her. She'd be fine. She was fine, she reminded herself, as her fingers tightened around Jake's.

"I'm good, yeah, thanks. Focusing on my breath, and on a task, keeps me calm. Besides, we won't be down here that long, right? And this is too important to me. I *want* to be here. That's worth the risk."

"All right. If you're sure." He squeezed her fingers back.

She nodded.

Jake flashed his light around. "Hand-dug in here. Musta had to do some maneuvering to get in those ceiling cross beams." He looked up at the low ceiling. "After 250 years, this won't exactly be a feat of sound structural engineering, either."

Vanessa took a step forward and brushed her fingertips against a pile of debris—large clods of dirt, stones and pieces of wood. "There was a pretty big cave-in at some point." She crouched down. "The way's mostly blocked. But it looks like this beam fell sideways. Makes a small opening on the ground."

Jake crouched down beside Vanessa to more closely examine it.

But as he did, something crunched under his foot. He shone his light on the ground.

"That's really old paper. May I?"

"Be my guest," Jake said as he lifted his foot and Vanessa reached down to carefully pick up the torn and smudged page.

8 September 1780

I have done it — the flag is complete. And he shall never know. Though he has taken my hand, he shall never have my heart. That's why I have given the flag to 310's proprietor for safekeeping. Lord C— m can never associate such an act with me, his betrothed.

And I derive all the more satisfaction because of it. For with one stroke of a pen, he cut down my true love. But with the flourish of my needle, Patriots all across the Colonies will be united under these colors.

Live free or die.

Jake whistled as he finished reading.

"I know, right? She never gave up. And I'm not, either." Vanessa narrowed her eyes as she lowered to her hands and knees to study the small opening. "We could be on the verge of a major discovery. Whatever she hid is down here somewhere."

"It's just a matter of getting through there." He jerked his chin at the opening. "Doesn't look very big though. I've squeezed into my share of tiny spaces but this is..."

Vanessa turned to Jake, a gleam in her eyes. "Let's shine some light through the opening and see if we can see what's in there."

"Right."

Just then another shower of dirt rained down on them from overhead.

Vanessa's pulse jumped, but she closed her eyes a moment to steady herself. They could be uncovering the find of a lifetime, she reminded herself. She could do this. She *would* do this. Dust drifted onto her as she shifted to lay flat on her stomach. Jake moved in to lay beside her so they could both see into the opening.

As Vanessa's eyes adjusted to the gloom, she noticed the space in front of her didn't extend very far. Maybe ten feet.

"Looks like there's not really much here," she said.

"You mean no treasure chests heaped with gold and diamonds?" Jake replied.

Vanessa coughed on another cloud of dust as she inched forward on her elbows. "Not that I can see—"

But the angle of the beam from Jake's light glanced off something that caught Vanessa's eye. "Hold your light steady," she said as she reached into the space, a determined tilt to her chin. They'd be out of here soon...

"What is it?" Jake asked.

"Not sure," she replied, as her fingers closed around the object. Once she retracted her arm, she brushed at the dirt. "Looks like rusted metal or something..."

Another stream of dirt sifted down on them both, shoulder to shoulder. This time Jake coughed.

"Careful there," Jake said.

Vanessa's heart jumped at the concern in his tone.

"It looks like," her voice rose in excitement, "...a bridle." She felt a bolt of adrenaline. Could they be getting closer?

"Huh," Jake said.

Vanessa held up a snaffle bit that a few flakes of rotted leather still clung to. "It's really small, though," she added.

"Pony?" Jake said.

Vanessa shook her head. "Too small for that. I think...it's from a toy horse."

"Maybe the horse is still here. Let's dig a little deeper." Jake reached his arm in beside Vanessa's.

As they worked in silence for a few minutes, Vanessa chose to ignore the slight tremble in her hands and the increased pounding of her heart as she dug. This was fine. She'd be out of here in no time and—

Another stream of dirt rained down. Had that been more than before? She shook off the jolt of panic. Focused on the digging. She was going to find answers.

Her fingers scrabbled against something solid. Like...wood? Adrenaline shot through her.

Wow. She stared at it, with a strange sort of certainty. This could be it, couldn't it? All her time, all her effort, could pay off big right now, really and truly. All the answer they'd been searching for could finally be *right here*. And she'd be the one to discover it. Her and Jake. Another spike of giddiness, combined with adrenaline, washed through her.

She swiped the back of her hand across her forehead as she began madly clearing away the dirt from around the object. She shone her headlamp down on it.

"Oh, wow, Jake!" she said with a laugh. "It's a rocking horse."

"But it's stuck." Vanessa leaned on her elbows as she tried and failed to get a hold on the wooden horse. "And *just* out of reach. If I can get a tad farther inside..."

"Sit tight. This isn't stable. Let's try this together."

But Vanessa didn't wait for Jake. She put action to words and started to wriggle forward. Larger pieces of dirt rained down on her.

Jake's gut clenched. Vanessa had no experience with this sort of thing, and if small spaces made her sometimes nervous... But then again, it was all too easy to get carried away by adrenaline in the heat of the moment. He'd bet she was running on pure adrenaline, and not thinking properly.

He opened his mouth to stop her but a cloud of dust kicked up and he coughed instead.

By the time he blinked away the grit from his eyes, she was nearly halfway inside. "Now I can reach it." Her voice sounded muffled but excited.

Jake's heart pounded. "Careful..."

"I've got it, I've got it."

A thin stream of dirt hit Jake on the back of the neck.

"Good," Jake said in a steady voice he didn't quite feel. "Now, if you hold onto it and move back out toward me very slowly, I think we can use our combined force to pull it free..."

He put his hands on her waist as she began to wriggle back toward him. But as she did, there was rumble and shudder. The subway. Jake swore under his breath. At the same time, a bigger cascade of dirt and debris streamed down on them both with her movements. There was a cracking noise. The beam.

He clamped an arm across her body. If he could just get her out of the—

"It's working," Vanessa said in an excited voice. "Pull harder."

"Vanessa," Jake said in her ear, "forget about the damn horse. We need to leave. This whole thing's gonna go." There was another rumble. More dirt fell.

He locked both arms around her waist and put everything he had into pulling her backward.

If they didn't get out now, the whole thing would collapse around them and—his heart lurched—he'd never get a chance to say how he truly felt to her.

"I can't just leave this here!" More dirt fell, and small stones followed larger stones.

"Vanessa," he said between clenched teeth as he gave one final hard pull. "you have to."

"No," she said.

With one last hard yank, the pair of them tumbled back onto the hard-packed dirt, just as the rest of the debris pounded down onto the spot they'd occupied a second ago. The wooden horse landed with a clatter beside them.

His mind raced as he held Vanessa's wild-eyed gaze. He'd been scared to lose her. Him, Jake Ford, afraid? Yes. He'd been afraid to put his heart back on the line. That's what he didn't—couldn't—admit to himself before this moment. But it was true—he was afraid to risk it all for love, and lose again. But what sort of life would he be living if he didn't take that emotional chance? Not one he wanted to live, that was for sure.

Without another second's pause, Jake jumped to his feet. "The rest of this could collapse any second." He yanked Vanessa, who looked a little dazed, up after him.

"But the rocking horse—"

"Just go." Jake gave Vanessa a gentle but firm push up through the trap door opening. She stumbled on the first step but made her way up the stairs.

On the other side, Vanessa dusted herself off and turned back toward the opening. But Jake wasn't there.

"Jake?" she called.

No reply.

VANESSA WHIPPED OUT her cell phone and was about to dial 911 when Jake's head poked through the hole, streaked with dirt and grime.

"Jake," she breathed, her eyes shiny, "are you ok—" She sprang toward him, and cut off the rest of her own sentence with a tight hug that he returned even more fiercely.

After a moment, he held up the rocking horse. "Should we see what secrets this thing has?"

They carefully moved away from the trap door opening and into the middle of the tack room.

Vanessa had forgotten completely about the cameras until they set the rocking horse, caked in centuries of grime, onto the flagstones. But she found she was too excited to care as she sank to her knees beside Jake, who crouched by the child's toy.

Vanessa swiped dust off the horse's head and ran her fingers over the faded paint. "There's a chunk out of the poor thing's forehead, though."

"Looks like it," Jake said as he cleaned off the rest of the horse's body. The horse had once been painted chestnut, with three white socks and a tear-drop shaped blaze on its forehead.

"But it's pretty sturdily built." He rapped his knuckles against the horse's head.

Vanessa helped him wipe the dust and dirt off the remainder of the horse.

"If I'm not mistaken," Carrie stepped forward to examine the rocking horse. "This is a John Townsend piece."

"Who's that?" Jake said.

"Colonial cabinetmaker out of Newport, Rhode Island. His side of the Townsend family moved from the Oyster Bay area in the early 1700s."

"So he could be some sort of relative to Robert and Sally Townsend," Vanessa mused.

"Probably somewhere in the family tree there's a connection," the other woman said. "Though usually he didn't work in children's toys."

Jake began to systematically rap his knuckles against the rocking horse: head, neck, withers. He moved a bit farther down the horse's back. "That...." He met Vanessa's gaze.

"...Sounds hollow," she finished for him.

"Townsend had a reputation for putting secret compartments into some of his cabinetry." Carrie volunteered. "If this one's like that, then there must be a concealed lever somewhere."

"It'd be a matter of triggering the mechanism, then," Jake murmured.

Vanessa's eyes fixed on the groove on horse's forehead. "I think I know the answer."

She reached into her jeans pocket and pulled out one of the garnet earrings.

"Knew there was a reason I felt the urge to grab these earlier," she said as she fit one of the garnet earring into the groove. As she pressed it flush with the wood, there was a faint click.

"Look at that," Jake exclaimed. "The blaze is teardrop shaped. So are 355's earrings."

A concealed door on the horse's belly had popped open on its hinges. Gently, Vanessa and Jake laid the rocking horse on its side.

"You can do the honors," Jake said to Vanessa.

She reached forward. "There's nothing here," she said as she felt around inside. "It's not—Oh." Her eyes widened. Her fingers closed around what felt like heavy thick material of some sort.

She tugged gently.

"Wow," Jake whispered as she slowly extracted the material.

Red, white and blue.

"The flag," Jake murmured. He reached out to help Vanessa. The wool was moth-eaten in places, disintegrated in others, but in the places where the material still hung together, the colors remained bright. Jake touched a fingertip to one of the red stripes. "Her cloak."

"Wow." Vanessa whispered. "I bet the white and blue are other pieces of her clothing repurposed to make the flag."

As they gently put the flag aside, something solid slipped from the folds and thudded to the floor. A cloth bag and a leather-bound book.

Jake let out a long, low whistle as Vanessa gently loosened the bag's ties to reveal a mound of glossy pearls.

She gasped, wide-eyed as she met Jake's stunned gaze.

"They were here, all this time." He blinked rapidly, and dashed the back of his hand across his eyes.

Vanessa put a hand on his shoulder and squeezed. "We found them," she whispered joyfully, a huge smile on her face. "And look," she pointed to the book's inside cover.

To Miss Henrietta Mason, on the occasion of her birthday. November 28, 1774.

"This is Agent 355's diary—the entries are all in the same hand as the other pages, too." Vanessa said, her voice rising in excitement as she carefully turned pages.

"Looks like her last name was Mason, after all," Jake murmured.

"It does," Vanessa agreed.

"She must have lived in what's now your museum," Jake added.

"Probably so. I'll have to cross-reference this name with the genealogy databases to see if I can find out more about where she came from and exactly how she's related, but I think you're right." Vanessa's gaze fell on the final entry.

3 November 1780

This, the day of my wedding, should be the happiest of my life. But I cannot say 'tis so. However, I shall not allow myself more than a moment of weakness, for my duties to the Cause have not quite been completed.

Geoffrey has been awarded a commendation for his role in the events of 3 September. As such, we shall make our way to Halifax, the headquarters of the British forces in North America, as my new husband has been transferred there.

Last evening, he presented me, quite proudly, with my bridal gift. An ornately carved mahogany box, with numerous large pearls. He must have recalled my remarking upon them, and wished to present me with the spoils of war.

'Twas my intent to bring these to 721 at once, but Geoffrey's departure has been hastened by his recent duty call at Halifax. As his wife, I must accompany him. So I have secreted the cache, and a part of my diary, in the belly of my favorite childhood toy, crafted by Sally's relation.

Certain other important pages, I have taken the precaution to separate from this book & tucked them behind loosened stones in our larder.

'Tis too risky to directly convey to any other ring members what I have done. Instead, I have chosen this more secretive method in the hopes that the hints I have left behind might be discovered in due course and be of use to the Culper members who still fight for the cause.

I shall pray that my departure shall not impede the quest for liberty.

"Except the pearls were never found," Vanessa murmured as she lifted her eyes from the page to Jake.

"No," he said as he put a hand on hers. "Until now."

"But what she was striving for was not lost."

He reached a hand up and brushed a smudge of dirt off of Vanessa's cheek. She smiled at him. "No, it wasn't."

"And since she loved horses, it makes sense she'd hide the valuables inside a rocking horse."

"Certainly not a place many would think to look," Jake said.

"And—"

Vanessa's phone suddenly rang. She looked at the ID. Roseanne, from the museum board. "I should probably answer this," she said as a knot formed in her chest. "Hello, Vanessa speaking."

"Vanessa, hi. We've made our decision."

Vanessa's stomach clenched but she made herself take a deep breath.

"And well, it wasn't exactly a clear-cut answer."

"What do you mean?" Vanessa clutched the phone.

"I mean that the vote was very close."

Vanessa swallowed.

"But," Roseanne said, "your argument was compelling enough that the appeal for a loan extension passed by the narrowest of margins."

Vanessa closed her eyes and exhaled slowly.

"Thank you," she whispered. Her eyes snapped open. A big grin spread across her face as she glanced first at the pearls, then at Henrietta's diary and finally at Jake's face. "I have some news I think that the museum board will love to hear."

JAKE'S PHONE BEEPED while Vanessa was on her call. He read the screen: Sara.

The Early Morning Show interview got a positive response. Your damage control is working. Oh, and since you and Bryce have been busy, I did some digging into the footage situation. They apologized about the delay and said because of the software update, the files had somehow been put into another user's folder. They've transferred them back to our editing suite.

Jake stared down at his phone, tension draining from his entire body. He closed his eyes briefly as he exhaled long and slow.

So glad to hear it on both counts, he replied. A huge grin split his face as he continued. *You'll never guess what we found!! We've located the pearls and the flag—in an antique rocking horse, no less—viewers are going to love this! Let's arrange a meeting ASAP to discuss.*

What?! That's incredible! Congratulations to you & the crew! Call me as soon as you can.

Jake, Vanessa, and the rest of his team, along with Carrie, left the dim stables and stepped back out into the daylight with the rocking horse. After Jake had a brief chat with Carrie, he made a quick call back to

Sara.

Then he turned to his team. "Sara says 'Congratulations!', guys. Dinner's on me tonight." He gave everyone high fives.

"Looks like this'll be a great start to our second season, hey?" Bryce said, as he slapped Jake on the back.

"Think so, man. I think so."

Finally, Jake approached Vanessa, who stood by the door texting. "How'd the call go with the board?"

She looked up and beamed. "Finding these pearls, and 355's identity, means the museum won't have to close after all. In fact, I just discussed it with the board, and they're eager to have me get right on a display about 355 and her involvement with the lost pearl cache."

"That's amazing, Vanessa—congratulations!" Jake high fived her.

She laughed. "I know, right? I can't believe it. But it's true. We really did it."

"Yes," Jake murmured, as he held her gaze, "we did."

Vanessa's heart fluttered.

After a moment, she said, "So what did your boss have to say about our finds?"

Jake laughed. "She's over the moon—

we're working on getting the final cut in to her as soon as possible. It's looking like we'll actually be a day or two ahead of schedule with our deadline."

"I'm so happy for you, Jake." Vanessa grinned at him. "And you know what else?"

"What's that?" Jake nudged her.

"I've finally figured out how to make this exhibit about Agent 355 really memorable for people."

"Oh?"

Vanessa nodded. "I'm thinking why not let the public experience the same thing we did on the treasure hunt?"

"I like where you're going with this."

Vanessa grinned. "We'd display all the documents, all the objects, and let the visitors to the exhibit solve the clues and find the pearls. Have it spread throughout the museum's main floor."

"That's fantastic." Jake smiled back at her and took a step closer. "There's something else I need to tell you."

VANESSA'S HEART SKIPPED a beat at the intent look in Jake's eyes. She took a breath as she tucked her phone into her pocket. "There's something else I want to say, too."

"Okay," he said.

"I just wanted to say I'm sorry again—about our fight at the gala."

Jake took her hand. "You don't need to apologize a second time."

"Thanks. I guess I just..." She sighed.

He squeezed her hand.

She squared her shoulders. "Eric had never acknowledged my work—or me. No matter what I did or how hard I tried, I was never enough, in his eyes. So I kept trying and trying to prove to him that I *was* enough for him by showing him all the hard work and effort I put into my job. But it didn't work. After we'd broken up, I started to figure out his behavior wasn't about me." She swallowed hard. "When you and I first met, I thought on the surface, you were the same as Eric. But as you and I spent more time together, I started to think differently. There was still that little voice in the back of my mind, though, that claimed you two were the same. I got scared, thought I hadn't learned, after all. And that's what came out at the gala."

She ducked her head and a strand of her hair fell forward.

"Oh, Vanessa," Jake murmured. He tucked her hair gently behind her ear, his fingertips warm on her face.

For a moment, neither spoke.

"I didn't see things very clearly either," Jake said, his voice husky. "Before we uncovered this treasure together."

Vanessa caught her breath at the look in Jake's eyes.

"I'm sorry about how I acted at the gala, too. I shouldn't have gone off like that. But I..." He cleared his throat. Blinked a few times. "I thought that with my kind of lifestyle, I couldn't have both freedom *and* love. That I didn't deserve it somehow"

He spoke even more slowly now, as if carefully weighing each word. "I was afraid that if I made a deep connection with someone..." He reached out and stroked her cheek, "...that it would fall apart."

"I used the excuse," he winced, "of not wanting to get entangled in a long distance relationship, to keep myself blind to the fact that I was simply...afraid that I'd get left again—" he heaved a sigh. "—and scared I'd be the reason for it."

He paused. "It's funny, what you don't see even when it's staring you in the face. Your fears are the biggest blind spot that you have."

He put one arm around her waist. "But if you aren't risking, you aren't really living. That's the first thing I learned from this job. And I realized today, back in the cellar, that I need to apply that to my love life, too. I shouldn't be afraid to take a leap just because I don't know quite where I'll land. Like *Indiana Jones and the Temple of Doom*. Where he's standing at the edge of that abyss, he has no idea if he's going to plunge to certain death. But he steps out..."

"...and there's something there," Vanessa whispered as she interlaced their fingers and squeezed.

"I want to take that leap with you, Vanessa." He cupped Vanessa's face with his palm. "Because you're different than anyone else I've met before, in all of my travels."

He tugged her nearer to him, and she could feel his warmth radiate toward her. Her heartbeat accelerated as she slid her hands up his chest. "I feel the same way, Jake."

"I'm glad to hear it," Jake said, his lips inches from hers. "Speaking of travel, I know you said you'd like to do a bit more of it, so I was thinking..." His eyes glowed. "How would you like to come with me on my next travel adventure?"

She laughed as she slid her arms around his neck. "That would be amazing. Yes, I'd love to! I'll ask for some vacation time and arrange for a temp after my exhibit opens."

"Perfect."

"But you know, there's one little mystery we didn't solve," Vanessa said.

"What's that?"

"We never found out who sent me that first letter of Henrietta's."

"No, we didn't. But Aaron at the library *did* say that the Culpers could still exist. Maybe one of them sent it to you."

"Ooo, I like that idea. They wanted to secretly help us find out 355's identity."

"Well, we have, so their little nudge worked." Jake stroked his thumb across Vanessa's cheek. "In fact, it seems like it worked on more than one level,"

"Maybe that was their ploy all along." Vanessa whispered. She was rewarded with a flare of joy that kindled in his gaze at her words.

"I bet it was," Jake murmured just before their lips met, "because you and I, we've discovered not only priceless pearls, we've also uncovered the hidden treasure of the heart."

Epilogue

THE TROPICAL EVENING breeze, filled with the scent of hibiscus and a hint of saltwater, whipped Vanessa's ponytail around and she knew she'd probably need a hairbrush the second they got out of the open-top Jeep, but she was too happy to care.

"Having fun yet?" Jake grinned at her as he slung one arm over her shoulders and steered with the other hand.

"Jake, you'd better watch the road!" she said between giggles.

"What road?" He laughed and gestured to the barely visible track through the Costa Rican jungle that they were currently navigating.

"True, there isn't really a road at all."

"Gotta love secret back ways to hidden beaches." He wiggled his eyebrows at her, and her heart zinged.

"Why yes, as a matter of fact, I do."

"I should hope so," he teased. "This little trek *was* your idea." Jake swerved to avoid a large chunk of rock.

Vanessa laughed again and settled Jake's sunglasses onto her face.

"Are you ever going to give me back my sunglasses?" Jake said, but Vanessa knew he was joking.

"How could I? They're a piece of history."

Jake grinned. "Very true. That was a historic moment, the first time you stole them from me when I asked you to be my girlfriend." He shot Vanessa a sideways glance that looked somehow...nervous?

Vanessa gave a mental shrug. Probably just a remnant of her jet lag.

"Time flies, doesn't it? Can't believe that was a little over ten months ago. But who's counting?"

"Obviously you are." She nudged him. "But you're right. It doesn't seem like that long ago since we found the pearls, and then had our first trip together to Morocco."

"Pretty amazing, wasn't it?"

"Definitely. I hadn't realized there are so many layers of history in that place."

"Probably why it made such a good second episode for the second season."

"Which started off with a bang, I'd say."

"I know. It's incredible just how well that 355 episode did. Sara and the whole network were celebrating for days."

Vanessa laughed. "So did Kali, and the entire museum board. Funding has been taken care of for the next few years, because of the money the exhibit is bringing in. And now that her husband's condition has stabilized, Kali's been so great about giving me regular time off."

"Which means we get to spend even more time together." Jake squeezed Vanessa's hand.

"Yes. But you know, I don't even mind our occasional separations with the long-distance element."

"It's working for us, and helps keep things interesting, for sure," Jake winked.

Another large rock loomed up, and Jake put both hands back on the wheel as the Jeep crept up and over the larger outcropping.

"Think we're almost here," Jake said.

Something in Jake's tone made her

heart skipped a beat. Was he...planning something?

Jake downshifted and the Jeep rumbled over the last bit of trail. Vanessa unbuckled her seatbelt as Jake turned off the ignition and pulled the parking brake.

"We got here just in time," she said. "The guidebook mentioned this spot was the best place in the whole region to view the sunset."

Jake unbuckled his seatbelt and then grabbed the beach towels and a small cooler they'd packed from the back seat. He held up the cooler. "And the perfect place for dessert."

She took the beach towels from him, and tucked them under her arm. "Come on."

But just then, Jake's cell phone rang. He glanced at the caller ID. "I should probably take this. It's Sara."

"Sure," Vanessa said. "Wouldn't want you to miss some prime treasure hunting opportunity."

Jake grinned. "I knew you'd understand. Hello?"

"Yep, we're having a great time. Just got here a few days ago and—what?"

Vanessa took a deep breath of the softly scented evening breeze. This place was almost magical. Sometimes it felt like she was dreaming, getting to do some much travel with Jake.

"Oh, really?" he said, "That's amazing. Yes. In South America, then?" He paused. "Uh-huh. Sure, I'll run it by Bryce, and we can get things ready to go when Vanessa and I get stateside again. Mmm-hmmm. Okay, sounds good. Talk soon. Bye."

Jake hung up and slid the phone into his pocket.

Vanessa turned to him with a smile. "Okay, I know that tone of voice. What sort of exciting thing have you guys dug up this time?"

Jake's eyes sparkled. "Sara has the next episode idea all lined up in South America. Something about an emerald..."

"Ooo, sounds intriguing."

"I'll fill you in on the details later. But," Jake interlaced his fingers with hers. "That can wait. Right now, we have a sunset to watch."

He interlaced his fingers with hers and they walked together the last few feet of the jungle path.

Vanessa stepped out from the dense jungle foliage onto the smooth white sand, and gasped.

"It's...stunning."

"Just like you," Jake murmured in her ear as he slide his arms around her waist and kissed the side of her neck. Vanessa shivered with happiness.

The white sand stretched out in front of them, and a group of palm trees swayed in the quiet, framing the expanse of warm turquoise waters. Pinks and purples of the sunset sky were beginning to meld into the water.

"But there's something else I wanted to show you," he said.

Vanessa looked around. "I don't see—"

Jake tugged her hand. "It's just over here..." He led her to the group of palms near the water's edge.

Vanessa's jaw dropped as they came around the corner. "Oh, Jake," she breathed. Her eyes widened as she took in the flickering semi-circle of tall taper candles, the fuchsia flower petals sprinkled around, and the pile of jewel-toned silk pillows.

Her heart fizzed at the intense look in

Jake's eyes as he sat on one of the pillows then pulled her gently down beside him.

"Vanessa," he murmured, "these past months have been...amazing." He paused. "More than I could've ever hoped for, or thought possible. We've been able to make things work so well between us, and I love that. I love how we just get each other, how we have this mutual respect and admiration for each other that's..." he swallowed "...beyond anything I could've imagined before I met you. I love this, I love what we have together, and I love you." He blinked a few times.

Vanessa's eyes filled at his expression, and she reached out and softly brushed her fingertips against his face.

She gasped as Jake reached into his pocket, pulled out a small black velvet box and opened it.

"That's why," he continued, his voice husky, "I want to make sure you're always in my life. Vanessa, will you marry me?"

The expression in his blue-green gaze seemed to look into her very soul, and she knew, in that moment, that her journey together with him had just begun.

Vanessa threw her arms around Jake's

neck as happy tears streamed down her face. "Yes, yes, I will, Jake. I'd marry you in a second. I love you, I love us, and I'd love to have you in my life forever."

Jake slid the ring on her finger and then sealed his promise with a kiss.

Thanks for reading!

If you enjoyed this book, please leave a review at your favorite retailer. Reviews help readers find new authors!

Want more treasure hunts and romance?

Travel to South America in *Lost Treasure of Love*, book 2 in the *Passport to Romance & Relics* series.

Visit
www.books2read.com/losttreasureoflove
or your local bookstore to get your copy!

GET YOUR FREE SWEET ROMANCE HERE!

Will Sara find true love?

Before she was Jake's boss, Sara was a savvy TV reporter determined to not give up on her dreams, or true love...

Don't miss this **exclusive collection** of **three sweet** contemporary **romance** novellas I wrote **just for you!** Includes:

- **Passport to Romance & Relics** – prequel novella, Sara & Todd's story

You won't find this collection available in any store! But it's yours FREE when you sign up to hear from me.

Go here to get started:
www.jessicaeissfeldt.com/yourfreegift

Discover other series by
JESSICA EISSFELDT

PRINCE EDWARD ISLAND LOVE LETTERS & LEGENDS

A bad boy charmer and a good-girl academic hunt for hidden treasure and uncover once-in-a-lifetime love...

A sassy jewelry designer & her ex search for lost pirate treasure & get a second chance at true love...

A feisty journalist & a quiet piano tuner decipher clues to long-forgotten World War II treasure, and each other's hearts...

Acknowledgments

Maren Woodward: New York City scouting consultant

Sabrina Volman: beta reader with a fantastic eye for detail

Steven Novak: excellent cover designer

Paul Savette of BB Ebooks: amazing book formatter

Author's Note

When I first found out about the Culper spy ring, I was intrigued, and decided to focus it on for book one of *Passport to Romance & Relics*.

But there are no known records that point to the identity of Agent 355, so all the documentation that appears in this novel are products of my imagination.

The original Culper codebook, devised by Major Benjamin Tallmage, is, in real life, archived at the Library of Congress, on loose sheets, not within a ledger book, as I've depicted. I've also taken the liberty of imaging that it might've been loaned out for Vanessa's fundraiser gala. Also, the codebook actually ends at number 763, but I've taken the liberty of adding the number 764 to mean 'inn.' I also made up their using the anagram code method. But you never know—they could have!

In the Ford Mansion, there are recreations of Colonial life as it would've most likely appeared during the Revolutionary time period when Washington made his headquarters there. But to my knowledge, there are no original documents—only recreations—there. However, for the sake of this plot, I made up a display with Washington's desk and his original documents, for Jake and Vanessa to discover.

According to historical documents, Agent 355 is first mentioned in a letter from Woodhull to Townsend dated August 1779. However, for the sake of this plot, I've changed the timeline of when Agent 355 might've joined the Culpers, so it fit with the arrival of the French fleet at Newport, RI in July of 1780. (From my research, it wasn't clear exactly when she did join the spy network.)

I've taken poetic license with the Townsend lineage, too. The Therese Smith character is completely fictional, as is the story of the cloak, thimble and needle. Also, Sally Townsend, to my knowledge, didn't work at her brother's shop.

The New York Public Library's manuscripts and archives division keeps individuals' papers. For the sake of this plot, I interpreted that mean diaries, too, so I made up Sally Townsend's journal for Vanessa and Jake to read.

And finally, I took poetic license with what the manuscripts and archives division of NYPL would allow, in terms of Jake and Vanessa being able to conduct the invisible ink test on the antique letter.

Bibliography

Kilmead, Brian and Yaeger, Don. *George Washington's Secret Sex: the spy ring that saved the American Revolution* (New York, Sentinel—published by The Penguin Group, 2013)

Marsh, Sarah Glenn. *Anna Strong: a daughter of the American Revolution* (New York, Abrams Books for Young Readers, 2020)

Tallmadge, Benjamin. *Memoir of Colonel Benjamin Tallmadge Prepared by Himself at the Request of His Children* (Gillian Press, 1904. Reprinted 2016, publisher unknown)

—— *Collecting Guide: American Furniture* Christie's.

—— *Inside The New York Public Library: The Steven A. Schwarzman Building.* The New York Public Library. September 30, 2014.

—— *Long Island History: The Culper Spy Ring.* Long Island History With Mr. Simonson. July 3, 2020.

—— *Morristown National Historic Park: Washington's Headquarters.* America's Parks. October 29, 2017.

—— *Revolutionary Spies: women spies of the American Revolution.* National Women's History Museum. November 9, 2017.

—— *Walking Pearl Street.* Forgotten New York. July 3, 2016.